D0406439

THE TRUTH HURTS

Also by Rebecca Reid

PERFECT LIARS

THE TRUTH HURTS

A Novel

Rebecca Reid

HARPER ⬤ PERENNIAL

NEW YORK • LONDON • TORONTO • SYDNEY • NEW DELHI • AUCKLAND

HARPER ◉ PERENNIAL

Originally published in the United Kingdom in 2019 by Corgi Books, an imprint of Transworld Publishers.

HarperCollins books may be purchased for educational, business, or sales promotional use. For information, please email the Special Markets Department at SPsales@harpercollins.com.

FIRST U.S. EDITION

Library of Congress Cataloging-in-Publication Data has been applied for.

ISBN 978-0-06-299758-6

20 21 22 23 24   LSC   10 9 8 7 6 5 4 3 2 1

For Marcus

THE TRUTH HURTS

"Ready, Mrs. Spencer?" he asked.

No, she thought. *Not ready at all.*

"Yes. Go ahead." She wanted the crowd assembled behind them to hear her.

It was a noise like nothing she had ever heard. A bang would be the easiest way to describe it, but it was more than that. Shattering. Cracking. Hundreds of years of history and memories collapsing as the wrecking ball swung into the house.

Her house.

She watched the honey-colored walls fold in on themselves, watched as the ball smashed through room after room. The crowd gasped with each swing.

It really looked like a doll's house now. You could see right in, the rooms rudely naked without the front of the house. It was almost comical, the huge porcelain bath of the blue bathroom exposed to the elements. And then, with another swing of the ball, that was gone too. Poppy tried not to wince; she tried to look as though this was what she wanted. She had to put on a show for the people who had come to watch.

This was entertainment for them.

She'd dressed carefully that morning, choosing the beautifully cut trench coat and heeled boots as protection against them just as much as the cold winter air.

I want this, Poppy told herself. *This is how I win.*

Clouds of beige dust filled the air, her home reduced to nothing.

Odd to think that once upon a time she had worried about stains on the sofa or marks on the carpet.

"Are you all right?" asked the man with the clipboard.

She must be pale underneath all of the makeup. She nodded again. "Yes. Fine."

"Most people don't like to watch demolitions," he said. His suit was cheap. Shiny. The kind of thing Drew would have despised.

"No?"

"Upsetting, I suppose. Seeing your home go."

Poppy pulled her coat around her. He had no idea. "It's the right thing to do."

Those were the official words. The words she had said to the local council, to people in the village who asked about it. To the local paper when they rang to discuss her generosity.

It was a gift to the community, she claimed. A lovely grassy park full of climbing frames and swings, somewhere for local children to play together.

It was a way of changing a tragic place into a place of enjoyment. Of hope. And no one seemed to question it. After all, how could Poppy really be expected to go on living there, after what had happened?

CHAPTER 1

Five Months Earlier

"Right, they're now officially six hours late," Poppy said into the phone. "I am the only person in Ibiza who's desperate to go to bed." She pulled her legs up underneath her, her bare feet a little cold.

"Have you called them?" Gina's voice, though hundreds of miles away, was comfortingly familiar. Poppy could see her, phone to her ear, tangled up in her duvet, curls tied up on the top of her head. For the hundredth time that week she wished that Gina was here.

"No, I hadn't thought of that, I've just been trying to reach them with my mind," she sniped.

Gina didn't answer.

"Sorry," Poppy said. "I'm just pissed off."

"I can tell."

"It's the third time this week."

"You need to say something to her when they get back."

Poppy raised her eyebrows at the phone. Maybe Gina's boss, who adored her, might take kindly to being told off by the nanny, but Mrs. Henderson made Cruella de Vil look like Maria von Trapp.

"Have you started playing that game where you work

out how much they're actually paying you per hour?" asked Gina. "That's when you know it's bad."

"We're down to £3.70," Poppy said. Eighteen hours a day, six days a week, for four hundred quid. She'd done the calculation on her phone after the kids had gone to bed.

Gina hissed through her teeth. "That's bad. My worst was the Paris trip with the Gardiners. Seven kids, fifty quid for fourteen hours a day. And they made me keep the receipts so they could check I wasn't buying my lunch or museum tickets with theirs. I might have actually lost money that week."

Poppy used her finger to hook a piece of ice from her glass of water. It slipped, falling back in. She tried again, craving the splintering of the ice on her back molars. It slipped again. "Why are rich people so stingy?" she asked.

"I don't know, babe," said Gina, yawning. "I need to hit the hay."

"No-o," Poppy whined. "I've cleaned the kitchen twice. I've laid the table for breakfast. I need you to entertain me . . ."

"Go to sleep."

Gina was right, of course. The youngest Henderson, little Lola, would be awake in four hours, and if Poppy didn't snatch some sleep before then she'd find herself snappy and short-tempered all day. "I'm not supposed to."

"That woman is a psycho. Ignore her. Go to bed."

"OK, OK. Abandon me."

"Call me tomorrow. Tell me all about how you calmly explained to them that you need notice if you're going to be babysitting late nights."

"Yeah, yeah, yeah. Night."

Gina made a loud kissing noise and then the line went dead.

Poppy could go to bed. Of course she could. But if Mrs. Henderson came back sober enough to realize that Poppy had slept on the job, she'd lose her temper. Her husband might earn a million quid a year in the City, but she wasn't above docking Poppy's pay over crimes like needing sleep. Poppy tipped her head back, looking up at the sky. The stars were incredible here. It was hard to believe that it was the same orange sky she looked out over every night from her tiny room in the Hendersons' London house.

She had hoped that the cool air out here by the pool would wake her up. It wasn't working. She could feel her eyelids pulling downward. She picked up her glass and walked barefoot back into the house, sliding the huge glass doors closed and locking them behind her. She padded upstairs, putting her head around Rafe's bedroom door first. He slept, just as he always did, perfectly still and clutching a plastic gun, his round face and rosebud lips betraying none of the aggression that would fill the house once he woke up tomorrow morning.

Damson next, Poppy's favorite. She had decided years ago that parents weren't allowed to have favorites, but nannies definitely were. Damson slept like her brother, perfectly still. Her iPad was in the bed next to her, still playing an audiobook of *The Secret Garden*. Poppy leaned over to turn it off and gently stroked the little girl's cheek. Damson hadn't been allowed a single ice cream all holiday because her parents had decided that those cheeks were too round.

Damson hadn't questioned it, or made a fuss, but watching her stoic little face while her siblings wolfed down ice cream hurt Poppy's heart.

Last, Lola, curled into a little ball in her huge white bedroom. Poppy had spent every day of the holiday so far worrying that Lola would touch something white with chocolatey hands. Childproof didn't seem to have been high on the agenda when they had booked this place.

The blankey that Mrs. Henderson insisted Lola adored was a puddle on the floor. Just yesterday, Mrs. Henderson had posted on Instagram about how little Lola had told the first-class air hostess that she could have a cuddle with blankey during turbulence. The story, like everything else that woman posted, was pure fiction. As Poppy bent down to retrieve an old cup from the bedside table, a beam of white light pressed through the pale curtains of Lola's bedroom. So, they had finally come home. She glanced at the watch on her left wrist. Twenty past two. They'd said they would be home at eight.

"Oh, Poppy," husked Mrs. Henderson, looking up as Poppy came into the kitchen. "Could you undo this?" She held her wrist out. On it was a delicate, sparkling bracelet with a fiddly clasp. Poppy looked behind her, scanning the stark white living space for Mr. Henderson, wondering why he hadn't been asked to help. Mrs. Henderson seemed to see where she was looking.

"Mr. Henderson decided to stay on at the party. But I couldn't bear to wake up away from the children, so I came home." She gave Poppy a wide smile. Six years working for the Hendersons had taught Poppy to read between the lines. This was a warning shot. Mrs. Henderson knew that she was late, she just didn't expect long-suffering Poppy to challenge her on it.

But, sleep-deprived and defensive of the children, Poppy had finally run out of patience.

"You know, Mrs. Henderson," said Poppy as she unclasped the bracelet, "the kids were really hard to settle tonight. You told them you'd be home by eight. They kept asking when you'd be back."

Mrs. Henderson raised her eyebrows. "I'm sorry?"

No, you're not, thought Poppy. "The kids. You said that it was just a drinks party. That you'd be home by eight. Rafe and Damson didn't want to go to bed because they thought they'd get to see you when you got home."

Taking one heavy jewel from her earlobe, Mrs. Henderson smirked. "Poppy, I don't expect to have my movements policed by you."

Poppy leaned on the kitchen counter, trying to keep her cool. "I realize that, I'm just saying they were worried. And I did call a couple of times but you didn't pick up . . ." She trailed off. Mrs. Henderson was taking a bottle of San Pellegrino from the fridge and walking out toward the staircase. "Mrs. Henderson," Poppy heard herself saying, her volume louder than she had intended, "please will you listen to me?"

Mrs. Henderson turned at the foot of the stairs. Not for the first time, Poppy drank in the thinness of her limbs, the depth of her tan.

"Poppy," said Mrs. Henderson slowly, as if English was Poppy's fifth language, "you're tired. I don't think you're entirely in control of what you're saying. Go to bed."

"I'm tired because I get up at six with Lola every day and you won't let me sleep when I'm here alone with them."

"I do not pay you to sleep," said Mrs. Henderson in a voice that could freeze ice. "I pay you to look after my children."

"And I do look after them! I do a hell of a lot more looking after them than either you or your husband do." Poppy felt the words falling from her lips, everything she'd wanted to say for months. "But it's not fair on them or me when you just waltz home six hours late without calling." Her volume had climbed higher and now she was shouting. At the top of the stairs, Damson appeared.

"Mamma?" she said to her mother's back.

"Now look what you've done!" said Mrs. Henderson.

"Everything's fine, Damson," said Poppy, forcing herself to smile. "Just go back to bed, OK?"

"Where's Papa?" she asked.

"Out," said Mrs. Henderson, without turning to look at her daughter. Poppy could feel the anger rising like bile. She grappled to keep a hold of it. She didn't do this. She didn't lose her temper, or tell people how to raise their children. She looked after the kids and she didn't interfere. That was her job. That was the only way that this ever worked.

"Go back to bed, Damson," said Poppy gently. "I'll see you in the morning. We're going to look at the rock pools, remember?"

Damson's face unrumpled. She seemed mollified. "OK. Night night," she said, trailing back to her bedroom.

"Now that you've woken the children up and disrupted my evening, have you finished?" said Mrs. Henderson.

Poppy sank both rows of teeth into either side of her tongue, focusing on the sharp sting of pain. Of course she wasn't done. She wanted to tell Mrs. Henderson that she was a bitch, that her children weren't fashion accessories, and let her know that Mr. Henderson had slid his hand down the back of her jeans at Lola's birthday party last month. But she bit her tongue. She loved these kids, and God knows it had been hard enough to find a nannying job in the first place. She couldn't afford to lose this one. She had to keep her temper.

"Yes," said Poppy slowly. "But it would be really helpful if next time you could call me to let me know that you're going to be late."

"Next time?" Mrs. Henderson laughed, starting to ascend the glass stairs. "Poppy, you're fired."

"What?"

"You didn't think that you could talk to me like that and still keep your job?"

It was hard to find words. It was as if there were too many of them, all fighting to exit her mouth at the same time.

"Fired?" she repeated quietly.

"Yes. Off you go," said Mrs. Henderson as she reached the top of the stairs.

"Now?" asked Poppy, astounded that even Mrs. Henderson could be this vile. "You want me to go now? At two in the morning? I don't have anywhere to go. What about the kids?"

Mrs. Henderson shook her head. "I think you've done quite enough to upset the children."

"Please," said Poppy. "I'll go in the morning. Let me say goodbye to them?"

Mrs. Henderson smiled. "I don't think that would help anyone."

"What about my stuff?"

"The maid will pack it. I will let you know when you can

come and pick it up, at a time when the children and I are out, so that you don't cause any more distress. And you can arrange to collect your things from the London house when we're back."

Poppy didn't know how to salvage this. She gave herself a fast, angry talking-to. She had nowhere to go, almost no money and it was the middle of the night. She shouldn't have lost her temper; she shouldn't have picked a fight. Forcing her mouth to form the words, almost choking on the humiliation, Poppy put on a gentle voice. "Mrs. Henderson, I—I'm sorry I said anything. Let's just go to bed. Let's talk about it in the morning—"

Mrs. Henderson shook her head.

"Please?"

"I'm very tired, Poppy, and this is becoming undignified. Just leave."

Rage, pure hot rage, swelled up in Poppy's stomach. "Fine."

Hoping Mrs. Henderson wouldn't notice what she was doing, she swept the Range Rover keys her employer had dropped on the side into her hand. Reaching the door, she was relieved to see she'd left her handbag hanging up. But her relief gave way to panic when she went into the hall and realized that her feet were bare and that the only shoes by the front door were the strappy gold heels that Mrs. Henderson had kicked off on arrival. She couldn't face the indignity of asking to be allowed to go to her room and get her own shoes. And even if Mrs. Henderson allowed it, if she realized Poppy had the car keys, Poppy would end up walking an hour on the side of the road to the nearest town.

Sighing, Poppy yanked the heels onto her feet. They were still warm and slightly damp from Mrs. Henderson's feet.

She allowed herself a look back at the house, a second to think of the kids, whom she had pretty much raised for the last six years, and then slid into the driving seat, thanking her lucky stars that she hadn't drunk an illicit beer earlier. There was no way Mrs. Henderson had driven home sober. But, Poppy thought as she took the car in a sharp U-turn and out of the drive, the rules were different for people like her.

CHAPTER 2

Pepito's was on the side of the road and full of Spanish teenagers, but it was open, and it was still serving, which was all that mattered. Poppy found the last table left outside, ordered herself a beer and then, because tonight had gone to hell anyway, asked a guy at the table next to her if she could nick a cigarette. She drew the smoke into her lungs, reveling in the burn at the back of her throat. She liked watching the ash creep toward her fingers. The beer was cold and had a thick wedge of lime shoved in the top. It was what she needed. It was a shame that she could barely afford it. The noise of the place was soothing after the silence of the Henderson house.

Steadying herself, she pulled her purse open. She had twenty-two euros in cash. Three credit cards—two maxed out and one with a hundred quid left on it. She had checked her online banking two days ago, putting her fingers over the screen and working up to looking at the number; when she'd eventually managed it she'd heard herself make a sort of yelping noise. How was it possible that she was so utterly broke all of the time? The Hendersons owed her several hundred in expenses—she'd paid for Rafe's sailing lessons and lunch for all four of them all week. She tried to reassure herself that once she got paid, once they paid her back, things would look healthier. But then Mrs. Henderson always had a lax attitude to repayment: what were the chances that they'd bother to reimburse her now? Would they even give her her final month's salary?

The teenagers next to her roared with laughter. She looked over at them, crammed around the table, sitting on each other's laps, talking so fast she couldn't pick out a single word and all interrupting each other, clinking beer bottles and gesticulating wildly. How long had it been since she had sat in a group of friends and laughed? She couldn't remember.

This wasn't the time to get introspective. She pulled out her phone and snapped a picture of herself, her head parallel to the Pepito's sign, pulling an exaggerated sad face.

Got fired. Sitting in a bar, working out my next move. Back in England asap. Can I crash on your sofa? she wrote, and pressed send.

Gina wouldn't be awake, but she would see it in the morning. Gina had a sweet deal, a "nanny flat" in the basement of the house her bosses lived in. Was there any chance she could ask Gina to lend her a couple of hundred quid to get her home too? Probably not. Gina was just as broke as she was. Poppy ran her finger down the list of contacts in her phone, scanning for someone who would lend her money. There was no one. Her eyes settled briefly on *Mum* and she dismissed the idea immediately. Even if her mum had the cash, there was no way she'd hand it over. Poppy didn't have a number for her father.

Next, she typed out a message to Damson, who had been

given the most recent iPhone for her eighth birthday. Would she see it before her mother intervened? It was worth a try.

Darling Dam, I'm sorry that I didn't say goodbye. I'll miss you lots and lots. Give Lola a big squeeze from me and tell Rafe that I'll miss him too. PS. Don't worry about the argument earlier. Everything is OK. All my love, Poppy.

Writing the penultimate line was almost impossible. She had to force her fingers to press the buttons. But it mattered. Damson needed to think that her mother was on her side. She was going to end up fucked up enough as it was. Poppy couldn't bear to make it worse. Poppy had been with the Hendersons since Damson was two, and she'd always assumed that she'd stick around until Lola was packed off to boarding school in ten years' time. She'd thought that she'd be there to guide Damson through spots and periods and boyfriends. Now someone else would get to do that, and Poppy would have to hope against hope that she'd find another Mrs. Henderson, someone who would hire her without asking too many questions.

What next? Grimly, like looking down at a cut, knowing that once you saw the blood it would start hurting, she searched for flights on her phone. Ibiza to London in the middle of summer with twenty-four hours' notice was, unsurprisingly, ruinous. The cheapest one, with two stops and a final destination in Manchester—two hundred miles from home—was three hundred quid. She slumped forward, letting her forehead touch the cool table. She'd have to sleep in the Range Rover on the side of the road, and then beg her final salary and the money the Hendersons owed her when she dropped it back tomorrow. Oh God, she'd have to go back in Mrs. Henderson's shoes. Despair swelling up in her chest, she scanned the restaurant for a waiter. The money situation was bad enough as it was. Another four euros for a second beer couldn't make much of a difference at this point.

"*Uno más, por favor,*" she said to a passing waiter, gesturing to her empty beer bottle. He ignored her. She looked down at her sundress. Did she look that rough? The thought that finding someone here to go home with would be a lot less unpleasant than sleeping in the car had already crossed her mind.

She got up, squeezing through the drunken crowds, and ordered her drink at the bar. Stepping back onto the terrace minutes later with a cold bottle in her hand, she saw that her table had been taken by a man in a blue linen shirt, sitting with his back to her.

"*Lo siento,*" she said, realizing that she was rapidly running out of words in Spanish, "*es mi—*" She gestured to the chair where she had been sitting.

The man turned to look at Poppy. He was about forty, but the expensive kind of forty that came with good clothes and a comfortable life. He had green eyes, curly dark hair and a self-satisfied sort of smile.

"You got up," he said. His accent was cut-glass English. Poppy rolled her eyes. The last thing she wanted this evening was to get into another argument with a Henderson-type.

"Never mind," she said, reaching over to grab her bag. As she leaned over she caught the smell of him: the scented ironing water some maid must have used on his shirt. The expensive aftershave. It smelled good.

"You could join me. If that's the extent of your Spanish

I can't imagine you're going to be making conversation with anyone else in this place."

"Seeing as it's my table," said Poppy, pulling out a metal chair, "you'll be joining me. Not the other way around."

He smiled. "A shame. If you were joining me then I would have insisted on paying."

Poppy felt her lips curling into a smile. "In which case, perhaps I was mistaken."

He let out a low laugh. "I'm Drew."

"Poppy."

"Poppy," he repeated, smiling at her. "Is there any chance that you're hungry?"

She'd been too angry and worried earlier that evening to eat, and thinking about it, it had been hours since she'd had anything. She nodded. "Starving."

"What do you want to eat?" he asked.

"Everything," she replied, swigging from her beer.

Drew gestured for the waiter and, though Poppy wouldn't have admitted it for all the money on Ibiza, she was a little impressed by how fluent his Spanish was.

"What did you order?" she asked as the waiter walked away.

He smiled. "Everything."

"Everything" had turned out to be two bowls full of crisps, a surprisingly decent salad and a plate of cold meat. Poppy had wrapped crisps in Parma ham and shoved them grate-fully into her mouth. Drew seemed to find this amusing, but resisted her persuasion to try it. Once the plates were empty, Poppy leaned back in her chair, rolling her fourth bottle of beer between her hands. Drew pulled a packet of cigarettes from his pocket. "Do you mind?" he asked. Poppy pulled one out of the packet and stuck it between her lips.

"Light?" he asked.

She smirked. "They're so little use without one."

Drew took one out of the packet for himself and then clicked his lighter. "I didn't think people your age smoked. Aren't you all incredibly clean living?"

"My age?" She raised her eyebrows. "I'm twenty-eight. And it's been a rough night."

"We have that in common," Drew said.

"You're twenty-eight too?"

Drew gave her a sarcastic half laugh. "No."

"How old are you?"

"How old do you think?"

Poppy considered him, the expensive watch, the discreet logo on his shirt. "Forty-two," she decided. Drew looked wounded.

"Forty-three, but you could have done my vanity a favor and knocked a few years off your guess."

"Who says I didn't?"

"Poppy, I know we just met but I'm afraid I'm going to have to tell you, you're making my bad night even worse."

"Why was yours so shit?" asked Poppy, dragging her fingertip through a drop of condensation on the tabletop.

"A litany of reasons."

"I'll tell you mine if you tell me yours."

Drew put down his beer. "I was at a party up in the hills, and I looked out at the people and realized that I couldn't stand anyone there, and so I decided to leave."

"Turned your back on that life forever?"

Drew laughed. "Of course not. But it was nice to pretend I had that kind of integrity, even if it was just for tonight."

She smiled. "Well, you get points for honesty."

"How about you?" he asked.

"I got fired."

"Fired? From where?"

"My job."

"That's generally what fired means."

Poppy put her beer down. "Do you want to hear the story or not?"

He gestured for her to continue.

"For someone who talks like the queen you've got some serious blind spots in your etiquette."

"What were you doing for work?" he asked, ignoring her previous comment.

"Nannying," she said. She watched Drew's mouth open and close, smiling, clearly holding back a comment.

"What?" she asked, trying not to smile back.

"Nothing," he said.

"Go on."

"I was only going to say that it makes a lot of sense."

Poppy raised one eyebrow. "And why's that?"

"I can imagine you'd be very good at that. That's all."

Poppy tried to frown, but his grin was infectious. He was implying that she was bossy, but for some reason it didn't bother her.

"I was," she replied, copying his cut-glass accent. "More than adequate."

"And you liked it?"

"I like kids."

"Why's that?"

"Less judgmental than adults. More honest."

Drew laughed. "And if you were so good, why did they fire you?"

And so Poppy told him the story. Not just the edited highlights that she would have given Gina, and not just the version of it where she herself had acted perfectly and Mrs. Henderson was a cartoon villain. All of it. The part where she lost her temper, shouting and waking Damson up. Taking the car keys. When she reached the part about the shoes Drew started to laugh again. "Show me," he said.

Poppy dropped one high-heeled foot in his lap. The shoes were two sizes too big and probably cost more than Mrs. Henderson paid her in a week. But Drew wasn't looking at the shoes. He was looking at her legs. Poppy suddenly became self-conscious about the ugly red scar under her left knee where she'd tripped over some of Rafe's toys and fallen down the stairs, more noticeable against the tan she had picked up playing with the kids on the beach. She also had a feeling that she'd missed a patch when she'd shaved her legs earlier that week, rushing to finish before Lola started crying.

"You are officially my hero," said Drew, placing his hand lightly on her ankle. "If I ever decide to give it all up, I want you there with me to steal shoes and cars."

Poppy sighed. Telling Drew the story had made it feel like an anecdote, a funny story she could tell once she was settled back at home. Once she was safe. But she wasn't safe. She was in a bar on the side of a road with an extremely attractive, considerably older man and absolutely no plan. The Europop that had been playing in the background dropped in volume, and a fluorescent strip above the restaurant flooded their table with harsh yellow light. Looking around, Poppy realized that the huge group at the next table had gone and they were the only two people left out here.

"I think they're closing," she said as the shutters came down over the windows.

"I think you might be right," said Drew. "So, what next?"

Poppy sighed deeply. "No idea."

"I meant tonight, not in terms of the whole rest of your life."

"Still no idea," she said, realizing that her leg was still tangled in Drew's lap. She pulled it back, putting her knees to her chest. It was finally starting to get cold. No idea. None at all. Apart from sleeping in a car and then begging her ex-employers for enough money to get back to England. The realization washed over her. One night in a bar flirting with a good-looking guy didn't change anything. Sitting with Drew had made her bold, as though she was reflecting the light that came off him. But that couldn't last. She needed to stop drinking so she'd be under the limit to return the Range Rover tomorrow morning.

"I should probably go," she said, reaching for her bag. "It was nice to meet you."

Drew stood up. "You're leaving?"

She nodded. "Yeah. Like you said, I have no plan. I'm going to go sleep in the car and I'll take it back in the morning."

Drew looked upward, putting his hands behind his head. "You're not great with hints, are you?"

"What?"

He sighed. "I was trying to ask if you wanted to come back with me. But I didn't want to be . . ." He trailed off. "I have a spare room."

Poppy drank in the triangle of his body, wide shoulders tapering down to narrow waist. How long had it been? She couldn't put a number on it, so it must have been a long time. Mrs. Henderson didn't allow Poppy to have guests, and she had wanted her to babysit most nights. A warm, familiar feeling was stirring in the middle of her body.

"I'd like that." She smiled.

BEFORE

Caroline Walker had had no intention of hiring Agnes. In fact, by the time the doorbell rang that gray Thursday afternoon, she had already hired someone else. It was the same woman—or rather it might as well have been—that she always hired to take care of the kids for the summer holidays. Well meaning. Kindly. Dressed in black bootleg trousers and a printed blouse for the interview. Someone called Lorraine or Sandra or Sue. Capable, reliable, with thousands of hours of childcare experience. She had told the agency there was no need to send anyone else.

So it was a surprise when the doorbell rang, and standing on the doorstep wearing a red flowery dress and a denim jacket was Agnes. "I'm so, so sorry that I'm late," she rushed out as soon as the door opened. "My train got stuck in a tunnel for, like, an hour, and then I got lost." She held out a tube map. There was a faint trace of an accent in her voice, something Caroline couldn't place, and the hint of a track of mascara on her left cheek, as though she had been crying. Her face was so open and hopeful Caroline couldn't bring herself to say that it was a mistake, that the agency should have canceled the interview. That she had already hired someone else who wasn't so close in age to her eldest son, hadn't arrived an hour late to the interview and who knew how to get around London. So she'd invited her in.

"I love your kitchen," Agnes said as she trailed behind Caroline into the long, sunny room.

"Really?" replied Caroline, confused at the compliment. There was still cereal tracked over the counter and the cat was sitting unhygienically on the side, licking its paws. "It's a mess."

"It's great," Agnes said. Her enthusiasm sounded genuine.

Caroline half-heartedly ran Agnes through all of the basics of the house—taking the kids out for at least a couple of hours a day so her husband, who usually worked from home, could concentrate. Making sure that they didn't disturb him when he was working, though she was never quite sure how much of the day that actually was. Bedtime, bathtime, as little TV as possible—while making Agnes a cup of tea (Earl Grey with two sugars, requested with a faint blush); it wasn't as if she really needed to know much. This was a courtesy. She would ring the agency after she had gone and say that she'd been lovely, very sweet, but that they shouldn't have sent anyone, given that she had already hired the last woman they sent, and hope that they might give her a discount on their fee for the inconvenience.

"Can I meet the children?" Agnes asked. "Jack's fourteen, Ella's eight and Grace is four, right?"

"Yes, that's right."

"You work as a lawyer, and Mr. Walker is an architect. You do all your own childcare in term time, and you just need someone to fill in during the school holidays. Which is perfect for me, because I'm going back to uni in October."

Her face changed as she finished the sentence, as if she had realized what she was saying was a little presumptuous. She was so sweetly keen, Caroline couldn't help liking her.

"What are you reading at Durham?" she asked, wanting to reassure the girl that it was all right.

"History." She smiled. "I've only got one more year left. I can't believe how fast it's going."

"I remember that feeling," Caroline admitted. "Blink and you'll be living in the suburbs with kids and a husband." She gestured around her. Even as she said the words she wondered why she was saying them. An awkward pause filled the air between them.

"And you've got a dog, right? The advert said he'd need walking once a day."

Caroline pointed out to the garden where their lazy black Labrador was sunbathing. "You like dogs?" she asked Agnes. "That's Boo." Most of the previous nannies had regarded Boo as an inconvenience.

"I wasn't allowed to play with them when I was a kid," she said shyly. "My mum thought they were dirty. But I love them."

Even though it wasn't a real interview, she'd left Agnes upstairs to play with the kids. Cheeky, she knew that, but Jim had been away on his "boys' trip"—a stupid expression for a holiday filled with men in their late forties—for almost a week and she was exhausted. The chance for a couple of minutes of quiet was too much to resist. She'd shut herself in her little study, a blissful storage room that the children knew they were only allowed to enter if someone was bleeding or unconscious. She lost herself in her papers and, looking up, realized that she had left Agnes alone with the children for over an hour.

It hardly seemed fair to make her work like that when she wasn't going to get the job.

As she reached the hallway, she heard all four of them, laughing hysterically. Even Jack, who considered himself far too old to have to play with his little sisters. The noise was so pure, so joyful that she couldn't help joining in.

Later that evening, Ella, who was eight going on eighteen, crawled onto the sofa and rested her head on her mother's chest.

"We have to have Agnes, Mummy," she said.

Caroline sighed. "You think so?"

She nodded solemnly. "Jack and Grace say so too."

"You really liked her?"

"Mm-hmm."

"More than Sue?"

Ella fixed her with a look that said, "Are you fucking joking?"

"OK," said Caroline, unable to resist making her daughter's day. "We'll have Agnes."

CHAPTER 3

Poppy woke alone. She sat up, struggling for a moment to work out where she was, before her eyes rested on a blue linen shirt, thrown over the back of a chair. A tidal wave of anxiety swept over her. Her job. The Hendersons. The car. The shoes. Drew. Drew's house. Her tongue was dry and half stuck to the roof of her mouth.

A long window ran across the wall opposite the bed, looking out over the sea. Everything she could see was either cream, white or glass. It was a house for grown-ups.

The previous night started to develop in her mind. They had stood on the balcony and looked out over the dark sea. Drunk a bottle of wine. Talked about his job, his friends, why he was in Ibiza. Had she asked if he was married?

She stretched, running her hands over the smooth sheets. It was painfully tempting to go back to sleep, to drag out her time here as long as possible. It made the Hendersons' villa look mediocre. Which was no surprise, really. It was everything that his accent and confidence had led her to expect. Fleetingly she wondered how he'd cope if he had to spend a night in the windowless bedroom she lived in at the Hendersons' house. The Hendersons. Would they be awake yet? Would they have realized that the car was gone?

Bending down she found the pile of clothes she'd been wearing last night: knickers, bra, sandals and a pink cotton sundress. Mrs. Henderson had called her brave for wearing pink because it clashed with her hair. How could that have only been yesterday? She picked up the knickers. What was worse, dirty knickers or no knickers? She shoved them in her handbag and put the dress and bra on. Would Drew give her a lift back to the Hendersons' car?

They hadn't had sex. Poppy had wanted to. They'd fallen into the bed kissing, a tangle of limbs, his hands up her dress, on her back, twisting in her hair. But then he'd stopped. Told her that he wanted her. Badly. But that he wanted her to be sober, at least the first time. Poppy had pretended to be OK with that and then turned away, a pounding heartbeat between her legs. Once she heard his breathing slow, she had clamped her hand between her legs and brought herself to a shuddering climax. The second she finished she had been filled with guilt and self-loathing. She'd felt her skin grow hot, humiliated at the memory. What kind of a person got themselves off lying in bed next to a sleeping stranger? She'd fallen asleep afterward, drugged by her orgasm, the alcohol and the horrors of the day.

Wandering along the corridor, which also had one entirely glass wall overlooking the sea, Poppy wondered who cleaned all the windows in this place. It must be a nightmare. Outside on the terrace, wearing navy shorts and a white shirt, was Drew. He had one leg casually slung over the other and was reading the *Daily Telegraph*. How had he managed that? Mr. Henderson had whined every day about the lack of English newspapers over here, how reading it on his iPad just wasn't the same. Drew had a cup of coffee in one hand and a pair of Wayfarers over his eyes. He looked like the kind of guy who picked up a kid once every two weeks from the Henderson children's school and then acted like it made him father of the year. What had she been thinking last night? This was exactly the kind of man who patronized her when she served drinks at parties.

"Hey," she said, squinting into the sun, one hand shielding her eyes. "I'm going to go."

"Go?" He jumped to his feet. "Where?"

"Back to the car. I need to return it or they'll report it stolen. Do you have the number for a taxi?"

Drew was smiling a strange smile. Poppy tried not to express her frustration. He might have all the time in the world but she didn't. The angrier the Hendersons were the less likely they'd be to give her the money they owed her. If she got the car back quickly enough, she could get a flight. Get out of here.

"I'll take you to drop the car back," said Drew, draining his coffee and getting to his feet.

She shielded her eyes from the sun, squinting at him. So polished, so together. "Why?" she asked.

"I like you," he said, heading toward the car.

"Why?" she heard herself ask again, her walk almost a run to keep up with his pace.

It was a stupid question; she was fully aware of that. But she wanted an answer. She knew she was attractive enough, and younger than him. She understood why someone like him would want to sleep with someone like her. But this was more than that. He didn't sleep with her last night, although he so easily could have. And he could have brushed her off with a cup of coffee this morning, maybe even paid for her taxi if he really wanted to be nice.

Drew stopped, lifted her chin between his thumb and forefinger and kissed her on the lips. "Lots of reasons," he said. "Come on.

"Roof down?" he asked as he pulled out of the drive. Poppy nodded. The car was long and low and the leather seats were sticking to the backs of her bare thighs. He pushed a button and back went the canvas, exposing their skin to the blazing sunshine. Poppy pulled her scratched sunglasses from her handbag and tipped her head back, watching the bright blue sky sail past them. The roads turned sharply but Drew clearly liked to drive. Poppy felt safe with him. Illogically so. She noticed a sign hurtle past them.

"We missed the turn for San Sebastián," she called over the noise of the engine.

"We have a stop to make first," said Drew, without taking his eyes off the road.

"Where?" asked Poppy, suddenly nervous.

"It's a surprise."

"I don't like surprises."

"Don't you trust me?" he asked.

She studied his broken nose, high forehead, tanned forearms. "No," she called. "Of course not. I literally just met you. You're a complete stranger."

"You share beds with complete strangers often?"

She raised one eyebrow to show him what a stupid

question that was. He laughed. And for some reason, the speed or the sun or maybe just because of him, she found herself laughing too.

"Where are we going?" she asked as Drew locked the car. They were on a long wide street lined with stone buildings and cream awnings. She looked at the clock on the car's display, worried about the time, the car, the Hendersons. A vision of a Spanish-speaking policeman wielding handcuffs filled her mind.

"You're going to do me a favor," he said. He set off, walking fast.

"Favor?"

Drew smiled. "I'm going to go and sit at that café over there"—he gestured to a café with white tablecloths—"and you're going to go in there"—he pointed to a shop—"and then in there"—he pointed to a building next door. Poppy pulled her sunglasses up onto her head, studying Drew's face in the sunlight.

"What?" she asked.

He pointed again. "Dress shop. Hair salon."

"You remember the part about me being broke, right?"

"It's on me," said Drew, holding out a credit card. "It's a favor. Remember?"

"How is buying me a dress and a haircut a favor?"

"I've been thinking about those vile people you worked for all morning," said Drew, taking Poppy's hand. His skin was cool, his fingers long. "And I want to shut them up."

"This feels like a deleted scene from *Pretty Woman*."

"I've never seen it."

Poppy scrunched her nose in disbelief. "It's about a guy

who pays a hooker to be his girlfriend for a week. He even sends her out shopping on his card."

Drew raised his left eyebrow. "I'm not trying to buy you. I thought it might be fun to turn up with you looking ten million euros, throw them the keys and tell them to stuff their job."

"Drew, look, this is very sweet but I need to get the car back. They'll think I've stolen it."

"Text her and say you're bringing it back later."

"What if she calls the police?"

"You think she's going to call the police and tell them that her nanny borrowed the car and is bringing it back later?"

"Probably not."

"So stop worrying."

How amazing would it be to be the kind of person who could just stop worrying, the kind of person who didn't wake up every morning with their stomach in a tight knot, waiting to remember all the things they were stressing about before they fell asleep. Poppy stepped closer to him, catching another hint of his scent, as if by standing close enough to him she might absorb some of his attitude.

"Why do you want to do this?" she asked, her resolve weakening. Across the road, she could see a dress in the shop window. White, button-front with a Bardot neckline.

"I'm being childish," he replied. His face was bright with enthusiasm. He looked like a naughty teenager. "I don't often get the chance to say a great big fuck you to the kind of people I always have to play nice with."

"OK," she said, "I suppose I could do you one favor. After all, you put a roof over my head last night."

"You are the very emblem of generosity," he quipped.

The woman in the dress shop was straight out of Spanish central casting, olive-skinned with a sheet of shiny dark hair. She poured Poppy a cup of black coffee, which Poppy pretended to like, and pulled item after item off the rack. Painfully aware that she wasn't wearing any knickers, Poppy tried on the dresses, and found that in spite of herself, she was having fun. Maybe it was weird, but a hot guy wanted to buy her a dress. How often did that happen? Perhaps she should just enjoy it.

Eventually she and Juana, who deserved every penny of her commission, settled on the beautiful white dress from the window. Poppy hadn't worn anything white since the first time she picked up a toddler. Juana replaced Mrs. Henderson's stolen gold shoes with an even more expensive pair before wrapping Poppy's tired sundress and borrowed shoes in tissue paper and putting them in a fancy paper shopping bag.

Alba, the woman in the salon, went into raptures about Poppy's hair, praising the coppery color and the length as she scrubbed it clean. Poppy blushed a deep red when asked what products she used. She couldn't face telling Alba the truth, that her usual grooming consisted of a stolen squirt of L'Oréal Kids and wrapping her hair up in an old T-shirt. If she was really lucky she might get a couple of minutes to aim a hairdryer at it.

It wasn't that Poppy didn't care. Quite the opposite. Her mother had often told her off for being vain, and even confiscated her bedroom mirror because she was "too pleased" with her own face. But after six years of looking after three small children, she'd forgotten how to do much for herself.

Now when she went out with Gina she'd stick an eyeliner in the corner of her eye and tug it back and forth a few times, brush her teeth and throw some red lipstick on.

"There," said Alba, putting the hairdryer down. "You like?"

Her hair, usually tied in a knot on the top of her head, was gently waved, as though she'd been swimming in the sea and let it dry. Or rather, as though she was in a magazine where she was supposed to look as if she'd been swimming in the sea and let her hair dry naturally.

"I love it," said Poppy.

"Ready?" she called to Drew, who was reading the papers. He looked up, then slowly ran his eyes along her body, his mouth spreading into a wide smile.

So, he liked the dress. She tried not to return his grin. "Well?" she asked. "Can we go now?"

"You know, most women would probably say thank you," said Drew, and Poppy put the credit card down in front of him.

"I'm doing you a favor, remember?" said Poppy.

"You're quite right," said Drew, placing a twenty-euro note under his coffee cup. "How good of you to remind me. Shall we?"

"Yes," said Poppy, trying to ignore the fear that had returned to her guts. "We shall."

CHAPTER 4

"Nervous?" asked Drew as they sailed around the curve of the mountain.

"No," lied Poppy. "We need to go to the left at the top here, so I can pick up the Range Rover."

Drew shook his head. "We'll give them the keys. They can go collect it."

"What?"

"They can go and collect it themselves."

"You haven't met them. That's not the kind of thing they do. They—" She stopped herself.

"For someone who isn't nervous, you sound nervous," said Drew, keeping his eyes on the road. "They fired you. Why are you still worrying?"

"I'm not," snapped Poppy. She dug her nails into her leg, through the stiff white cotton of her new dress. "I just . . ."

Drew slowed down. "I'm sorry," he said, looking at Poppy. "I shouldn't be pushing you. You don't have to do anything you're not comfortable with. Do you want me to turn around? We can go back and get the car."

Poppy focused on her feet. Juana had sold her wedged

espadrilles with closed toes to hide her chipped toenail varnish. "I don't know," she said quietly.

"You're not as confident as you seem," said Drew matter-of-factly.

"Difficult to be confident when you don't know if you're getting your final paycheck."

"You'll get it."

"You don't know these people."

"I know their type. And I promise, you'll get your money. Where's all of last night's confidence?"

It was a good question. She sat up a little straighter, her eyes on the road, and said, "OK. I like your plan. Let's do your plan."

"Good," said Drew, turning into the drive. "It's this one, right?"

Poppy rang the doorbell.

After a short wait Mrs. Henderson came to the door. Watching the kaleidoscope of reactions on her face was even better than Poppy had hoped it would be. First there was the look of exhaustion, unquestionably caused by her first twelve hours of solid childcare in her entire time as a mother. Then shock at recognizing the girl in the white dress with the killer blow-dry was Poppy. And finally horror at the realization that Poppy had arrived with this incredibly good-looking man with an expensive watch and an even more expensive car.

"Poppy," she said, grinding the words out from between her subtly enhanced lips. "Can I help?"

Poppy had fully expected to freeze up. To throw the keys

at Mrs. Henderson and then run back to the car. But maybe the dress had magic powers, or some of Drew's cool cockiness had rubbed off on her on the drive.

"Can we come in?" And before she'd been given an answer, Poppy was through the door and settling herself on one of the high stools by the kitchen island, Drew next to her.

Mrs. Henderson followed them, blinking. She wore a jewel-green swimsuit with a sarong around her boyish hips.

"Can I offer you something to drink?" she said, her voice dripping with sarcasm.

"Yes please," said Drew, acting as if he thought she was being genuine. "Water would be great."

Poppy tried not to squeal with joy as a dazed-looking Mrs. Henderson took a San Pellegrino from the fridge and placed it on the counter.

"So?" said Mrs. Henderson, pulling herself up to her full height. "Can I help you?"

"I brought these back," said Poppy, passing the shoes back in the box that Juana had so kindly given her.

"And these," added Drew, putting the Range Rover keys on the counter.

"You're lucky you did," said Mrs. Henderson. "Hengist wanted to report it stolen but I managed to talk him out of it." She clearly wanted to add the words "you're welcome."

"Well, as you can imagine, Poppy assumed you wanted her to take the car," said Drew evenly. "She didn't think there was any way that you would throw a young woman out of your house into the night without any kind of transport?"

"Of course," Mrs. Henderson said eventually.

"And then *of course* there's Poppy's final payment?" Drew smiled.

Mrs. Henderson looked him up and down and then glanced at Poppy. "I'll need to discuss it with Hengist."

Poppy could feel Drew watching her. "I can tell you how much I'm owed," she said, more boldly than she felt. It had been easy to stand up to her before, when she'd been stewing in her anger for hours, exhausted and defensive of the kids. But it was far harder to talk about money, especially in front of Drew, who wouldn't give a second thought to a few hundred quid. "It's this month, plus expenses. And I'm supposed to get one month's pay."

"Yes," Mrs. Henderson replied, her voice robotic. She reached for her handbag and pulled out a checkbook. "Of course," she said as she scribbled along the lines.

"Thank you." Poppy took the check and shoved it into her bag.

"We haven't been introduced yet, by the way," said Drew, reaching his hand across the counter. "I'm Drew Spencer."

Mrs. Henderson blinked slowly, and then fixed her face into a pleasant expression. "Amanda Henderson," she replied. "I know you by reputation, of course. You probably know my husband, Hengist?"

Drew gave her an impassive look. "Quite possibly, if he's in finance. Forgive me. I'm not great with names. Darling, we should get going."

Poppy got to her feet. "Mrs. Henderson, are the kids here? Can I say goodbye?"

"They're not here," she replied. "Hengist took them out

to give me a break." She looked at Drew with a martyred expression. "Three kids. I'm so lucky that Hengist does so much."

Poppy managed not to laugh. She wasn't entirely sure that Lola would even be able to pick her father out of a lineup. He'd spent about ten hours with her since she had been delivered by scheduled C-section three years ago.

"Why don't you leave them a note?" asked Mrs. Henderson.

"Really?" Perhaps Mrs. H was hedging her bets, thinking that if Poppy and Drew worked out they'd be an addition to her dinner-party set.

"Of course. They're going to miss you," said Mrs. Henderson, as if she had forgotten how this whole thing had happened. "Come with me. There's a notepad in here. Drew—Poppy's bag is in that room over there." She gestured at the tiny room where Poppy had been sleeping.

Poppy followed Mrs. Henderson into the side room that Mr. Henderson had been using as a study. Mrs. Henderson handed her a pad and a pen. "There you are. I'll make sure they get it."

Poppy sat down and scribbled a note to each of the children, telling them how much she would miss them and how wonderful it had been to look after them. When she was finished she handed the pad back to Mrs. Henderson, who had been standing and looking at her phone with uncharacteristic patience.

"Thank you," said Poppy. "Genuinely. I hated the idea that I wouldn't get to say goodbye."

"Of course. Now if you've finished, I presume you and

your . . ." She trailed off, dramatically unable to find the word to describe Drew. ". . . will be leaving."

"Yes," said Poppy, trying not to rock the boat, fully aware that Mrs. Henderson could become a hurricane in a matter of minutes. "Thank you again."

"Oh, and Poppy?" said Mrs. Henderson. Poppy turned to see her standing like a spider in the middle of a web. She dropped her voice. "Enjoy it while it lasts."

Drew was standing in the kitchen with her suitcase. "Ready?" he asked.

Poppy nodded.

"Catch," said Drew, throwing her the car keys. Poppy kept the surprise from her face and instead turned to Mrs. Henderson, giving her a wide smile, refusing to show that her words had rattled her.

"I'll send someone to pick up my things in London," she said.

Mrs. Henderson did not reply.

CHAPTER 5

Poppy and Drew walked calmly out of the front door, and then legged it, wheezing with laughter, as soon as they were out of sight of the house. It took Poppy several attempts to start the car, but eventually it roared to life and she curved her hand around the gear stick, sliding it into first gear and putting glorious distance between her and Mrs. Henderson. They sped through the warm air without speaking for a few minutes. Drew casually placed his hand on her thigh, saying nothing.

"Where are we going?" he asked Poppy after a couple of miles of curved road, sea on one side and mountain on the other.

Poppy spotted a rest area, where the pavement gave way to a sandy hollow. She braked sharply and pulled in. "Here," she said.

Drew looked nonplussed. "Here?"

Before he could ask anything else, Poppy had twisted the keys in the ignition, climbed onto Drew's lap and met his lips with hers. She kissed him hungrily, feeling him straining through his shorts.

"You want this?" he asked, undoing his belt.

"You have to ask?"

"Condom?"

She shook her head. "I'm on the pill."

"No knickers," said Drew with a half smile as she pulled her dress up around her waist.

"No knickers," she replied as she pushed herself down and, without meaning to, gasped at the relief of having him inside her. She ground herself against him, moving entirely selfishly, wrapping her arms around his neck and squeezing her eyes shut. Drew let her take control, meeting her movements. He reached to stroke her nipples but seemed to notice her tense at his touch and dropped his hands back to her thighs, where he gripped her flesh. Poppy moved faster and eventually moaned as she came. Seconds later, clearly tipped over the edge by Poppy's ecstasy, he gave a low whimper into her ear.

"Fuck." He laughed as she untangled herself from him, tipping back into the driver's seat.

"Fuck," she replied, pulling her dress down. The familiar feeling of guilt was washing over her, forcing her to question how her face had looked, whether she'd sounded stupid, what he would think of her now. It was the same guilty feeling she always got after sex, as if she'd done something dirty and wrong.

"So, Poppy," said Drew, doing up his belt. "What now?"

"I don't know," she replied, trying to sound composed.

"You should probably pay that check in," he said. Was he about to tell her that he'd had fun but that he was done with her, that he wanted to drop her off in town?

"Yes," she said, her voice bright. "Yes, I should. Is there any chance you might give me a lift to the bank?"

"Of course," he said, sounding strangely detached. "You can drive if you like."

"Good," she said. "Thank you."

The bank took ages, and the air conditioning was broken. The woman behind the window needed hours to decide whether she could do anything with this English check, but for once Poppy wasn't angered by the slowness. Every moment that the ancient woman with the blue eye shadow in the creases of her eyelids wasted was longer standing next to Drew and feeling his body near hers, absorbing his confidence and imagining that she'd be able to wrap her thighs around his waist again.

After the check was paid in they walked slowly back to the car. "Thank you for everything," Poppy said, her eyes on the road.

"You're welcome," he replied.

Poppy reached up and kissed his cheek, darkened with a little stubble. A weirdly formal thing to do, given that she'd been moaning into his ear a couple of hours earlier.

"You know," he said, running his hand down the small of her back. "That check will take a few days to clear."

"Three," said Poppy. "The woman in the bank said three."

"If you wanted," said Drew, "you could stay with me for a few days. Just until it clears. So you can book your flight."

Poppy resisted the temptation to throw her arms around his neck. Three whole days together, three whole days in his world, just them and the house and the sea.

"OK," she replied, smiling at the ground. "Just until the check clears."

BEFORE

Jim was not impressed to hear that his wife had fired the sensible middle-aged nanny they'd chosen together.

"Don't you think I should have had some say in it?" he asked, standing in the kitchen with his suitcase by his feet.

"You were away," countered Caroline. "And the kids wanted her. They're the ones who are going to be spending time with her, after all."

"And what about me?"

"You want a nanny?" Caroline stifled a laugh as she turned back to the kitchen counter. "Do you want a glass of wine?"

"It's not funny, Caro. A week ago, we'd agreed on a qualified professional who was going to be living out, and I get back and you've replaced her with a teenager who's living in the spare room."

Caroline poured herself a glass of wine. The kitchen had been immaculate since Agnes had started. Maybe it was because she was young, maybe she was trying harder than usual, but that first day Caroline had come home to a clean kitchen, two kids in bed and one doing a puzzle at the kitchen table. Agnes might not have any qualifications but

43

as far as Caroline was concerned, she was a fucking miracle worker.

"She's not a teenager. She's twenty-one," Caroline said, pulling out a chair and sitting at the kitchen table. "And she has to live in because her family live in the arse end of nowhere."

"How do you know that she'll be able to cope? The point of paying for this is that I can get on with work without the kids running in to see me every thirty seconds. I need someone who can keep them quiet and out of the way. You wouldn't want them running into your office every five minutes and interrupting you . . ."

It had been literally years since Jim had worked on a real project, so long that Caroline couldn't help thinking that if he was so anti Agnes taking charge of the children, perhaps he could consider doing it himself rather than sitting in his study mucking about on the internet. But saying any of that might trigger one of Jim's low periods, blocking him off from her and the kids for days, maybe even weeks. So she bit her tongue. "I know, Jim. She's great with them—you'll see."

"It's easy for you—your work stops when you leave the office, but when you work from home—"

"Easy?" Caroline raised her left eyebrow. "That's a new one."

"Not easy," Jim conceded, pouring himself a glass.

"Easier than architecture?"

"Oh Jesus, don't start this."

"I'm not starting anything."

"I'm just saying, they can't pound on my study door every time they bang their knee."

44

"I don't think that'll be a problem," said Caroline with a little smile. "You should see them with her."

A knock at the kitchen door saw them both jerk their heads up. It would be Agnes, Caroline realized with dismay. How much had she heard?

"You don't need to knock," called Caroline toward the door. Agnes appeared from behind it, her hands balled. Caroline's maternal instincts weren't always up to much—the smell of newborn babies or the size of children's shoes left her cold. But Agnes's worried face made every motherly nerve in her body twinge. She watched her husband as he took her in. His face was still set. If he was swayed by her long hair and limbs, by her wide mouth and Disney princess eyes, he wasn't showing it. Her friends would tell her that she was mad to bring someone who looked like that into their home. But Jim wasn't clichéd enough to try it on with the nanny.

"Sorry," said Agnes. Caroline had noticed how often she started sentences that way. She wanted to tell her to stop, that she shouldn't apologize, that there were plenty of people in the world who'd walk all over her without an invitation, that it was madness to give them one. But perhaps she was already used to being walked all over.

Agnes had moved in with just one suitcase and a tote bag. To Caroline, she had looked overwhelmed by her new room.

"I just wanted to say that Jack's watching a film and the others are asleep, so I was going to go out and grab something to eat."

"You don't want to eat with us?" Caroline asked.

Agnes looked surprised. "I didn't, uh—"

Caroline caught Jim's eye and gave him a look that said, in no uncertain terms: "Tell her she can eat with us, or else."

"Agnes." He smiled, offering his hand. "I'm so pleased to meet you. I'm Jim Walker. The dad."

She smiled, not quite meeting his eyes. "Nice to meet you," she replied. "Are you sure that you don't mind me eating with you?"

"We insist," said Caroline. "Glass of wine?"

CHAPTER 6

The sun was slipping into the sea as Poppy and Drew finished supper. Soon the pink-orange stains it had trailed across the sky would be reduced to inky darkness. It had been more than three weeks since the "three days until the check clears" deadline had sailed past, neither of them saying anything. Instead they had settled into a blissful routine.

Poppy spent most of her mornings on the sun-drenched terrace, sitting on the painted wooden chair, watching the sky change and reading one of the hundreds of books that lined the walls of the living room. In the afternoons, they'd go down to the beach and swim, Drew doing methodical strokes through the waves while Poppy kicked around in the shallows. Then they'd jump into the car and drive to the village, evening sun on their shoulders, and buy food and wine for that night. They never shopped for more than a day or two in advance, as if they were worried that this, whatever it was, had a shorter lifespan than the peaches or bread that they bought, as if anything more permanent might jinx the little world they had built. Every time Drew's phone buzzed, every time he took a phone call, Poppy assumed it would all end. But somehow, after four weeks of paradise, it still hadn't.

Poppy stretched backward, throwing her arms out and sighing.

"I'm so full," she moaned. "I'm never eating again." She had roasted figs, drizzled with balsamic vinegar and honey, and served them with the burrata recipe she'd made for countless Henderson dinner parties but never actually got to eat. Drew had praised the food before it had even reached his lips, just as he did every time she cooked. He seemed somehow surprised that she wanted to make food, that she wanted to choose things at the market and bring them home and prepare them, rather than going out.

"You said that last night," said Drew. "And if I remember rightly, the night before as well." He topped up her glass. They'd spent ages earlier in a little cave of a wine shop picking the perfect red wine. Drew had laughed when Poppy had told him that she knew it was expensive because it didn't taste of anything until you swallowed it.

Drew had put on weight since she had been staying at the house. It suited him. He was still slim, but his hips were a little less angular now, and his face no longer drawn. The first time she'd stripped his clothes off she had been surprised by how lithe his body was, just skin and muscle, no softness at all. After a couple of weeks together, she had understood why. It was as if he wouldn't eat unless she reminded him to, as if there was nothing else reminding him to do so. The stirrings in her stomach that said "bread" or "olives" or "pizza" didn't seem to exist for Drew. She suspected, though she hadn't asked, that back in London his life would consist of black coffee for breakfast, nothing for lunch and a client dinner in the evening, most of it left on the plate so that his mouth could keep convincing whoever he was talking to, uninterrupted by food.

A silence settled. "I'm going to get fat if we keep doing this," she said, and then stopped abruptly. Any mention of time was forbidden. An unspoken rule that they'd both abided by, in case they broke the spell. "And then you won't fancy me," she added, trying to distract him.

Poppy sank her back molars into the soft flesh of her cheek, waiting for Drew to speak, wishing she could reach backward and catch the words "if we keep doing this" from the air.

Drew got up and stood behind her, facing out over the sea and kissing her neck. "You could put on fifteen stone and I'd still fancy you." He gently bit her ear.

He'd never kick her out, he was far too nice for that. But the summer would end eventually. They couldn't stay here, driving the car around from wine shop to food market to ruined castle every day, cooking and laughing and drinking every night. This was a holiday. And what she had said had brought that reality into sharp focus.

"What if we did keep doing this?" said Drew, sitting back down.

"What?"

"What if we kept doing this?"

Poppy sat upright, searching Drew's face across the table, unsure what to say, unsure whether she had mistaken his meaning. "You want to keep seeing each other?"

He nodded and she felt her lips pull at the corners.

"For as long as you could put up with me, yes."

"How long do you have the house for?" she asked, trying not to let the thudding inside her chest control her answers.

"Until the end of the month," he said.

"So forever until then?"

"Well, then we'd go somewhere else."

"Together?"

"I'd hoped so, yes."

"Like, boyfriend and girlfriend?"

Drew took a steady breath. "Or, if you were interested, like husband and wife."

Poppy had been about to put her wine glass back on the table when Drew spoke. It fell the last inch and hit the table sideways, spilling wine over the scrubbed wood. She jumped up, stammering her apologies, and grabbed at a napkin to mop it up.

"Sorry," she said. "That was so stupid. Sorry, sorry."

Drew came around to stand next to her and put his hand over hers, on top of the wine-soaked napkin. "Poppy," he said. "Stop."

"I just want to clean it up."

"If it's too much—we don't have to. It was only a suggestion. I know it's madness. We've known each other less than a month. I just . . ." He paused. "Forgive the crassness of the wording but I can't help thinking that when you know, you know. And I realize that I'm a lot older than you, and you might not even want to get married, but I thought . . ." He paused again, looking into her face, still so confusingly calm. ". . . I would ask."

Poppy searched his expression, the tension between his eyebrows, the tightness around his mouth. He slept horribly. She'd never told him, never admitted that she noticed it, but every night he twisted in the sheets, clearly a long way from peace. Poppy wasn't stupid. She hadn't reached adulthood without realizing that handsome rich men didn't just stumble into your life, buy you dresses and then offer to marry you. There would be something. There would be a reason. Probably lots of reasons. She tipped her head up and kissed Drew's lips.

"Can I think about it?" she asked.

He looked relieved. "You're not angry with me for asking?"

"Of course not." She smiled. "I just need a bit of girl chat. Can I borrow your phone to call Gina?" Mrs. Henderson had, unsurprisingly, canceled the contract on her phone, which had been the one perk of her job. She would have to get a new one when she got back to England, but for the moment there was something freeing about the idea that no one could get in touch with her.

"Sure," he said. "But we should get you a new phone at some point." He handed her his shiny black phone and she swiped at the display, marveling not for the first time that he had told her his passcode. The last guy she had dated, Josh, still covered his phone with one hand after six months when he typed the code in.

She typed the number in, one she'd called a hundred times before from the Hendersons' "Nanny Phone." *Maybe: Gina Green*, said the screen.

"That's weird," she called out to the terrace, wandering back toward Drew.

"What's weird?"

"Your phone knows who Gina is," she said, turning the

phone around to show him the screen. "How does it do that?"

Drew laughed. "It's terrifying, right? You call her a couple of times from my phone and it somehow knows who she is. The robots are coming for us!" He laughed and picked up a book to read as she went inside.

Gina answered on the third ring. "How's it going?" she exploded as soon as she realized it was Poppy. "Is he still perfect? How's the sex? Can you *please* send me pictures of the house?"

"He's still perfect," Poppy said. She could hear the smile in her own voice. She couldn't help reveling in the feeling of, for the first time in as long as she could remember, having something that someone else was even a little envious of. "And I think I have news."

Gina was quiet.

"Gee?" she asked.

"Sorry, sorry," said Gina. "Mum wants me to come down to dinner."

"How is she?" asked Poppy. Gina's family lived in Crystal Palace, and she spent half her weekends there, allowing her mother to fawn all over her. Every time Poppy visited there seemed to be a new cousin or auntie whom she had never met, all squashed into the tiny terraced house. They were loud, funny, warm and kind. Sometimes Gina would invite her to spend the weekend, and spend the whole time apologizing for the mess and the noise, not realizing that was exactly why Poppy had come.

"She's being a right bitch today, keeps asking why I don't

have a boyfriend and why I haven't had a pay raise for a while. What's going on with you?"

"I think he asked me to marry him," she said.

Gina squealed. "Marry him! Are you joking?"

Poppy sat down on the sofa, playing with the fringe on one of the cushions. "I know."

"So, what are you going to say?"

"Say?"

"About getting married."

Poppy paused, trying to work out whether she really didn't know, or whether she felt like she had to pretend not to know. She decided it was the former. "I can't say yes, can I?" she asked.

"Why not?" asked Gina. "You're into him, right?"

Gina had once told Poppy off for being easy when she'd given a guy her phone number on a night out. She was the queen of game-playing. The ultimate commitment-phobe. Her enthusiasm was a surprise. "I think so," Poppy said, tangling her fingers in the fringe, "yes."

"And he's good to you?"

Good? He was better to her than anyone in the world ever had been. He listened when she spoke. Never talked over her or interrupted. He watched her, noticing her moods. If she was cold he got her a sweater. He said he liked the way she sounded when she sang. "Yes," she said. "He's good to me."

"Then why the fuck not?"

"Because I've known him less than a month? Because it's mad? Because . . ." She paused. "A month, Gina. You can't marry people you've known for a month."

"Not a normal month, though. You've been together 24/7. That's like months in dating time."

"I guess." Gina was right about that. Every single moment, waking and sleeping, they had been together. Talking about history and doing the crossword, or just sitting in oddly comfortable silence.

"My auntie Jasmine married my uncle after a month."

"Didn't she need a visa?"

"It worked out great."

"They got divorced, didn't they?"

Gina laughed. "Yeah, but she got her visa."

"Well, I don't need a visa, and I can't marry him. Not after a month." Saying the words out loud didn't help convince her.

"You don't want to?"

Poppy didn't answer. If things were less strange, if she wasn't on the phone, hundreds of miles away from anywhere she had any right to call home, she might have laughed.

Of course she wanted to. It had been a long time since she had wanted anything more.

"I just don't understand why he wants to," she said, looking at herself in the mirror. Her eyes went straight to the trifecta of flaws she disliked in herself the most: the width of the bridge of her nose, the heavy smattering of freckles that covered her body and the curve of her stomach, which appeared as soon as she ate anything. She wasn't hideous, she knew that. But she wasn't the kind of remarkable person who made someone drop everything. She wasn't the type of woman whom people proposed to after a matter of weeks. She wasn't special. "Why me?" she said into the phone.

"You're looking for reasons not to be happy," Gina said, after letting the silence speak for her.

"All right, Oprah."

"I'm serious. You sound happy when you're with him."

"I am," she admitted.

There was a sound of a baby crying from Gina's end. "Look. He's gorgeous. He's rich. He's kind to you. He's good in bed and he wants to put a ring on it. Just enjoy it. You would be absolutely fucking mental to say no."

"OK," said Poppy, catching sight of her reflection in a framed painting on the wall. Her face layered over the painting. "OK."

"I have to go," said Gina as the volume of the crying escalated and a woman's voice shouted over it. "Speak soon? I want to hear everything. Go live your fairy tale, you lucky bitch. You deserve it."

"Do I, though?" The words came out before she could stop them.

"Yes," Gina said, her voice unusually gentle. "Yes. What happened . . . wasn't your fault. And it was years ago. You slaved away for the Hendersons, you hardly had a day off in years. You've served your time. You deserve to be happy."

Poppy jabbed at the red circle on the phone and wandered back out to the terrace, her sandals clapping against the stone floor. She stood, one hand on the door frame, looking at Drew's turned back a meter or so away from where she stood—the same way she had seen him for the first time at the bar on the side of the road. His shoulders were a quarter of an inch higher than usual. A sign, she had noticed, that he was worrying. Perhaps he wasn't as cool about this as he had seemed.

She nodded, smiling and surprised by tears pricking in the corners of her eyes.

Drew turned around, a smile breaking across his face like a sunrise. "Is that a yes?" He pulled her into his arms, wrapping himself around her. "Really?"

"Yes," repeated Poppy. "Yes."

She relaxed her torso into his, breathing him in. This was a fresh start, she repeated inside her head. A new beginning. Maybe it had been long enough.

Maybe she had served her time.

Maybe she did deserve this.

CHAPTER 7

The waiter poured the pale pink liquid into both glasses and Poppy watched. It looked like she felt. Fizzy. The stem of the glass was long and slender between her fingers. She'd never understood before what people meant when they said something felt like a dream. But sitting here, on the cobbled street, with a heavy linen napkin in her lap and her soon-to-be husband—that word still sounded like it belonged to someone else—she was terrified that at any moment it would all shatter away into nothingness. Would she roll over in a minute and find Damson Henderson crying because Rafe wouldn't let her change the TV channel?

"Are you nervous?" asked Drew.

She looked up. "No," she said, not entirely honestly. "I just can't quite believe we're going to do it."

"And you're sure you don't want your family here?"

She looked down into her lap. Crumbs had settled in the napkin. There were people she wished were there to witness the wedding, but their presence was impossible. Her family, however, would only have ruined it.

How was she supposed to explain this, to Drew of all people? Perfect, gilded Drew who was so good at everything and so easy with everyone, who made waiters laugh and always knew exactly which fork to use.

Drew had offered to fly them out, he'd offered to wait and have the wedding in England so that they could be there. And if he had been shocked by Poppy's refusal, he hadn't shown it.

How could she have told him that even if they had their wedding in England, the chances were her family still would have declined the invitation? Seeing Poppy happy wouldn't sit well with any of them.

"Yes," she said. "Very sure."

Drew took a piece of bread from the silver basket in the middle of the table and tore it into pieces, taking butter from the little white dish and spreading it with his knife. The local courthouse had told them to arrive at 3:30 p.m. They had an hour and a half to sit here, drinking champagne and looking at each other before they went across the road to make the biggest commitment of their lives.

"I was thinking," said Drew lightly, "I wanted to run something past you."

Poppy put her glass down on the table, trying not to look worried. "Oh?"

Drew shifted in his seat, leaning forward and taking her hands between his. Poppy's chest constricted.

"We've had a pretty spectacular few weeks together, right?"

Poppy nodded. "Getting married after a month levels of spectacular, yes."

"I've been thinking about what it is that's made things so special between us."

Poppy smiled. "Lots of wine and food and sex?"

Drew nodded. "Agreed. But I think there's something else too."

Poppy's chest was thudding. Something about his calm voice or the way his thumb was stroking her hand frightened her. "What else?" she asked.

"I think it's because since we've been together we've been focusing on the here and now."

Poppy's heart quickened. *Please don't tell me you've changed your mind.* "Right?"

"In previous relationships, I've found that 'the Past'"— he said the words with a smile, drawing them out—"was something of an anchor, dragging us down. Creating arguments, drawing focus, that sort of thing. So I wondered if, given that we've been rather unconventional in all sorts of ways already, you might be open to trying something with me."

What the hell was he about to ask her to do?

Drew went on: "An agreement that we don't talk about the past."

Poppy tried to slow the thoughts down in her head so that she could catch one—any one—and process it properly. "At all?" she asked eventually, because she had to say something.

"At all," Drew replied. "The way I see it, everything that happened to you until I met you brought you to me. And vice versa. And we can both agree that us meeting was a pretty great thing. So as long as we don't keep any secrets from each other going forward, I figure I don't need to know every breakup and argument and fight you've ever had with an ex. In fact, I don't want to know anything that you don't want to tell me. Family, friends—anything. As far as I'm concerned, it's not relevant. I don't believe that total transparency is always the way toward happiness."

When Poppy was six she had found a twenty-pound note on the ground. She'd been out with her dad, doing the food shopping, and it had fluttered along the street and landed on her shoe. All the rest of that week Poppy had carried the money around in her pocket, not quite able to believe that she was capable of such glorious, magical luck.

She looked across the road to the courthouse where their wedding would happen in just over an hour. Drew noticed where she was looking. "Oh, darling," he said, "I didn't mean—of course we're doing this, whatever happens. It was just a suggestion . . ."

Poppy considered Drew. His long fingers, his olive skin, his straight white teeth. She'd worked for a "perfect" family long enough to know that behind the Instagram posts and family holidays there were always cracks. Always mistresses or affairs or bored lonely housewives wishing they'd never had kids. The shinier something looked on the outside, the more rotten it usually was within.

This wasn't like the twenty-pound note. It wasn't pure, one-sided good fortune. There would, of course, be a reason that Drew had suggested this agreement. Something significant, probably. An ex-wife. An ex-family? A current one, even. Or maybe something else. A white-collar crime, perhaps. Time in a cushy, gentle prison. Nothing violent, but embarrassing nonetheless.

Something impossible to explain, even to herself, told her that what she would stand to gain from this arrangement was far greater than anything she might lose.

"I like it," she said softly. It was as though someone had untwisted the knot inside her chest. She felt more than relief; she felt calm.

Drew looked delighted. "Really?"

For the first time in a long time, the white noise in the back of her head had quieted. This was her chance to leave it all behind. To never have to have the conversations she dreaded the most.

"Yes. It feels so enlightened and European." She smiled. "Are you sure you're not secretly French?"

Drew laughed. "I draw the line at having to keep a mistress in the third arrondissement."

"Agreed," said Poppy. "No mistresses."

"No mistresses. And no secrets. But everything that happened before we met isn't important."

She nodded her head. "I won't ask you, but you'll tell me what I should know. Right?"

Drew shifted in his chair and Poppy could imagine perfectly what he would look like in a business meeting. His back was straight, his hands folded neatly on the table and something about his voice changed. "All right. What should you know? Well. As you know, my family were killed in a car accident when I was eight. I went to boarding school and I spent the holidays with my grandparents who are also now dead. I went to university in America, I've lived in the City since I was twenty-eight, I've had a couple of long-term girlfriends but mostly I've been married to my job. That's it."

The waiter arrived carrying huge white plates of food and made a fuss about arranging them on the table. She watched Drew as he stayed perfectly still, allowing the little performance to take place in front of him, not stammering *"gracias"* every ten seconds like she did.

"Your turn," he said, spearing a little potato on his fork. Would she ever stop finding the way he ate astonishing? It was like he was performing surgery, methodically putting together neat forkfuls of food, perfectly balanced with a piece of everything on the plate. His manners were beautiful, the kind of manners that she had been expected to coax out of unruly children so that they could sail through life, never having to worry about getting anything wrong.

She took a deep breath. "I grew up in Kent; my mother and my sister still live there. Teresa's younger than me, and she has a daughter. My dad left when I was eight. Mum never really got over it. She didn't want me to see him anymore, so I didn't. Then she got very into church, and she was sort of different. She'd always been religious, but suddenly it was like everything that made us happy was a sin." Drew made a face and she returned it, relieved to see that he wasn't harboring similar tendencies. She had absolutely no idea what Drew thought about religion, let alone whether he believed in God.

Next she would have to say the hard bit. She paused, picking up a stem of asparagus. She bit through the fresh green flesh, steadying herself for what would come next.

"I went to Durham to study history and then I ended up working as a nanny."

There it was. Like jumping into a cold swimming pool, horrible for a moment and then like nothing at all.

Drew reached over and took the bottle from the silver ice bucket, which Poppy knew would annoy the waiter. The bottle trailed drops of water onto the white tablecloth. It was so highly starched that the water beaded on it, unable to sink in.

"People usually ask questions at that point," Poppy said. "About why I ended up being a nanny. They think it's weird, after Durham and everything."

"That wouldn't adhere to our agreement."

"Adhere?" Poppy laughed.

"What?"

"You just talk like a grown-up. Not like anyone else I've ever dated."

Drew smiled, but said nothing and Poppy realized as the words reached him that she had made a mistake—conscious that she had stumbled over their new rule by mentioning something from the past. Was that allowed? "I like it," she added, feeling the back of her neck getting hot.

"Good." Drew continued to smile, seemingly unconcerned by her cock-up.

Poppy returned her focus to her plate, not sure how to fill the silence and smarting from her mistake. This must have been what it was like for newlyweds in the olden days, still strangers to each other, unsure exactly what to say next. Everything Poppy could think of to break the silence was a question that might violate their newly minted rule.

"Now," said Drew, reaching inside his jacket. "I have a present for you."

"A present?" she asked. How long had it been since she'd had a present that wasn't a wonky handmade card from one of the children?

"A wedding present," he said, sliding the envelope across the table.

"But we're not technically married yet."

"Does that mean you don't want to open it?"

"Absolutely not." She slid her finger under the flap of the envelope and pulled out a sheaf of papers. The first page read, in bold capitals, "THURSDAY HOUSE." It was some kind of legal document.

"What is it?" she asked Drew.

"Keep going," he said.

The second page was stiff photographic paper, and on it was a picture of a house. A perfect yellow stone house, square and symmetrical, with purple wisteria growing up the outside and a pale green front door. It sat in a wide gravel drive, surrounded by tall trees and green fields.

"It's a house?"

"It's our house," said Drew.

Poppy put the papers back on the table. "Our house?"

"I bought it," he said. "For us."

She picked the picture back up and ran her finger over the wide windows. "For us?"

Drew's face tightened. "If it's not where you want to live, or if it's too much, we don't have to live there. It can be a country house, or we can rent it out, or—"

"It's perfect," she said. "Where is it?"

Drew's face relaxed again. "Wiltshire," he said. "Near Bath and Bristol. An hour or so from London on the train."

"You bought it for us?" said Poppy, still feeling dazed.

"I mentioned to a friend that we'd like to see some houses when we got back to England, and I thought it would take months, but he sent me the details of this one and when I saw the name, I knew. It was meant for us. I was so sure you'd like it."

"Thursday House," she repeated. Visions of thick cream writing paper with "Drew & Poppy Spencer, Thursday House" printed on it in navy-blue ink filled her mind.

"It just seemed right," said Drew. "I met you on a Thursday."

In a moment Poppy was next to Drew's seat, kissing him and twisting her arms around him.

"You're sure you like it?"

Poppy laughed. What must Drew's life have been like for him to think being bought a house could be a bad thing—something she could be cross about. Poppy had assumed, just like everyone else she knew, that she would never own anything, let alone something enormous, something beautiful.

"You bought me a house as a wedding present," she said. "I've been living in someone else's storage room for years. In what world would I not like it?"

"That," Drew said, pulling Poppy onto his lap, apparently unconcerned about the people in the restaurant looking at them, "is quite a relief."

BEFORE

The Walkers lived in a leafy corner of north London, on a square with a garden in the middle. The area had everything people told estate agents they were looking for. Good schools, clean streets. A community. They had barbecues on the green; in the summer children ran in and out of each other's houses. It was like living in an era that hardly existed anymore.

It was a warm Tuesday morning and Mel, somewhere between a friend and a neighbor, had popped round for a cup of tea, which inevitably meant she wanted gossip.

"She's amazing," Mel said as they sat at the kitchen table and looked out into the garden. Agnes was chasing the children around with the hose. They squealed as she sprayed them. "So much energy."

Caroline knew what was coming. "Yeah," she agreed. "Oh, to be twenty-one again. That's why they tell you to get the kids thing over and done with as early as you can."

Mel snorted. "Yeah, just as long as you've found Mr. Right, got your career sorted and bought a house first."

Caroline sighed. "Too bloody right."

"She's pretty too."

"Who?"

"Who do you think? Her." She pointed outside, toward Agnes.

"Oh, Agnes? Yes," said Caroline, getting up to put the milk back in the fridge. "She is." She hoped her tone wouldn't invite any further comment.

"Patrick was saying it last night."

"About Agnes?"

Mel nodded. "Saying how brave you were."

Caroline's skin prickled with irritation as she sat back down. "Brave?"

"You know!" Her labored laugh suggested that the conversation wasn't going quite the way that Mel had hoped.

"No?"

"Brave! Hiring a nanny like her?"

"Because she doesn't have any formal qualifications?" Caroline's tone was harsher than she'd intended.

Mel looked down into her mug, saying nothing.

"Or because my husband won't be able to resist screwing her?"

Mel's cheeks stained dark pink. "You know that's not what I was saying."

"So what were you saying?"

"Oh God, I don't know." Mel got to her feet and reached for her sensible parka. She wore the same thing they all did. Jeans, Converse, drapey T-shirt, hair tied up in a mum-bun. When did that happen? When did they accidentally start wearing a uniform? "I've got to go and pick up Bella from ballet. I didn't mean anything by it, OK? I just . . . Patrick can be a bit of a lech so I'd be nervous putting temptation in his way. But obviously Jim isn't like that, so it's not a problem. She's clearly great. I'm probably just jealous that you've got help for the summer and I've still got baby sick in my hair from yesterday."

"Don't." Caroline relented. "I'm being over-sensitive. I'm just a bit tired of hearing people worrying that Jim's going to cheat because there's a younger woman in the house."

"Course not," said Mel. She leaned forward to bump her cheek against Caroline's. "You two are good. And she's not that pretty."

Caroline raised one eyebrow, but resisted pushing Mel on the subject. It wasn't her fault that Mel was so insecure about her own husband.

CHAPTER 8

The first three weeks of Poppy and Drew's marriage were bliss. They spent their wedding night in a hotel in town, in a room that had floor-to-ceiling windows and a bath in the middle of the bedroom. The next day they had gone to a spa up in the mountains to be polished and smoothed and by the time they came back to the cliff house Poppy had almost begun to believe that this was who she was now. Occasionally she would catch sight of herself in a window and pause, though she knew it was the kind of vanity her mother would have despised. Her hair, which had been tied in a bun every day for the last six years, was shiny from the expensive products in Drew's bathroom. Her skin glowed from all the sleep and sun; her hips were a little softer. It was as if someone had put a filter on her.

Poppy lay stretched, brown and slick with oil, on the hot stone by the pool. It was a Wednesday afternoon, not that days mattered much to them, and she was naked but for a pair of pink bikini bottoms. A shadow fell across her torso. She put her book down and looked up at Drew, olive-skinned in a pair of blue swimming shorts. "What are you reading?" he asked.

"*Jane Eyre*," she said. "I found it on one of the shelves inside."

"Any good?"

"You haven't read it?" She sat up, instinctively reaching for her white cotton kaftan, still not quite used to being so very naked in front of another person during daylight.

"No, I don't think so."

"I thought everyone had to read it at school?"

"Not me." Drew slid his feet into a pair of sandals. "I thought I might go down to the market to get something for supper. Any cravings for tonight?"

"Maybe sea bass?" Poppy got to her feet. "If you wait for me to change I'll come too." She gathered her things, turning for the house. "What did you read at school?"

"I don't remember," he replied, following her into the house. "Shall I just go to the market? It'll close before long."

Poppy scanned the room for her shoes. Maybe they were upstairs. "How can you not remember?" she called as she ran up the stairs. "You must have done a Brontë or an Austen or something. Everyone does."

He didn't reply. In their bedroom Poppy pulled a sundress on over her naked chest and pulled her hair into a ponytail. "Drew?" she called again. He didn't reply, so she went to the hall, leaning down over the banister. He was standing still, tapping his foot.

"What's wrong?"

"Nothing."

"You're being weird."

"I'm just keen to get going."

"Is it the book thing?"

"No."

Poppy walked halfway down the stairs and sat on a step. "Why won't you tell me what books you did at school?"

"Why does it matter?"

It matters because you won't tell me, she wanted to say. "It doesn't matter," she said. "It's just weird that you're being so secretive."

"I thought we had an agreement?" The words were staccato, like machine-gun fire. Poppy flinched at them, moving back on the step where she sat.

"Sorry," Drew added, seconds later. "I didn't mean—"

"It's OK," Poppy replied, too quickly. "I just didn't realize. I thought . . . I wasn't asking you about how many people you've slept with or anything. Nothing, like, important. I didn't think . . ." She trailed off. "I didn't think stuff like school would be a big deal."

"We did *Othello*, I think," Drew said, pulling himself upward. "And *Great Expectations*."

Poppy nodded, trying to be pleased with the information.

"Listen, do you mind if I go to the market alone? I could use a few minutes. I'd like the drive . . ." He left the end of the sentence open.

Poppy pulled her face into a smile. "Of course. You go. I need to shower this oil off anyway."

She stood in the shower for a long time. Drew must have gotten home while she was still scrubbing at her skin because when she came back into the bedroom, swathed in a huge white towel, Drew was sitting on the bed.

"I'm sorry," he said, before she could speak.

"Me too," she replied.

"Do you want to talk about it?"

Poppy shook her head. "Is that OK?"

"No one's going to make us."

"You're supposed to, aren't you?"

"Says who?"

"I don't know. Therapists. Magazines. People."

Drew stood up and gently took the towel from her head, letting her warm wet hair down onto her shoulders, heavy on her back. "I won't tell if you don't."

There were so many things that she needed to ask him. About whether the "rules" really did mean she couldn't ask about school or books or how he learned to ride a bike, because that wasn't what she had thought the deal was at all. But as he kissed her, she didn't want to ask. She didn't want to throw grenades into the warm, safe peace that existed between them. So she didn't.

That evening Poppy took her shiny new phone into the guest bathroom and called her mother. She had chosen the time carefully. After six thirty, which was supper time, but before 8 p.m. Anyone who phoned after 8 p.m. had better be ringing with news of a serious emergency. Poppy had once had a phone call from a boy she was seeing at half past nine. Her mother had refused to speak to her for three days.

The phone rang six times before her mother answered. Poppy didn't need to hear her voice to know it was her. Her breathing, hundreds of miles away, was all it took.

"Hello?" came her mother's voice.

"Mum. It's me."

Her mother said nothing.

"It's Poppy."

Still nothing.

"Mum? It's Agnes."

A pause, and then a breath. "Agnes. Hello."

"Hi."

Poppy drummed her foot on the stone floor, begging for some inspiration as to what she should say next. "How are you?" she said eventually.

"I'm fine."

"And Teresa?" Asking after her sister usually worked. Her mother liked to talk about her.

"She's well."

"Good."

It was clear that her mother wasn't going to ask how she was. Poppy was sweating; she could feel pricking under her arms and down her spine. "I just wanted to ring to tell you that I got married."

The silence was, if anything, even louder than before.

"That's all. He's called Drew," Poppy ventured. "He works in finance."

More silence.

"Mum," Poppy said, her voice shaking. "Please say something."

"Congratulations," said her mother finally. "Was that everything? I need to get on."

"Yes," said Poppy, trying to keep the break out of her voice. "That's all."

The dial tone told her that her mother had hung up.

Poppy turned on the shower to cover the noise, then buried her face in a thick white towel and allowed herself a brief, shameful sob. Why did she still care what Karen thought? Why did it still matter to her? All her cruel words and vindictive punishments, all the judgment and the mind games, and yet she could still reduce Poppy to a sobbing mess with just a few words.

Eventually she got to her feet, took three long deep breaths and filled the sink with cold water. Just as she had a hundred times before when she needed to hide the fact she had been crying, she sank her face into the coldness and opened her eyes underwater. Eventually, when her lungs started to burn, she allowed herself to come up for air.

"Where have you been?" Drew smiled from his seat on the terrace where he was reading a book.

"Just in the bathroom."

"Are you OK? You look . . ." He trailed off.

"Of course."

"You're not upset about earlier? I really am sorry—"

"No," she interrupted. "Really. I'm fine."

Drew didn't look like he believed her, but instead of pushing it he poured her a glass of wine. "Are you going to beat me at Scrabble or cards this evening?" he asked.

Poppy laughed. "Just as long as you're ready to lose, I don't mind either way."

CHAPTER 9

Drew had a habit of going into the smallest bedroom, on his phone, and staying there for half an hour or so. Poppy, trying to seem cool and relaxed, didn't want to say anything. But the intensity of the phone calls, the length, the secrecy: all of it worried her. Drew's words at their pre-wedding lunch played over and over again in her ears. "I don't believe that total transparency is always the way toward happiness."

Panicked, she had called Gina, who had been infuriatingly sensible and asked her what Drew claimed to be doing. "Working," Poppy had said.

"If he says he's working, he's working," said Gina, as if nothing could have been simpler. "He married you, for Christ's sake. What more does the poor fucker have to do to convince you that he's serious about you? Get a picture of your face tattooed on his back?"

"I just have this feeling," Poppy tried. But Gina had been distracted and noncommittal, so Poppy made the right noises and thanked Gina for her advice and hung up the phone feeling just as wretched as ever.

"What do you keep doing in there?" she burst out one

night during their last week in Ibiza, when Drew exited the bedroom, a smile on his face and the red line of his phone etched into his cheek.

"Working," he said, looking surprised.

"On what?" Poppy demanded.

Drew's face clouded. He walked silently to the kitchen, poured two glasses of wine and took a seat on the terrace. Poppy followed dumbly behind him, mimicking his movements.

"I don't get it," Poppy announced.

After a while, looking out over the sea, Drew turned to her. "You look cold," he said.

"I'm not," she lied. But summer was undeniably almost over, and the breeze coming over the sea was cool, pricking at her skin. Drew pulled off his sweater and gave it to her, still saying nothing. She didn't want to talk about being cold. She wanted him to explain what he had been doing.

"I'm sorry," she said eventually. "I just don't understand what's going on. Why are you suddenly in there all the time? Why won't you tell me what you're doing?"

Drew shook his head. "Don't be sorry. It's understandable."

"I am. Sorry, I mean."

"Why?"

"I've been paranoid. I shouldn't care."

Drew shook his head. "No, you haven't."

Poppy felt a tightness wrapping around her throat. So there was something. Something he had been trying to hide from her. That nasty little voice, which sounded just like her sister's, the one that had been saying "too good to be true" over and over again since the night that she met

Drew, was right. It was all too good to be true. She couldn't have this. It wasn't for her.

"What is it?" she asked weakly, wishing that she could be a better version of herself in this moment, a bolder, braver one who didn't need to know what the story was.

"I've been making calls to England," said Drew slowly.

Poppy nodded. "To who in England?"

"My friend Ralph," he said.

"Ralph?" replied Poppy, her eyes wide.

Drew seemed to catch her meaning, to understand what she thought. "It's not like that," he said. "He's been helping me to arrange things."

"What things?" she asked.

Drew drank a long sip from his glass and then put his hands behind his head. "Life, Poppy. Having your things picked up from the Hendersons', having my things brought up from my London flat, having it prepared for rental."

"So?" asked Poppy, unable to understand how this could possibly have been a secret.

"I've been having the house sorted out too. Getting my cars brought up, the place opened, cleaned. Some furniture for some of the rooms. I just . . ." He trailed off.

"What?" she asked, more confused than before.

"I wanted it to be perfect."

Poppy gave a half cry, half laugh. "What on earth are you talking about? Why did you keep it all a secret?"

Drew's face was a picture of misery. "I thought it would be a nice surprise," he said.

Poppy's half laugh turned into a full one. "You are the most ridiculous man I have ever met in my entire life, Drew. Utterly and completely ridiculous."

Drew looked confused. "What do you mean?"

Poppy reached upward and kissed his forehead. "You should have just told me. I thought you were having an affair or something."

It was Drew's turn to laugh now. "An affair? We've been married less than a month."

Drew got to his feet, holding Poppy in his arms. "Drew!" she shrieked. "Be careful! If you drop me I'll break something." But he ignored her protests, which they both knew were only for effect, and carried her inside where he threw her onto the huge sofa.

"Promise there's no one else?" she whispered as she lay, brown against the white fabric, her head resting on his chest.

"No one but you," said Drew, stroking her hair. "Why would I want anyone else when I've got you?"

Poppy nuzzled into his skin. *You wouldn't be the first person*, she wanted to say. But those stories belonged to the past, and they had agreed that the past could not and would not follow them into their new life together. So she said nothing, and kissed Drew hungrily instead.

The room was only half lit now; the sun had slid into the sea hours ago and the air felt cool.

Poppy shifted her body, wrapping it against Drew's.

"Poppy?"

"Yes?"

"I've noticed something."

"What have you noticed, darling?"

Poppy liked this game, where they talked as though they were in a 1950s sitcom.

"Why do you close your eyes when you orgasm?"

Poppy sat up, putting a cushion in front of her body. She could feel the tell-tale rush of blood that meant her chest had gone a mottled red. "I'm sorry?"

Drew smiled, clearly not unhappy with the reaction he had provoked. "I'm sorry too. I didn't mean to shock you."

"I'm not shocked. I'm just surprised. I didn't know I did that."

"You didn't?"

She shook her head. "Every time?"

"Every time. It's like you need to pretend that I'm not there."

That part was true. It was certainly true; there was no doubt about that. It didn't matter how much Drew's body turned her on, how much the feeling of his hands on her skin made her desperate for him inside her; if she wanted to come she needed to magic herself away to somewhere else and imagine that all of it was happening to another person. She just hadn't realized that he had noticed it. No one else ever had.

She sighed. "I don't know. Catholic upbringing, I guess."

"Even the Catholics don't disapprove of sex within marriage."

Poppy plumped the pillow in front of her stomach, running her hand over the smooth fabric. "I suppose I didn't have the best introduction to sex."

"No?"

This was dangerously close to asking about the past. She wondered how curious Drew was. How far he would push to find out. What he might offer in return.

"No," she replied. She'd read once that therapists have a

trick where they say nothing and force you to speak because you want to fill the silence. She watched Drew, wondering whether that could possibly work on him. He didn't seem the type to be bothered by silence.

"What happened?" he said, after a while. Was he allowed to ask that? she wondered.

"It's embarrassing," she replied, dodging the question.

Drew ran his hand up her thigh. "I'm unshockable."

She took a deep breath. "When I was younger, my mother caught me . . ." She paused, taking a breath. A run-up. ". . . touching myself." She looked up at Drew through her eyelashes, trying to gauge his reaction. So far if he was horrified he wasn't showing it. But then, he never did. He seemed unshocked.

"She got angry," she went on, unsure how to say the next part. She had only ever told this story to one person before, and he had howled in outrage.

"What happened?"

"She hit me."

"Your mother hit you?"

Technically another question about the past. Her blood was up now. He looked worried. Worried enough to keep ignoring the rule?

"Yes," she said. "It happened quite a lot."

"My God."

He clearly thought the story was over, and she considered letting him be right. But then the only man she had ever told this story to would remain the only man she had ever told this story to, and that felt wrong. "And she told her priest," she whispered.

Drew sat up straight, his face a picture of horror. "She told your priest!"

"She made me go and see him. I had to talk to him about it and stuff." Her neck and face were burning with the memory of it: sitting on a pew, looking the old man in the eye and telling him what she had been caught doing, watching his gaze, sure he was looking at her hands, guessing which fingers she had used. She'd prayed there would be a confessional like there always was in films, so that she could hide her face while she said the words. But there wasn't. She'd had to look him straight in the eye while she told him that she was bad and broken and dirty.

"That's horrific," said Drew. "Why would anyone do that to a child?"

Poppy tensed, feeling the need to defend her mother that always came when she tried to talk about her childhood. "She's religious. She thought it was a sin."

"Do you see much of your mother?" he asked, stroking her hair.

"No, not really," said Poppy. "She was great when I was little, but then my dad left. And she got obsessed with church."

Drew nodded. "They've got a lot to answer for."

"Was your school religious?"

The silence was screamingly loud. Had it been an accident, or had she asked on purpose? She couldn't quite decide. Could he really refuse to answer her question when she had just told him that story? Adrenaline thumped in her bloodstream; she felt almost high on the excitement of pushing against the rule as she asked, "Drew?"

"Yes," he replied. "Do you want a glass of wine?"

"Catholic?" She felt his body tense. Did that mean yes? Or was it just a reaction to her asking the question?

"I'm going to open that bottle of red we bought yesterday," Drew said eventually. "Unless you'd prefer white?"

"Did you like it? Boarding school?" She could tell he didn't want her to ask; she wasn't stupid. But she couldn't stop herself. It was as if someone else were pushing the words out from her lips.

"Poppy . . ." His tone was a warning.

"I just—" She wanted to tell him that she hated it. That it felt unfair to give him little slices of her life and get nothing back, that she regretted agreeing to this game, that she didn't know if she could live a life where she didn't know where her husband went to school or who his childhood hero was or when he had his first kiss. She didn't need to know about his adult years, the ones where whatever he was running from would have happened. She just wanted to know little, stupid, inconsequential things, the kind of things she offered up to him with ease. But asking would mean fighting, and in her experience fighting sometimes meant leaving. So, as ever, her lips sealed themselves. She stared up into the darkness, listening to his breathing, telling herself over and over again that it was OK, or that at least it was going to be OK. "Sorry," she said, hanging her head. "I know."

Drew relaxed back on the sofa and put his arm around her shoulders. "I spoke to Ralph earlier. He said that the house will be ready the week after next."

The house. Their house. Poppy felt her mouth widen into a smile.

"Do you feel ready to go home?" he asked. "I'm extending the lease here for a week but we can stay longer, if you like."

Poppy shook her head. "I want to go home," she said. "I want to go home with you."

CHAPTER 10

And so, two weeks later, Poppy and Drew sat in the back of a smart black car, sliding along the motorway and then off into twisting lanes under green canopies. Poppy lay her head on Drew's shoulder, her hand resting on his thigh. His wedding ring glinted in the sunlight and her arms were evenly brown. They must look, she thought, like such a couple.

"Have you ever been to Wiltshire before?" asked Drew.

"No," she said. "But I'm in love with it already. Look over there!" The car was at the summit of a huge hill, looking down over a valley; sitting in the crook of the valley was a yellow house. "Is that it?" she asked excitedly, leaning over and putting her finger to Drew's window so that he couldn't miss it.

"Yes!" He laughed. "That's it."

The car slowed, the driver taking the driveway meter by meter for fear of a puncture.

"I don't know why I'm nervous," she said. "I already know what it looks like."

Drew squeezed her hand. "I feel a bit nervous too." They

rounded the bend and there, in front of them, was the house.

Poppy caught her breath. It was so symmetrical it looked like a child's drawing. The door was wide and pale green, matching the window frames. How many windows? She counted eight. All high and mullioned with square panes. She squinted, trying to see through them, trying to see inside the perfect doll's house. Wisteria dripped over the porch, brushing the huge front door. She turned to Drew to tell him how she loved it, how it was the single greatest thing any person had ever done for any other person. But the words weren't there. So instead she squeezed his hand and smiled. Drew seemed to understand. She was surprised, given how stoic Drew's reactions were to almost everything else, to see that he looked emotional too.

"Are you OK?" she asked.

"Of course," he said. "I just can't quite believe that it's all happening."

Me neither, thought Poppy.

The night Mrs. Henderson had fired her, the night that had felt like the end of the world, had turned out to be, without doubt, the luckiest day of her life.

. Drew pushed the front door open. He stepped into the entrance hall and stood, stock-still, looking up at the high ceiling, the staircase, and the rooms that surrounded him. It looked like he was trying to fill his lungs with the smell of the house. It was funny, she thought. One day she'd walk in here and she wouldn't be able to smell it anymore, their house smell. Drew turned slowly. For a moment Poppy wondered if he even really knew that she was there. And then, as if he had caught himself doing something awful, his head jerked.

"Shall we explore?" he asked. "Or eat?"

"Eat?" she said. "Don't we need to shop?"

He laughed. "Ralph had food delivered earlier today."

Poppy gave a little whistle. "Whatever you're giving Ralph for helping you out, double it. He's a fucking star. But I'm not hungry. How could we be when we've got all of this to look around?"

The entrance hall was dominated by a huge staircase, the floor had a worn Persian carpet and along the wall ran a long sideboard. The wall bore a huge landscape in a gold frame.

"They left all their furniture?" asked Poppy.

"Ralph said they didn't want any of it. Threw it all in with the price of the house. The mattresses are new—Ralph had them delivered. But we don't have to keep any of it—we'll want to make it our own."

Poppy took a left turn and wandered into a huge green and yellow drawing room. "This is incredible," she called back.

"There in a moment," Drew replied.

Poppy wandered around the room, running her fingers over the mantelpiece. There were dark rectangles on the walls where photographs or paintings must have hung, blocking the walls from the light. Who would the photographs have been of? she wondered.

She took out her phone and snapped a picture of the room. She started to send it to Gina but stopped herself. It felt too much like showing off. The old, familiar ache for

Caroline pulled at her chest. Would she ever stop reaching to dial her number when something important happened?

At the far end of the room there was a huge mirror in a gold frame, mounted on the wall. The glass was speckled with age, and when Poppy looked in it she realized it must be ancient. It was warmly flattering. Softened by age, making her reflection prettier than she was. How many people must have looked in this mirror over the years? Teenage daughters of the house running in here to check their dresses before going to a party. Guests glancing over their shoulders to check that their hair was still perfect. She'd look in the mirror to admire a baby bump one day. And she'd show her children—Drew's children—their own reflections in it. Maybe she'd be looking in that mirror when she saw her first gray hair, or noticed the lines around her eyes deepen. It was a warm, comforting sort of thought.

She ran her hand over the surface, brushing off a fine layer of dust with the sleeve of her top. Before Poppy realized what was happening there was a snap and the mirror had fallen straight down the wall and hit the floor. She jumped back, as though she had burned herself. The mirror tipped forward, slamming onto the floorboards with a sickening smash. Poppy stood perfectly still, looking at the dull brown back to the frame, rooted to the spot.

"Poppy?" Drew yelled from another room. "What was that?" She heard his feet on the stairs and then he was behind her, putting his arms around her.

"Are you OK?"

She couldn't move. "I hardly touched it," she whispered.

Drew hugged her tightly. "Thank God you're all right. You could have been really hurt."

"I'm so sorry."

Drew's eyebrows lowered. "Don't apologize."

"It's such bad luck. You don't think it's some kind of sign? Like an omen?"

"On the contrary," said Drew. "It's incredibly good luck. You could have been hurt, and you're fine."

"I'm really sorry," she said again.

Drew took her hand and led her out of the room. "Stop apologizing," he said. "It's not your fault. It's an old house. Things break. It doesn't matter." He looked at her, holding her gaze. "It is not an omen."

"What are we going to do with all this space?" Poppy asked as they explored the house, room by room.

"Fill it with babies," said Drew, smiling. "One in each bedroom."

"There are eight bedrooms!" objected Poppy. "Think of my poor vagina." But her heart swelled with the idea of children, her own children.

They ran, like kids playing hide-and-seek, along the wide hall, opening doors and looking inside them. Either side of the front door were huge white doors, one leading to the drawing room and the other to a library. Poppy left the doors open, dragged the dust sheets off sofas and tables and then ran into the next room.

"You're a nightmare," said Drew, standing behind her with a dust sheet.

"But we don't need those anymore," she said, pulling it from him. "We live here now!"

"I suppose you're right," he said. "Come on, let's go upstairs."

Upstairs was arranged around a square landing, with a huge staircase in the middle. "This is the master bedroom," he said, pushing the door open.

The carpet was a little faded and the curtains had seen better days. It was like the house had given and given to its previous owners and now it was exhausted. But the room was huge, the ceiling so high Poppy had no idea how they would ever manage to change a lightbulb, and a bay window so enormous that when Poppy threw herself onto the bed, she could look out across miles and miles of sky.

"You like it?" said Drew, standing by the doorway.

She nodded. "I love it."

Something low in her gut shifted as she said it. A feeling like Christmas being over or Sunday night, like the taste in your mouth after you ate something sugary. But that was stupid. The house was perfect. She was just unsettled by the mirror, nervous and superstitious. Everything was fine. She repeated the words over and over inside her head.

"Good," he said, turning back onto the landing. Poppy got to her feet, following him.

"How did you know?" she asked. "How did you know how beautiful it would be?"

Drew threw open another door to a slightly smaller room, which looked out across the fields. "I had a feeling."

She followed Drew back downstairs and outside, trailing behind him as they walked around the garden. Everything had clearly been in full flower a couple of weeks ago. Now stems bent slightly, the weight of heavy, blowsy flowers dragging them down. The edge of the neat green lawn immediately outside the house was lined with a wall of lavender. It smelled sweet and light and nothing like the lavender fragrance her mother sprayed in the drawers of their house. Fat bees buzzed over it, drunk on pollen.

Poppy saw that there was a big wooden table on the lawn. The kind of table that other people would have sat around for family barbecues and summer parties. Happy, laughing people who had belonged here, but who were somewhere else now.

Something about it pricked at her, giving her just the smallest, almost unnoticeable sense of unease.

"They left so much stuff. It's weird. Like they just disappeared. Why would they do that?"

"Ralph said it was easier for them to leave their things than to get rid of them," said Drew. "They emigrated, didn't want the hassle of shipping it all. We don't need to keep anything that isn't to your taste. Ralph arranged for new bed linens and towels, all the basics, and had it all cleaned. I thought while we got started it would make life easier."

Poppy nodded. "Why did they go abroad?"

"No idea. You're sure you like it?" he asked as they went back into the house, using the side door. There was a rack next to it, filled with left-behind rubber boots. Long walks in the snow, children shrieking with snowballs, red noses. Woolly hats. A small hand in hers, belonging to someone who thought of her only as Mummy.

"It's perfect," she said. And it was true. The house was perfect. Big. Very, very big. But perfect. And what else could she possibly say?

It wasn't that she didn't like it. It was a feeling so much

more complicated than that. A twisty, ephemeral feeling that she didn't belong here.

"Let's eat something," she said, wondering if supper and a big glass of wine might do something to calm the twisting of her stomach.

The kitchen smelled like paraffin and wood polish. On the wooden table at the far end, squashed against the back wall, there was a package, wrapped up in old-fashioned parcel paper. "What's that?" she asked.

"Why don't you open it?"

"It's for me?"

"For us," he said, "but you should open it."

She ran her finger under the layer of brown paper, splitting the Sellotape from the paper and pulling it away. Inside was a long cream rectangular box. She looked up. "It's a box."

"It is indeed," Drew said. "Open it."

"Am I going to like it?"

"You really don't like surprises, do you?"

She laughed. "I'm starting to feel better about them." She lifted the lid off; there was a little resistance from the box. Inside was a layer of tissue paper. She pulled it away and lying in the box was a sign, pale green wood like the front door, with the words *Thursday House* carved into it. She beamed at Drew. "It's perfect."

"You should take it out of the box," said Drew.

"Why? I wasn't going to put it up this evening."

"Just do it." Drew had an expression on his face, one of Poppy's favorites. A quirk at the side of his lips and a little creasing around his eyes.

"All right," she said. She lifted the sign out of the box and underneath it there was a red leather box. A jewelry box.

"What is it?" she asked, knowing the answer. Drew didn't reply, he just gestured at her to open it. So she did. And sitting in the box was a ring. A fat round diamond with two smaller diamonds either side of it, on a warm gold band. She picked it up, marveling at it.

"I didn't think a sign for the house was very exciting on its own," said Drew.

Poppy slid it onto her finger, still speechless, and held her hand up to the light. It sat on top of the simple gold band she'd chosen for their wedding, rudely beautiful in the light.

"I didn't think it was fair that you missed out on the engagement ring, even if we weren't ever really engaged." Drew ran his hands around her waist, down her hips and into the back pockets of her jeans. "You look even more beautiful in England than you did on Ibiza," he said.

Poppy shook her head, trying to dislodge the shards of worry that had worked their way in. She looked down at her hand. It was beautiful. The most beautiful piece of jewelry that she had ever seen in her life.

"I love it," she said truthfully. "And I love you."

It wasn't the first time she had said it. She'd whispered it back to him when he'd told her weeks ago. But it was the first time that she had known without any doubt that it was true.

BEFORE

Late afternoon was Caroline's favorite part of the day. Homework was done, shoes were by the front door ready for school and a brief sense of calm descended before the bedtime rush of baths and stories. She felt no guilt about letting the girls watch TV while Jack messed around on his phone so that she could get supper ready in the kitchen. It was her little half-hour respite, between five thirty and six, to cook and clean and stand in the warm yellow kitchen, listening to the radio and not to anyone. So, when the kitchen door opened, she steeled herself to tell whoever it was to bugger off and leave her be. But it was Agnes.

"Can I help?" she asked.

"No, no, it's fine. You've had them all afternoon. Why don't you go and relax for a bit?"

She looked crestfallen. Something shifted inside Caroline. The more she got to know Agnes the younger she seemed. "Or you can come and sit with me while I sort supper out?"

Agnes took a seat at the breakfast bar, her fingers dancing over the marble worktop.

"Can I ask something?" she said eventually, her eyes

firmly planted on the floor. She wrapped a strand of hair around her finger.

Knowing from previous experience with Jack that these conversations were much less painful with a focus, Caroline took a bag of potatoes out of the vegetable rack. "Of course you can," she said. "Give me a hand with these?"

Agnes seemed relieved.

"So, what was the question?"

"When Ella got upset earlier . . ."

"Threw a tantrum."

Agnes smiled. "Yes. That."

"What about it?"

"What do you do when she gets like that?"

Caroline sat down at the breakfast bar. "You don't need to worry about that stuff—disciplining them. If they're playing up you tell Jim or me and we'll sort it out."

"I know." Agnes's neck was red. "I was wondering what you guys do, though."

Why was she asking this? Something about her question felt uneasy, but Caroline sensed it was important, and costing her a great deal to ask. "Well, it depends really. If she's really upset I'll try to talk to her about what's going on. Otherwise, if she's just pushing the boundaries to see what she can get away with then I'll put her on a time-out. When they're older, like Jack, it's more about taking away privileges like screen time or pocket money."

"You don't hit them?"

Caroline sat up, her muscles tensing. "No, we don't ever hit them. You haven't—"

"No, no, I wouldn't, I haven't—" Agnes sounded horrified. Relief flooded Caroline. She realized that she had never said that. She had never expressly forbidden any of her nannies to hit her children, just assuming they knew that in this day and age it was impossible.

"Is that—" Agnes stopped. She was clearly trying to seem offhand, casual. "Is that normal, not hitting them?"

Something about her tone made Caroline sure that these were questions she had been working her way up to asking. "I think so," Caroline said, trying to be measured. "Maybe when Jim and I were kids some parents did. But surely by the time you were a child parents weren't still—" She stopped, noticing that the potato Agnes had been peeling had slipped out of her hand. "Did your parents?"

"Mum," she said. "My dad left when I was little. We don't see him anymore."

"Did your mum hit you?"

Agnes nodded.

"Often?"

She nodded again.

"Darling, I'm not sure that sounds quite right. Maybe you should talk to her about it? She was on her own, had two of you. Sounds like she was under a lot of stress. She might have done things she's not proud of . . ."

"Mum is quite old-fashioned," Agnes replied, her eyes cast down. She looked nervous, as if she thought her mother might be able to hear her.

"Oh?"

"Catholic."

Caroline sensed that she needed to change the subject for the moment, leaving the door open to come back to it. "Ah. Hence Agnes."

She nodded again. "I was born on St. Agnes' Day. I wish

I could have been born any other day of the year. Everyone at my school laughed at it."

"You don't like your name?"

She raised one eyebrow. "Do you?"

Caroline wasn't sure what to say. No, she didn't like it. It was heavy and old-fashioned and didn't suit this sweet, lost young woman. "Jim uses his middle name instead," she volunteered, avoiding the question.

"Really? What's his first name?"

"Steven."

"He doesn't seem like a Steven."

"No," Caroline agreed. "When we met at university he was going by Jim; his middle name is James. And it stuck."

Agnes finished peeling the potatoes and took the pan to the sink, filling it with water. "Could I do that?"

"I don't see why not. What's your middle name?"

"Poppy."

Caroline smiled. "Well, that's much better. Suits you down to the ground."

"I can really do that? Just start using it?"

"Yep."

"I don't think that my mum would like that."

"Well," Caroline said, knowing that she was stepping over an invisible motherly line that should have remained uncrossed. "You're an adult. You don't have to ask her, or tell her. You can just do it."

CHAPTER 11

A week after they moved into Thursday House, Poppy sat on the bed in the master bedroom, painting her toenails. She lay back against the mass of pillows, wiggling her toes and admiring her handiwork. It was a bright orange color called Hopeful Harlot. She'd seen it on their trip to Bath that morning. She'd almost put it back when the register had displayed the price, twenty-seven pounds, but Drew had just swiped a card over the reader and they'd carried on toward lunch at a restaurant on a rooftop.

A noise caught her ear. She screwed the lid back onto the bottle, as if stopping what she was doing would enable her to hear better, and pulled open the bedroom door. Music, unquestionably music. Pretty, watery notes filling the house. She wandered down the stairs, watching her feet hit each step, and followed the sound, finding her way to the drawing room, the huge yellow and green room at the front of the house. It was one of Poppy's favorites. The uncomfortable, formal furniture favored by whoever had lived here before worked in here in a way that it just didn't in the smaller rooms.

She stopped in the door frame. The piano—a huge

mahogany thing that she'd given little thought to—had been under a dust sheet when they arrived. Now Drew sat with his back to her, drawing his fingers across the piano keys, apparently without effort. Was it like that for everything he did? Did he ever have to try? He'd picked up a wife and a house in a matter of months, things most people spent years doing. Maybe that was how it worked for him.

"Jesus Christ," she heard herself say.

Drew stopped and looked up. "Not a fan of Debussy?"

"You don't see it, do you?" The words came out heavier than she wanted them to. Clunky.

"What?"

"Your whole life is like the picture that comes free with the photo frame. Just, you know. Perfect. And you've simply dropped me in the middle of it. I don't get it."

Drew extended an arm toward her. She sat down next to him on the piano stool, trying to take up as little space as possible.

"I'm not perfect. No one is perfect. I promise you, I've made all sorts of fuck-ups. But is it really such a bad thing that we've got a nice house? A nice life?"

"It's not bad, it's just . . . a lot."

Drew laughed and pulled her toward him. "I know."

She leaned into him, feeling the warmth of his skin through his shirt.

"I need to talk to you about something," said Drew, pulling the wooden lid over the keys.

Poppy felt her muscles tighten. "Oh?"

"It's nothing bad," he countered. "Come with me?"

Poppy followed behind him, eyes focused on the back of his head, telling herself that it wouldn't always be like this, that she would learn to relax. They'd only been married a month and a half. Known each other less than three.

"This is going to be an awkward conversation," said Drew as they reached the study. He stood behind the desk, which sat like a leather-topped island between them. She felt a pricking under her arms, like she was starting to sweat. What was he about to say?

"Oh?" she said, forcing her face to stay neutral.

Drew took an envelope out of his desk drawer and passed it over to her. A thick white one with a window. The kind of letter that banks and businesses sent.

What had he found out? She could hear the blood thumping in her head.

"What is it?"

"Open it."

So she did. And out came three little plastic rectangles with A P SPENCER written on them.

"Credit cards?" she said, the hammering of her heart slowing as her eyebrows knitted together in confusion.

Drew stood up, taking the cards from her and laying them on the desk. He pointed at the first one. It was granite-colored. "Credit card. You use that for any major purchases, say anything over a few thousand pounds. The limit is thirty thousand."

Poppy put her head to one side. "What the fuck?"

Drew put his hands up. "I told you. Awkward conversation. Just hear me out, OK?"

"OK."

"I'll be back at work next week, so stands to reason that you need money to do whatever you want—decorate the house, see friends, go into town, whatever. So, the credit card is for major purchases, anything over a few grand goes on there. This one"—he pointed at the green one—"is your debit card. It comes out of our main account. That's for everyday stuff, getting cash out, petrol, food shopping, that sort of stuff. There's about three hundred thousand pounds in there at the moment."

Poppy nodded, her eyes wide. "And that one?" She pointed to the gold one.

"That's your private account."

"I already have a private account."

"I know, and you should keep that one. But I thought it might be nice for you to have access to some private money, away from the joint accounts. Not that I'll be checking up on you, but if you want to do something private or treat a friend or anything like that, that's what that account is for. I've put some money in there, ten grand, and if you want more you can transfer it over from our joint debit account. There's a list of passwords in the envelope, which I'm told is a deeply unsafe thing to do, so best if you don't lose it."

Poppy picked up the cards. "Should I give you some big soul-searching speech about how I can't possibly take this because I haven't earned it and it's not mine?"

Drew laughed. "You can if you want. But you know how I feel about this. It's our money. So it's not worth it. And," he went on, seeming emboldened by her response, "I thought it might be worth paying off any existing debt."

"Debt?"

"Yes, Poppy, debt. It's when you owe someone money and they charge you interest," he teased.

"I know what debt is, you nob."

"Good. So I'll put you in touch with James Griffiths. He handles my finances—our finances—and he'll talk you through the process of getting rid of anything like student loans or overdrafts."

She shook her head. There was an odd sort of lightness inside the cavity of her chest. The idea that there would be no more red-stamped letters, no more panic-inducing phone calls from unknown numbers.

She felt her face lifting into a huge smile, one that she had no control over. "Why are you doing this?"

"Because there's no point you accumulating interest on loans that could easily be paid off, and it's better for your credit rating to start using . . ." He paused. "Oh. You mean this?" He gestured between the two of them. "You really don't see it, do you?"

Poppy put her head to one side. "What you see in me? No. I can't say I do, really. I mean, I know I'm young, and the sex is good . . ."

Drew laughed. "Do you want the speech?"

"The speech?"

"About all the reasons I fell in love with you and why I'm never letting you go?"

She shook her head. Maybe she did want it. But not now. Not after he'd just given her so much. She smiled. "I know it's the sex stuff."

"Yes." He laughed. "It's the sex stuff."

She stretched up to kiss him. "Do you know where the best place to shop for a private jet is?"

"Oh, it's always more efficient to rent planes than to buy them," started Drew. He caught sight of her expression and laughed again. "God," he said. "Before I met you, I swear I only laughed once or twice a year."

Poppy rested her head on his chest. "I think technically that was a comment about the past," she teased.

"You're quite right," he said. "My mistake."

BEFORE

"I think we should ask Poppy to join us for the party tonight," Caroline told Jim as she chopped garlic.

"Really?" asked Jim.

"You don't think so?"

"Well." Jim straightened up from where he'd been playing fridge Tetris, trying to make the huge weekly shopping fit. "She's probably got plans."

Caroline shook her head. "No, I asked her yesterday. She's in tonight. I hate the idea of her sitting in her room on her own while we're all down here."

"Is it strange that she doesn't have a social life of her own?"

Scraping the knife along the board, Caroline swept the garlic onto the raw chicken, which would soon look delicious but right now was a little stomach-turning. "She does, but her friends are all either traveling or doing high-powered internships. She goes for drinks with them after work sometimes."

"Shouldn't she be doing that? Interning or something?"

"With what money?"

"Money?"

"Her parents don't live in London, Jim. Internships don't pay."

"All right, all right." He put his hands up, as if she was holding a gun at him. "Why are you so defensive of her?"

Caroline snorted. "I'm not. It's just . . ." She trailed off, hoping he might interject with something. Prove he knew her at least a little better than she thought he did.

Jim hated this game; she knew that. Any attempt to encourage him to reach a conclusion on his own rather than having it explained to him was dubbed "playing games"—something Jim maintained that he never did. He let out a long sigh. Was this going to trigger a low? She'd never known anyone who was subsumed by misery like Jim was. Of course, she would never call it sulking, not to his face. She felt guilty for thinking it, tried to chase up some sympathy from the recesses of her mind. But sometimes, when his dark moods meant she had to do everything for him, the kids and herself, it was hard to find. In the old days, before they had kids, he could go days without getting out of bed if he was in one of his bad patches.

He'd been better since they'd had kids, making a superhuman effort some of the time. But starting any kind of fight was a risk—he could flip into a bad place at the drop of a hat. It might not last as long as it had when he was younger, but she still couldn't risk it, not when they were about to have friends over. And anyway, these good periods were precious. She didn't want to waste time arguing when they had already lost so many days to his misery.

"I feel protective of her, all right?" she explained, putting the chopping board in the dishwasher. Poppy always washed it by hand, so that the wood didn't warp in the hot water, but

Caroline thought life was too short. You could buy another chopping board, but there was no money in the world that would bring back the wasted seconds that trickled down the drain with the garlicky water. "She clearly doesn't get on with her mum; her dad bailed years ago. She's young and she's alone in London, and I want to make sure she's OK."

Jim crossed the kitchen and, to Caroline's surprise, wrapped his arms around her. "I'm sorry," he said.

"Sorry?"

"I know I don't always get these things. I know you wish I did."

Caroline relaxed her body, letting her head rest on his chest. He was so comfortingly, wonderfully solid. Over six feet, with a sturdy trunk. Muscle, covered with fat but still muscle. He would swing the kids around, one on each arm, while they screamed with laughter. Sleeping next to his heavy warmth every night, knowing he was always there, silent and still, was one of the great joys of her life. She shouldn't be so impatient with him.

"I know it's hard for you. Thanks for trying," Caroline said.

It had been months since he'd had a proper bad patch. Their counselor had told Caroline that she had to learn to relax into this new status quo, that things wouldn't go back to the way that they used to be. To believe that things were going to be OK.

"We don't have to ask her," she said into his chest. "I just thought it might be friendly." She felt Jim drop a kiss on top of her head.

"Of course we should ask her," he said, as if it had been his idea from the very beginning.

CHAPTER 12

On Sunday morning Poppy woke to find the other side of the bed empty. Drew was already dressed, sitting on a velvet chair in the corner of the room with an espresso cup in his hand.

"Good morning," she sighed, twisting her body into a delicious stretch.

"Good morning." Drew smiled, folding the paper down. "What shall we do today? Last day before I have to abandon you for work, worst luck."

"Let's go into the village."

"What village?" he asked.

"Linfield, duh."

"Why would we go into Linfield?"

"Because it's where we live?" said Poppy, getting out of bed and pulling on a dressing gown. "And I want to see it."

"There's nothing there," said Drew. "I've been down there before. Post office, bloody huge war memorial and the kind of village shop that's only open six hours a week."

Poppy rolled her eyes. "Well, if there's nothing there then it won't take us very long to see, will it?"

"We could go into Bath. Or . . ." he said, running his

hands over the silky fabric of her dressing gown, "we could just spend the day in bed. Seems like a good use of my last day of freedom."

"Nice try," she said, pulling away. "We can go back to bed after we go to the village. Stop being a snob."

"I'm not a snob," he called to Poppy's turned back.

If Drew was annoyed about Poppy winning the argument, about coming to the village, he hid it well. They parked on a slab of road at the top of Linfield Hill. It overlooked a couple of broken swings and a dirty slide.

"Enjoying the beautiful view?" asked Drew.

"See? Snob," she replied, searching the vista for something that might disprove Drew's view that Linfield was shit. "Come on, there's bound to be a pub on the High Street."

Drew bristled. Poppy was starting to realize that he didn't do the word no. At least not when it came to her. It was like she was supposed to know what he wanted, or didn't want. And she could feel from the way his forearms had tensed, from the lines between his eyebrows, that he didn't want to go out in search of the local pub.

"One drink," she said consolingly. "And then we can go home, or we can go somewhere else."

"There's supposed to be a great place over in Beech-brook," he said. "Ralph was raving about it."

"We don't want awards," said Poppy. "We want a local."

She pushed the door open and drank in the heavy scent of beer, bleach and fried food. A middle-aged woman in the far corner was wrapping metal cutlery in paper napkins. She glanced up and then went back to her work.

It was impossible to tell what color the carpet had been originally. Blue? Red? Decades of ash and booze had clearly settled into it, leaving a color that had no name and the faintest trace of a diamond pattern. The pub was empty but for a couple of blokes at a table in the back, looking down into their pints.

"I feel like I'm fourteen again," said Poppy. Drew raised his eyebrows disapprovingly. "Oh, you weren't in the pub at fourteen?" She was pushing her luck now, she knew that.

"No," he replied, a little smile on his lips.

"Did you prefer private wine tastings?" It was becoming a little game. Every time Drew let her get away with a question she would take as much as she could and stash it away, building up a private little gallery of details about him in her head. It was impossible to predict what he would allow her to push and what would turn him silent. But maybe one day she would be able to predict it.

To Poppy's relief, Drew returned her grin. "Yes, as a teenager I mostly went on vineyard crawls." Poppy giggled.

"What can I get you?" asked the woman, putting her stack of cutlery on a table with a few bottles of ketchup and brown sauce. Poppy leaned forward, putting her hands on the sticky counter.

"Peroni, please," she said.

"Two," said Drew. Their voices seemed to go dead in the padded quietness of the room, dulled by the overstuffed armchairs and ocean of sticky carpet.

"Visiting for the day?" asked the woman, pulling the glasses down from the shelf. She moved quickly, as if the bar was packed with customers braying for booze rather than one couple.

"No," said Poppy. "We just moved here." The barmaid's cleavage was hoisted by two white straps, visible under a black tank top. The straps made indents in her plump shoulders. Her red-black hair was scraped aggressively back from her face. She reminded Poppy of home.

The woman behind the bar beamed. "Oh, you should have said! Welcome to the village. When did you move in?" The beer crept up the long glass, a foamy white head forming at the top.

"About a week ago," said Drew. Was she imagining it, or did he flinch? "How much do I owe you?" He pulled his wallet from his jeans.

"Drew!" said Poppy, gently poking him in the side. "Sorry, my husband doesn't do small talk, apparently. We moved in on the eighth."

"Settling in all right?" asked the barmaid.

"It's gorgeous," said Poppy. "I love it. I'd been living in London for years."

"Bit of a change of pace." She chuckled. "I've been here twenty years, and by local standards that still makes me a newcomer. Whereabouts are you living?"

"Thursday House," said Poppy, enjoying the words on her tongue, reveling in the newness of it. "Over on Croft Lane."

The woman's face lost its brightness and she put both beers down unceremoniously on the counter. "Six pounds," she said.

Poppy, confused, reached into her bag to find her purse, but Drew was quicker, handing over a ten-pound note. "Keep the change," he said, his voice flat. Before Poppy could offer to help, Drew had taken the drinks and was through the door. Looking back over her shoulder at the barmaid's grim face, she followed him. Outside Drew found a bench, facing into the sun.

Poppy sat down. "That was weird."

Drew squinted into the sun, patting his pockets for his sunglasses. "Mm," he replied. "That's small towners for you."

"Are you still annoyed we didn't go into Bath?" she asked. Drew blinked, apparently surprised by the directness of her question.

"Not at all." He took a long drink from the pint glass. A bead of condensation slipped down it like a tear. "Though," he added, "I'm not sure this place is going to be getting a Michelin star any time soon."

"It's still so nice," she said, putting her feet up on the bench and leaning her weight on her hands. "I can't believe summer's nearly over."

"Long may it last," Drew replied, tipping his face up to the sun.

They sat in companionable silence, eyes closed under their sunglasses, enjoying the sun on their skin.

The pub door swung open and out walked a man with a ruddy face. He was wearing a navy-blue sweatshirt and had the kind of pregnant stomach that only came from several decades of hard drinking.

"All right?" He smiled, dragging a match over the little box in his hand and lighting a cigarette.

"Good, thanks," said Poppy. She felt his eyes on her bare legs and dropped them under the table, smoothing her skirt over her thighs.

"Here for the weekend?" he asked.

"No," said Poppy. "We just moved here."

He looked surprised. "Moved to Linfield?"

"Just outside," she said.

"Where?" asked the man. "I've lived here my whole life; I know it like the back of my hand." He held up the front of his hand and Poppy dropped her gaze, wishing she hadn't allowed this conversation to happen.

"Croft Lane," said Drew. Poppy noticed that his glass was nearly empty, not much more than a cloud of white foam at the bottom. Hers was still almost full. She took a long drink from it.

"Which house?" asked the man. Was it Poppy's imagination or had his tone changed?

"Thursday House," she replied. Too late she saw Drew's expression and realized he was willing her silently not to say the house's name. The man with the red face picked up his glass from their table. He was close enough that Poppy could smell him: fresh and stale beer mixed together. He opened his mouth, as if he was about to say something, and then seemed to think better of it. He turned on his heel, walked back up the stone steps and slammed the door behind him, rattling the glass in the window and shaking the whole frame of the pub.

"What was that about?" she murmured. She looked down at their legs, parallel to each other. Drew's tanned and hard, spread with blond hairs. Hers shorter and freckled.

"What?"

"Oh come on." She turned to face him, holding her beer between two hands. "What do you mean 'what'?"

"That bloke?"

"Yes, that bloke! Why didn't you want me to tell him where we live? How did you know he was going to lose his shit?"

Drew snorted. "Such an elegant turn of phrase."

"Seriously. What was that? Why does he hate us? And the barmaid."

Drew sighed and wound his arm around her. Not for the first time she reveled at the warmth that came from his body. "I thought this might happen."

"What might happen?" Poppy was frustrated now.

"Look." Drew sighed again. "There's no easy way to say this. But when you've got certain things, when you live somewhere like we do, when you're . . ." He trailed off.

"Rich," said Poppy.

"For want of a better word, yes. People don't always warm to you."

Poppy traced her finger down the outside of her glass. "You think he doesn't like us because we live at Thursday House?"

"These villages," said Drew, "they've got a way about them. If you live in the village you belong here. If you live in one of the big houses, you don't. It's a sort of 'us and them' thing."

"'Us and them,'" repeated Poppy slowly. "I've never been an 'us' before."

Drew squeezed her a little. "That's why I didn't want us to come. I didn't want you to be upset, to feel as if we're not liked here."

"They really don't like us because you've got money?"

"We," he corrected her.

"Sorry," she said.

"Don't apologize. I'm sorry. I didn't mean to snap. I just want you—need you—to realize that it's our house. Our money. That's what being married means."

Poppy nodded. "I know. At least, I know that's how it is for normal people. But this isn't exactly normal, is it?"

"Who would want to be normal?"

They laughed, and then Poppy's phone started to buzz on the table, angrily loud against the wood. She looked down at the display and recognized the number instantly.

"You're not going to answer?" asked Drew.

Poppy shook her head. "It's my mother." The screen went dark. "You must think I'm a complete bitch," she said, pulling at a strand of wood that had splintered off the table.

"Why would I think that?"

"Not wanting to speak to her."

"I'm sure you have your reasons."

"But with everything that happened to you—losing your family in the accident, growing up alone. It must seem so selfish not to want to talk to her."

Drew looked away. "Does she know that we're married?"

"Yes," she said, looking down at a bead of blood on her finger. "I called her from Ibiza. Told her what we'd done."

"What we'd done," said Drew. "You make it sound like a crime."

"As far as she's concerned . . ." Poppy trailed off. "No family, no church. To her, that's a crime."

Drew drank from his glass. "You didn't tell me that you'd spoken to her."

"Should I have done?"

Drew shrugged. "Why didn't you?"

"I didn't think you'd want me to tell you about it."

"Why?"

"I don't know," she said. "All that stuff about the past not mattering, about just starting again together, and ignoring everything that came before . . ."

"It's supposed to free us up, allow us to not get bogged down in every bad relationship or terrible university haircut. Not cut you off from your family."

"You sound pissed off."

"I'm not."

"Then why are you having a go at me?"

"I didn't think I was."

"Sorry." Poppy dropped her gaze. "I feel bad about avoiding my mum and I'm taking it out on you."

"You don't have to talk to her. Just because you're related to someone doesn't mean you're obliged to keep them in your life. I think sometimes you have to give up on the idea that someone is going to change."

Poppy nodded, not trusting herself to speak without crying.

The first time Poppy had been to Gina's house she had felt like she was being punched in the stomach. Watching Gina's siblings, nieces and cousins pile on top of her, hugging her. Seeing the adults ply her with food and tell her she was too thin. It was everything Poppy had read about in books, watched on TV and silently ached for. The love, the warmth, the noise. The solid safety of belonging to a unit. It was what she had searched for as a nanny, trying to insert herself into other people's families.

"You had a terrible university haircut?" She smiled up at him, composing herself.

"There are no surviving pictures."

"You're so lucky you went to university before the internet was invented."

"It was invented, thank you very much."

She and Drew would have children soon. No more standing on the outside of other people's families, trying to become a part of them. A proper family, the kind that no one could take away.

CHAPTER 13

Wednesday morning was bright, but cold.

"Do you want pancakes?" Poppy asked, hitching up the strap top of her pajamas and opening the fridge to find the milk.

Drew appeared from the hall, dressed in a shirt and trousers. He shook his head. "I have to be in London in a couple of hours." He looked tired.

Poppy dropped her spatula. "Do you really have to go?"

"Yes," said Drew. "I'm sorry. Have you seen my black shoes?"

"You said you might be able to work from home some of the time? I was on my own yesterday, and Monday, and there's still so much to do to get us properly moved in. And you're going away all of the week after next." She couldn't find the words to tell him the truth. That she hated being alone here.

Drew had found his shoes and was lacing them up. "Poppy, I've got to go to the station. I'll be back later. I'm sorry. But I've told you, you need extra hands—hire someone."

"And I've told you," she replied, wishing she were wearing something more impressive than shorts and a tank top while trying to assert herself to her husband, "that I will. But I just haven't yet. And I can't get it all ready by myself. You did say you'd help. I don't want to be—" *On my own here*, she was going to say. She stopped herself, realizing it would sound mad.

Drew picked up his bag. "Darling, I'd much rather stay here with you, but I have got to go." He kissed her forehead and disappeared through the kitchen door. Poppy stared at the space where he had stood.

The silence of the house seemed to swallow her. Trying to pull herself together, she put the kitchen radio on, fiddling for a station she recognized. It hummed with static and crackle. Drew had had it on Radio 4 earlier without any problem. She played with the dial on the side of it, but the crackling didn't stop. It was an old brown thing, left behind by the previous owners like so much of the stuff that filled her home. It must be twenty, thirty years old. Was that why it wasn't working? She felt for an antenna at the back and yanked it up. The radio emitted a scream of static, punishingly, painfully loud. She threw her hands up to her ears by instinct, and then pulled at the plug that connected it to the wall. Childish anger welled up inside her and she smacked her hand against the front of the radio. It hurt. The radio was, unsurprisingly, unaffected. The house rang with silence once again. Why was it that everything she tried, no matter how totally simple, seemed to go wrong?

Poppy picked up her phone and a bottle of water and went back upstairs to bed. She pulled the curtains closed, lay on her back and stared at the ceiling. If she could fall asleep for two hours then she could get up and shower.

Shave. Moisturize. That would take her up to lunchtime. Then she could make lunch—that would take an hour. After that she'd clean up—she could stretch that to an hour if she did it slowly—and then it would only be a few hours until Drew came home. Maybe she'd go into town and do some food shopping. The fridge and the cupboards were full, but there must be something they needed?

Drew had asked if she was bored. And she had said no. There was no way to admit to it without sounding painfully ungrateful. "Thanks for this mansion you bought us, thanks for making it so that I never have to work again, but actually I'm so lonely and bored that I almost miss being screamed at by Mrs. Henderson."

There was no point in sulking. She should do what he had told her to do: find someone to come and help out with everything that needed doing. The prospect of someone else moving around the house, making noises and chatting to her, was a comforting one.

Cleaner Linfield, she typed. There was a number, and a name. She tapped at the phone number and felt her heartbeat quicken as it rang. She loathed calling strangers. Poppy had never understood people who didn't hate the intimacy of someone else's voice on the other end, a stranger whom you had to connect with without being able to see them or glean anything about them.

"Hello?" came a voice.

"Um, hi, yes, sorry," she said, sitting up. "I found your number online. I'm looking for a cleaner."

"Right," said the woman at the other end, who sounded

like she was in the middle of doing something else. "How many bedrooms?"

"Eight," said Poppy, guiltily.

"Eight?"

"Yeah. We've just moved in. It's, um"—she paused—"quite a big place."

The woman laughed. "Sounds like you need help. Where are you?"

"Just outside of Linfield."

"Which road?"

"Croft Lane." The speaker on her phone crackled. "Hello?" she said.

"We don't have anyone available," the woman said, and the line went dead.

Turning onto her front and pulling a pillow under her elbows, she went back to Google, typing the same words. There was an agency, based in Bath. That would be better. More professional.

"Hello," she said when a woman picked up. "I'm looking for a cleaner." That was better. She'd planned what she was going to say while it rang. She sounded far more convincing; she would not be cut off this time.

"Name?"

"Mrs. Poppy Spencer," she said. The Spencer part had become second nature. It was the "Mrs." that felt like it belonged to someone else.

"Bedrooms?"

"Eight."

There was no reaction this time, just a pause while she noted the information. Poppy pictured her, sitting behind a desk with a headset on, looking at the clock and breaking down the day into manageable chunks. An hour until a cigarette break, three hours until lunch. Six hours until a coffee break. Eight until home time.

"Where are you based?"

Poppy recited the address once again.

"We've got someone who can come tomorrow. She's new to the company. Is that all right?"

"Yes, totally fine," Poppy replied, too quickly. "That's great, thanks so much."

There. She had achieved something. When Drew came home she would be able to tell him that she had hired a cleaner. Now all she had to do was fill the rest of the day.

BEFORE

A beam of sunlight fell across Caroline's computer screen, obscuring the words she was wrestling with. She got up, taking the shabby curtain in one hand and starting to pull it across the glass. Down in the garden she could see the children playing with the hose. The children and Poppy, she corrected herself. She had found herself thinking of them collectively as "the children" more and more lately.

Poppy wore denim jeans and a white bikini top printed with cherries. She was putting her thumb over the top of the hose to make the water spray sideways in all directions. The children were shrieking, running in and out of the water, which was always freezing. Jack was collecting water in his hands and throwing it at Poppy, aiming primarily at her chest. Caroline smiled to herself. This would inevitably be his first crush. Perhaps she had accidentally given him a type for life. Would all future girlfriends be redheaded and domestic? she wondered. The idea gave her a strange, jealous sort of ache in her chest. She tried to push it away. She refused to be one of those mothers who clung to her son, wanting him to be a little boy forever. His interest in Poppy was normal. Healthy.

It felt strange to watch them like this. She was seeing her children like other people did, how they behaved when they weren't aware of being watched by their mother. Were they this happy and carefree when they played with her? When was the last time that they had all messed around together? The ache in her chest doubled.

She could go downstairs and join in. But even as the thought occurred to her she knew it wasn't possible. This was the sort of rough, silly play that Mummy didn't do. This wasn't her domain. Her job was to be consistent. Reliable. Boring, even. That was what they needed from her.

At the end of the garden the door to Jim's shed opened. It wasn't a shed really; it had lights and power and heating, all installed at great expense because Jim claimed he needed his own space, that he couldn't concentrate in the house with the children shouting and interrupting. Caroline strained her eyes, trying to make out Jim's expression. Was he pissed off at the interruption? All three children stopped, looking at their father. Poppy dropped the hose. She looked terrified. Something in Caroline swelled, a raw animal instinct. What had happened to her before she came here to make her so afraid?

Suddenly all five of them were laughing. Jack picked up the hose and sprayed Jim. Jim took it back and sprayed Ella. Poppy, tentative, picked up the hose and aimed it meekly at Jim's feet. She looked bowled over by her own boldness. Jim chuckled, saying something that Caroline couldn't hear, and then picked Poppy up, throwing her upward. She squirmed and giggled.

Funny, Caroline thought, how he doesn't mind being interrupted to play outside with the kids when Poppy is around. She tried to convince herself it was perfectly natural that Jim wanted to play with them now, that it was sunny and warm and everyone was in a better mood than usual. But she couldn't shake the niggling memory of all the times he had slammed the door on her and locked himself away, claiming his work came first, that he couldn't be expected to be Mary Poppins and bring in a salary.

Jack ran toward his father, trying to pull Poppy out of his arms. Jim laughed and pulled away. He couldn't see it. He must be missing the expression of anger on Jack's face, his fury at his father for holding Poppy in a way that he couldn't. Caroline sighed. Jack hit his father's arms, pretending to be playful. Jim put Poppy down and rubbed his arm, saying something to Jack, the expression on his face no longer jovial. Jack turned from the garden and stormed into the kitchen. Caroline felt the slam of the door shudder through the house.

That night she sat in bed filing her fingernails while Jim padded around, looking for a book he was convinced they used to own.

"Jack was a little shit earlier," he said, bending down to look at the bottom shelf of their bookcase.

"Oh?" Caroline wasn't sure why she pretended not to have seen the whole scene unfold. "What happened?"

"We were playing in the garden, I picked Agnes—sorry, Poppy—up, and he went for me."

"Went for you?"

"Started punching me. We were play fighting but he really went at it."

Caroline nodded. "You know why, don't you?"

Jim looked up. "No?"

"He's got a thumping great crush on her."

Jim smiled. "Who could blame him?"

Caroline raised one eyebrow. "Careful."

"Poor kid. Unrequited love's a killer."

"You don't think we need to do anything?" said Caroline.

"Like what?"

"I don't know. Tell her not to be alone with him in his room or anything. In case he tries it on. I suppose if she were a bloke and Jack were a nearly fifteen-year-old girl wouldn't you have read the riot act?"

"There it is!" Jim pulled the book triumphantly from the shelf. "I knew we had it."

"Jim?"

"Yes?"

"What I just said. About Poppy and Jack. What do you think?"

"Oh. No, I don't think we need to. He's too shy to try anything, and even if he did, she'd come to us."

He flopped down heavily on the bed, lying on top of the duvet. Caroline looked down at his long, hairy legs. "All right," she said. "Goodnight. Love you."

"Love you too."

CHAPTER 14

By Thursday the prospect of another day alone in the house was unbearable. Poppy jumped every time there was a noise in another room, and wandered from room to room trying to shake the feeling that she was being watched. She put the TV or radio on in every possible room to try to drown out the silence and counted the hours until Drew came home. Every day she had resolved to talk to Drew about the house. She hoped that saying the words out loud might help: telling him that she didn't feel at home here without him, that she didn't feel like the house wanted her. Nothing worked for her like it did for him. Maybe that mirror hadn't been an omen, but a curse. But when Drew came home and lit up at the sight of the house, she lost her nerve. There was no way to explain her fear of a pile of bricks without sounding mad.

Poppy looked at the bedroom clock. It was 8:45 a.m. Gina would have just dropped the Winterson kids at school and would be wending her way back home with the youngest of her charges. They hadn't spoken properly since Poppy had gotten back to England. Her fear of showing off had stopped her from sending pictures or updates, but now that she thought about it, it was unlike Gina to go quiet on her.

To Poppy's surprise, Gina answered on the second ring.
"Uhuh?"

"Gina, it's me."

"Uhuh?"

"It's Poppy, you nightmare."

There was a shuffling noise and then Gina's voice, slightly less slurred. "Sorry, I just woke up."

"What? I thought term had started again?"

"It has."

"So who took the kids to school?"

"Fern." This registered as odd. Mrs. Winterson always, always left the house before the kids were up. She worked half the time on Harley Street and the other half volunteering with kids.

"Why wasn't Fern at work?"

"I'm off sick."

"You're sick?"

"Not sick sick. Booze flu. Why'd you call? I thought I'd lost you to the New Boyfriend Bermuda Triangle for at least another month."

To talk to you, she wanted to say. *You're my best friend. You're supposed to be interested in what's going on in my life. Since when did I need a reason?*

"Oh, it's nothing," she said. "Just to catch up, I guess."

"Bullshit. What's going on?"

"It's stupid." Poppy played with the edge of the duvet cover. "It's just a big house and I don't really know what to do with myself. I'm fine. I just feel like I'm playing pretend."

There was a rustling noise as Gina sat up in bed, a sign

that she was about to take Poppy's problem, however stupid it was, seriously. Poppy felt a warm rush of love for her.

"Have you done anything to the house yet?"

"I hired a cleaner. She's coming this afternoon."

"What about the décor? You've been talking about wanting to decorate your own place for as long as I've known you. Why aren't you doing it?"

"I'm going to, I just . . ." Just what? What was the reason? She didn't want Drew to think she was ungrateful for not loving the house just exactly as it came? She didn't know where to start? She was worried that she wouldn't do it right and Drew would be reminded that she didn't come from his world? Or maybe it was something deeper.

"You need to do something," Gina said. She sounded happier. Gina loved giving Poppy advice. Or maybe she loved giving everyone advice, Poppy was never quite sure. "Put your stamp on the place. You'll feel more like you belong there if you do."

"I guess." Poppy tried to summon some enthusiasm.

"Don't guess, do it. Pick one thing you don't like and change it. What's the problem?"

"What if Drew doesn't like it?"

"You don't like it right now, what's the difference?"

"He bought it."

"Is he shitty with you about this stuff?" Gina suddenly sounded concerned.

"No, no, not at all."

"You're sure? He doesn't get angry or anything?"

"No, God no," Poppy assured her. She was telling the truth. "He's never even raised his voice. I feel like if he came home and I'd painted the whole place black he'd be like, OK, your call. That's the problem, I guess."

Gina gave a dirty little laugh from the other end of the line. "You've found a filthy rich husband who doesn't complain. Pops, you need to relax, you've got it made."

Poppy laughed. "OK, OK. I'll try your thing. Love you."

Gina made a high-pitched kissing noise and hung up.

Poppy wandered down into the hall, barefoot in her pajamas, pushing doors open and looking into rooms. One change. That was what she had promised Gina.

Poppy spent the morning in Bath. She drove into town, parked with miraculous ease and then happened upon the most amazing home interiors shop she'd ever seen. Hushed and dark, it was crammed with beautiful things, all illuminated by warm gold light. Poppy wandered around the shop running her fingers over glass decanters and velvet cushions. Eventually she decided on the perfect lampshade. It was blue silk with a copper-gold interior. "Have you checked the size of the light fitting?" asked the slender girl behind the counter.

"Yes," Poppy lied. It would inevitably fit one of the lights in the house, though it would have been showing off to tell the girl that.

Delighted with herself, she'd taken the lampshade, wrapped in tissue and placed in a huge box, and driven back to the house full of good intentions. Gina was right. It was her home. She just needed to assert herself. Wrap the house around her and Drew, not the other way around.

CHAPTER 15

Poppy signaled, turning the car sharply into the drive and hoping that the display on the dashboard was wrong, that she wasn't back late. But of course it wasn't wrong, and standing on the front steps of the house was a teenage girl in black trousers and a T-shirt with "Merrie Maids" written on it.

"I'm so sorry," said Poppy, slamming the car door shut and taking her bags from the trunk. "I lost track of time. Have you been here long?"

The girl raised one heavily drawn-in eyebrow. "About ten minutes. Are you Poppy Spencer?"

"Yes," said Poppy, fumbling for her keys in her handbag. There was an unquestionable air of suspicion on the girl's face.

"I'm Kay-Lynne," the girl said.

"Nice to meet you, Caitlin."

"No, Kay-Lynne," said the girl, following her into the house.

"Oh, sorry." Poppy could hear her accent slipping back to its original, away from the rounded vowels she'd started copying all those years ago, wanting to sound like the rest of Caroline's family. "Nice to meet you."

"This is a big house."

"Yes." Poppy looked up, as if the hall were news to her. "Come to the kitchen, I'll make you a tea and we'll work out what we're doing?"

Kay-Lynne shrugged. "Sure."

Poppy put the kettle on and steadied herself. She was at least ten years older than this girl. This was her house. She lived here. She belonged here. Kay-Lynne was infuriatingly comfortable. The first time Poppy had visited a house for an interview she'd been so nervous she'd got on the wrong tube and cried all the way there. Kay-Lynne clearly didn't share that kind of nervousness. She went under the sink and started to look at Poppy's cleaning supplies. "I've got products in my bag that I can use," she said, standing up. "But that's an extra seven pounds."

"That's fine," said Poppy, pouring water into the cups. "Do you want milk and sugar?"

Kay-Lynne nodded. "How long have you lived here?"

"Nearly two weeks."

Kay-Lynne looked around. "You got everything unpacked quick."

"Lots of the furniture and things were left here by the previous owners."

Kay-Lynne had unpacked various brightly colored bottles and sponges. "Why?"

"They didn't want it, they were going abroad."

"Where to?"

"I don't know," said Poppy, feeling stupid. She took a seat

on the sofa by the window and pulled her legs up to her chest. Where *had* the previous owners gone?

"That's weird," Kay-Lynne said.

"I guess it is."

A silence settled between them, broken only by the intermittent spritzing of kitchen spray. Kay-Lynne was methodical and precise in the way that she cleaned, and the counters, which Poppy had thought were quite clean, were coming up with an unfamiliar shine.

"You've not had a cleaner before, have you?" said Kay-Lynne after a while.

Poppy flushed. "No, no, I haven't. Why?"

"Most people don't feel the need to sit there and talk to me."

"Sorry," Poppy apologized. "I just thought maybe you might want some help, and . . ." She grappled for something to say that didn't sound completely stupid. "And I used to be a nanny, and do cleaning, and sometimes I liked having company."

Kay-Lynne's thick eyebrows moved up toward her peroxide hair. "You were a nanny?"

Poppy nodded. "Six years."

"You still do that?"

She shook her head. "No, I'm not working at the moment. I'm going to finish getting us moved in and then I might retrain . . ."

"How long you been together?"

There was no way that Poppy was going to watch the firework-display reaction on Kay-Lynne's wide face that was inevitable if she told the truth. "Five years," she said. "We got married earlier this summer."

Kay-Lynne looked her up and down, pausing on her ring finger. "What does your husband do?"

"He's in finance."

"Banking?"

Yes? No? Poppy paused for a moment. "Yes," she said.

"Is he from round here originally?"

"No."

"Where's he from?"

Poppy cleared her throat, fumbling for something to say, anything other than *I don't know*. Literally anything. "London," she said eventually, her voice high and strange.

Kay-Lynne laughed. "You looked confused for a moment there! Mind you, when my mum and dad went to get registered to get married he got her birthday wrong when they asked him, and she went mental in front of the woman from the council . . ."

Poppy made the right faces and noises while Kay-Lynne cleaned and talked, but inside she was burning.

"Are you OK to get on if I go upstairs and do some work?" Poppy asked, already retreating toward her bedroom.

How was she supposed to go through the rest of her life looking like a complete fucking idiot every time someone asked her a question about her husband? How many times would she have to lie about where he came from or where he grew up or any of it? But what was the other option? Tell him that she had changed her mind? That she wanted to know everything about him, to savor every detail. And then what? Tell him what had happened with the Walkers and just hope that there was some tiny chance he loved her enough to overlook it?

No chance.

CHAPTER 16

Eventually, after delivering a monologue about how Poppy had the wrong kind of vacuum and too many stairs, Kay-Lynne left. Poppy said something half-hearted about having her back for five hours a week, all the time trying to think of a good excuse to never see her again, without having to lie to the agency and say she'd done a bad job. She had left the entire ground floor gleaming. But Poppy could barely look her in the eye while she handed over the cash, tipping embarrassingly generously in the hope it might distract from her awkwardness. She watched as Kay-Lynne drove away, and then closed the door, awash with relief.

She didn't need someone to help clean. She had cleaned people's houses for years. She was good at it. She could take control over this sodding house. She lived here. It belonged to her. Just like Gina said, as soon as she started making changes, it would feel like hers.

She found a stepladder in a dusty cupboard in the hall and dragged it into the little sitting room. It was the coziest room in the house, nestled by the kitchen, warm with a wood burner. The sofa in here was the only really comfortable one they had. This was where she and Drew watched telly, or lay reading their books. So it felt like the right place to start.

The joints of the stepladder screamed as she pulled it open, positioning it under the light. Then she carefully climbed it, testing each rung with her weight, until she could reach the lampshade. She reached up to unscrew the lightbulb, her feet awkwardly balanced on different steps. She clasped her hand around the bulb and began to screw it out of the socket. Out of nowhere, an enormous heat surged through her arm, through her body, knocking the air out of her. She wrenched her hand away, the movement sharp and instinctive. Beneath her the stepladder creaked. Panicking, she overcorrected, losing her balance and falling, taking the bulb with her. As well as the thud of her body hitting the floor, there was a delicate crunch as the lightbulb broke in her hand.

Slowly, she sat up. The pain in her right hand was insistent. A piece of glass stuck directly into the palm and a trickle of blood was seeping down her arm. Her wrist felt stiff and heavy and her shoulder ached. She pulled herself to her feet and went to the light switch, flicking it back and forward. She had switched it off. She wasn't stupid: she knew better than to try and remove a bulb while the light was still on. How had this happened?

She knew first aid, of course. You weren't allowed to look after expensive children without knowing how to fix them if they got broken. She pulled the glass out of her palm: one solid piece, luckily. The cut wasn't as deep as it could have been, so she raised the wound above her head, a tea towel grasped between her fingers, waiting for the pain to stop. Walking back into the sitting room, she gave the ladder a resentful kick, slamming the rubber toe of her Converse into it. *For fuck's sake.* There was blood on the carpet, and she needed to bandage her hand, so she'd have to tell Drew what had happened. She hated how useless she felt next to his calm capability. Changing a lightbulb was nothing. She had nursed other people's children through fevers, cooked four-course dinners for impossibly picky guests. She had cleaned, organized and managed an entire household. She wasn't like this. Or at least, she didn't used to be.

Something about this place seemed to sap her independence. It was as if she was too small, or too weak, to be able to wrestle with it.

Poppy's skin prickled when she heard Drew's key in the lock. She was sitting on the kitchen sofa, waiting for the roasted vegetables to finish in the oven.

"Hello, darling," he said, his smile lighting up his face. "I was going to ask how the new cleaner did but I don't think I need to. It looks incredible."

"Yeah, she was great. Really good."

"What happened to your hand?" he asked, catching sight of the bandage around it.

Mortified, she grimaced. "I'm a catastrophe."

He reached for her wrist, gently. "You're sure you don't need to go to hospital or anything? I could probably get someone down to check it out? Or you could come down to London with me tomorrow and see the doctor at work?"

"Honestly. I'm fine. It's my arse and my pride that are bruised."

"How did you do it?"

She started telling Drew about the creaking stepladder

but when she reached the part about the electric shock, she stopped. She told him she'd simply lost her balance instead.

"What made you decide to change the shade?" Drew asked.

"Gina said that I should try putting my stamp on the house." She paused, noticing Drew's raised eyebrows. "I called her this morning. I was feeling a bit out of sorts."

Drew looked hurt. "You could have called me."

"You were working."

"You can always call me, whatever I'm doing."

He got to his feet, took the lampshade from the kitchen table and disappeared into the little sitting room. After a couple of minutes, he called for her.

"Ta-da!" he said, flicking the light on. "It looks great. And bloody hell, it's clean in here. I'm glad you're making changes. You've got great taste. I even like your experimental carpet dyeing." He pointed at the splatters of her blood on the cream floor.

"Sorry," she said sulkily. "I didn't mean to."

"Hey." Drew nudged her gently in the ribs. "I was joking."

She let him wrap his arms around her and relaxed into his chest. "I'm sorry," she said. "I'm just embarrassed. I fucked up the first thing I tried to do here. I feel like . . ." She trailed off.

"What?"

She knew if she said the words out loud, if she told Drew that she had gotten it into her head that the house was fighting with her, he would think she was mad. So she didn't tell him. "I think we might need a new carpet," she said instead.

"Probably needed one anyway," Drew replied, looking back over his shoulder to the kitchen. "Whatever you're making smells great. Now, I reckon a large glass of wine might take the edge off the injury. What d'you reckon?"

She smiled. "Yes, doctor."

After supper Poppy stood at the sink, washing up the pan she had cooked the pasta in, her bandaged hand covered by yellow rubber gloves.

Drew came up behind her, winding his arms around her waist. "You're not unhappy here, are you?" he asked. "At Thursday House?"

Guilt flooded Poppy's bloodstream. She turned the tap on, rinsing suds off the water glasses. "Unhappy? No, of course not. Why would I be?"

"Well, you were living in London before. You're pretty isolated at this house. I worry sometimes that—" He stopped, taking a breath, and then went on. "I worry that you've gone from cooking and cleaning for them to cooking and cleaning for me."

Poppy reached out to put her hand on Drew's. "It's so, so different. This is my home. Our home."

She buried her head into his body, breathing his smell, just slightly sweaty from a day of London and the train, mixed with the tang of his deodorant, his aftershave and his skin.

"I was thinking," said Drew, "that we might have a party."

"A party?"

"Well," he said, "a weekend sort of thing. Have some friends down on a Friday evening through until Sunday morning."

Poppy smiled. She could feel her chest warming. "I'd like that," she said. "A weekend. Soon, maybe?"

Drew nodded. "Next month? We could get someone in

to do the heavy lifting, all the washing-up and bed-making and that rubbish. And someone to cook, of course."

"I'd like to cook," said Poppy, playing with a loose thread on her sweater.

Drew gave her a wide smile and Poppy thought, as she so often did when he smiled, how astonishingly perfect his teeth were. "You really don't have to."

"I want to," she said, turning back to the sink. She pulled the plug and watched the hot soapy water flood away. "Who are we going to invite? Let me grab a pen—we should work out who we're having. And where they'll sleep. And what I'm going to make."

She sat down at the kitchen table, pen poised. There was a strange look on Drew's face. "What?" she asked.

"Nothing."

"What's that face?"

He shook his head. "Nothing."

Poppy cocked her head to one side. "That's a 'now' face, not a face that you made before you met me, so I get to ask as many questions as I like," she teased.

"I just like seeing you happy," he said. "That's all."

Poppy pulled the lid off her pen. "I've literally never been happier than I am with you."

Her words sat between them for a moment. Drew dropped his gaze, as if he was embarrassed by her words. "I love you," he said after a moment.

"I love you too," she replied. "Now, who are we having? Ralph, obviously—we have to show him the house—he did so much to help get it sorted before we moved in. And then his wife—which one is she? Emma?" She scribbled on some thick cream paper, Drew's fountain pen heavy in her hand. "It's going to be amazing."

They spent the rest of the evening talking about plans for their weekend, Drew explaining which of his friends secretly resented the other and debating what to have for the Saturday-night main course, Poppy's body slotted neatly under Drew's arm.

"This is what it's like, being married, isn't it?" said Poppy as she blew out the candles on the kitchen table.

Drew smiled. "I suppose it is."

She reached up to kiss him. Behind him she could see the silhouette of the new lampshade, perfectly still in the sitting room. There was something off there. It was too big for the room, she saw now. The front rooms had double-height ceilings but this little room needed something smaller. There was something smug about it, as if the whole room was looking back at her and saying, "You shouldn't have tried to change things here."

BEFORE

It was the sticky, dry feeling on the back of her tongue that woke Caroline. She rolled onto her front, her head slopping over the pillow, and looked at the time. Just before 7 a.m. Miraculously, the children still seemed to be asleep. Or maybe they'd gone in to see Poppy that morning rather than bounding onto their parents' bed, demanding iPads and Netflix. She ran her hand over the side of the bed where Jim should have been. It was still warm, but he wasn't there. Had he gone downstairs to make breakfast for the kids, like an absolute saint? She pulled a sweater from the chair in the corner of their bedroom, where all clothes seemed to end up, and padded downstairs. The carpet was getting shabby on the landing, stained where years ago Jack had dropped green clay and it had been trodden in before anyone had cleaned it up.

Reaching the kitchen, she heard voices and, to her own surprise, paused. Poppy's voice. And Jim's. The noise of clinking glasses. A running tap. Had she started clearing up last night's dinner party? Guilt flooded her stomach. Poppy had helped so much last night. She shouldn't be down here,

140

clearing up already. Technically she didn't even work on the weekends.

"So you had fun?" She heard Jim's voice.

Poppy's reply was drowned by the noise of the tap. Caroline looked down at herself, at her blue cotton pajama bottoms and Jim's massive sweater over her T-shirt. She wasn't wearing a bra. She could feel last night's mascara, which she thought she had taken off, caked in her lashes. She knew it would have tinted the skin under her eyes.

"I'm sure they didn't," came Jim again. "Why would anyone have minded you being there?"

"I don't know," Poppy said. "I was surprised that you asked me. I'm your nanny."

"It's not *Downton Abbey*." He laughed. "Christ," he added, "did you ever watch that?"

"My mum loved it," she heard Poppy say. "Until there was a sex scene, and then we were all banned from watching it. She doesn't approve of sex on telly."

"For God's sake don't let her watch *Game of Thrones* then!"

They both laughed. Caroline shifted her weight, careful not to let the floorboards creak under her feet. She put her face to the crack between the door and the frame.

Jim and Poppy were standing next to each other at the sink. Poppy was fully dressed in jeans and a navy-blue fisherman's sweater, the sleeves rolled up to her elbows. In Caroline's imagination, she had been wearing little shorts and a tank top, fresh from her bed. Thighs marked with sheet creases. Caroline put her finger to her pulse, surprised at how viscerally her body reacted to watching her husband

141

standing next to this beautiful young woman. Poppy said something that Caroline didn't catch, and watched as Jim raised his hands toward her. Her breath caught in her throat. Jim's hand went upward, toward her face. It seemed to happen in slow motion. Was he about to push her hair from her face? Stroke her cheek? Run his index finger over the curve of her lip? All of the things he had done to her, Caroline, when they had first known each other flashed in front of her eyes like a slide show.

Unblinking, Caroline watched. But, as she did so, Jim's hand moved to the top of Poppy's head. He ruffled her hair. Poppy stepped back, batting his hand away. "Jack doesn't like it when you do that to him either!" She laughed, smoothing her hair back into place. Caroline's breathing slowed. She pushed the door open.

"Morning, love," said Jim, turning from the sink. "I hope you feel better than I do."

Caroline smiled, at her husband's warm, open face and at her own silliness. She was becoming everything Mel had predicted that she would, and that couldn't be allowed to happen. She was better than that.

"Poppy, it is not fair that you look that good after last night," she said, taking in the girl's fresh, pale skin as she flicked the kettle on.

Poppy smiled, drying up a glass. "I'm told hangovers get worse with every year. Seeing as I feel OK this morning, shall I take the kids to the park to give you two some time to go back to bed?"

Caroline and Jim exchanged a look. "You are an angel," said Jim.

"Sent from heaven," Caroline added.

"I'm really not. I just . . ." Poppy paused, dropping her gaze to the floor. "I really like being here with you guys."

"We love having you," said Caroline, truthfully.

"We really do," said Jim.

CHAPTER 17

When Poppy was growing up, her mother considered boredom a deep personal failing. Occasionally Poppy would complain of having nothing to do. On a good day, her mother would send her upstairs, telling her to play with her sister or read a book. On a good day, Karen would suggest a game. But on a bad day, she would hit her. Poppy knew Drew would never raise his voice, let alone his hand to her. But the idea of telling him, when he came home worn and tired from work and the long, hot train journey, that she was bored, felt ungrateful in the extreme. "How can you be bored?" asked the little voice in the back of her head that often sounded like her mother. "You've got everything." But the problem with Thursday House, not that Poppy would ever have admitted out loud that there was a problem, was that everything lovely it offered was designed to be enjoyed by more than one person. Poppy had swum, the only singular activity she could think of, every day that week, shivering in her swimsuit and pretending that autumn wasn't on its way. She had methodically plowed along the length of the pool and back, thinking about how good it was for her body and how it would make her feel happy. But it hadn't.

She'd found a load of dusty tennis rackets in the shed near the pool, so she had tried tennis on her own, knocking a ball back and forth against the wall, and working on her serve, hoping that if she got better she'd be more fun for Drew to play with. He'd acted as if he thought her game was endearing, her inability to return amusing. But she knew that would wear thin. Only she'd lost several balls and grown bored of running to pick them up and eventually lost interest. Eventually she'd collapsed onto the sofa of the little sitting room and binge-watched television with the curtains shut. If her mother could have seen her she would have been disgusted. "I'm a grown-up, I can do whatever I want," Poppy had said to herself, eating an ice pop. But it had done nothing to shake the sense of guilt she felt.

This morning, she would have a bath. That was the sort of thing she'd dreamed of, back in her Old Life, as she now thought of it. Lying in a long, hot bath all morning, reading and thinking and being quietly alone. She would make a mental list of everything that needed to be done before Drew's friends came for the weekend. She padded along to the biggest bathroom, which sat between two of the spare rooms. It was square and high-ceilinged, just like the rest of the house, bigger even than any bedroom she had ever had until moving here, with a wide window looking out over the fields. She took a deep, slow breath, spinning the metal taps and sending a cascade of water splashing against the porcelain. She watched as the water crept up the side of the bath. Her mother had been very clear that overly deep baths were a waste of hot water and an indulgence. She'd spoken fondly of how, during the war, people had painted black lines around the inside of their baths to show how much water it was acceptable to use. Poppy had always been a little surprised that her mother hadn't done so herself. She put one foot into the water, wincing at the heat, and pulled it back out. Too hot. And she'd forgotten her book. Pulling a towel around her, she turned the water off; she would go and get her book and come back when it had cooled down a bit.

Her book wasn't on the bedside table, so she picked her way down the stairs. The hall was cold. Toward the bottom of the stairs, she heard an unfamiliar noise. She stopped, hand on the banister rail. Slowly, she turned to look behind her, not sure what she was expecting to see. Nothing. Empty space, just stairs and wall and banisters peeling up to the landing. Was there a noise? She strained her ears, searching for something, the skin on the back of her arms suddenly tight. There was a feeling. A strange, scratchy feeling, as if someone's eyes were on her. Steadying herself, she stepped upward, taking the stairs one at a time. It was broad daylight. Nothing bad ever happened in daylight, she knew that. She'd watched thousands of scary films. She and her girlfriends at university had been obsessed with them, squeezing into a bedroom to terrify themselves with shadowy figures on someone's laptop screen.

The noise was coming from the bathroom, a determined, flat noise like running water. But she had turned the taps off. Unquestionably, she had turned them off.

Poppy pushed the bathroom door open and saw the wide tap spewing clouds of steam and a thick column of water. She rushed forward; seeing that the bath was almost half full she grabbed for the tap. She squeezed it, trying to turn it, but it was stuck. *Fuck*, she thought. *Fuck, fuck, fuck.* She grabbed for a towel and wrapped the tap with it, trying to make it turn. Nothing. It was jammed. She reached into the bath, feeling for the plug, but the water was so hot she heard herself yelp with pain.

Panicking, she reached for her phone and dialed Drew's number. He answered on the third ring. "Darling?" he said.

"The bath's going to overflow," she stammered. "I can't turn it off. It's so hot, I can't pull the plug . . ."

"Andrea," she heard Drew say, his voice quieter. "I need an emergency plumber at Thursday House, immediately." Even in her panic, even with her hair matted with steam and sweat she couldn't help thinking how different they were, how Drew summoned someone to fix the problem while she panicked.

"Is it overflowing yet?" he asked.

She shook her head.

"Poppy?"

"Not yet."

"That's good."

Poppy said nothing, watching the huge bath fill higher and higher, almost two-thirds of the way full now. What room was she above? She pictured the house, trying to work out what was below the bathroom. Oh Jesus, was it the drawing room? Was the bath going to tip a ton of scalding water over the piano that Drew loved? She felt her chest tightening, breath coming shorter and harder.

She pulled the towels off the towel rail, putting them on the floor around the bath in a futile attempt to soak up the water that would be spilling over in a matter of minutes.

She went across the hall to the guest bathroom and

pulled more towels from the rail. Was this going to help even at all?

"Do you know where the stopcock is?" came Drew's voice from the phone.

"No."

"I'll talk you through it. Go downstairs."

She took the stairs quickly, watching her bare feet.

"You need to go down to the cellar," said Drew. "I don't know if you'll get phone reception down there—it's under the stairs."

As she reached the hallway, a red van pulled into the drive. The words *Wilcock and Sons* were painted on the side.

"Drew, the plumber is here! I have to go—"

"Poppy, before you—" she heard Drew say as she hit the red button on the screen. Shit. Should she call him back? There wasn't time. He'd tell her later.

"Hi!" she called to the man by the van. "I'm Poppy Spencer, thank you so much for coming so fast. Do you mind coming up? It's just in here—"

The man was slender. Poppy wished he were bigger. More reassuring to look at. He moved slowly, taking a toolbox from the back seat and then following her. "Thank you so much for coming so quickly," she breathed again, steps two at a time under her feet. He didn't reply, his face grim. But he followed her into the bathroom and, as the water started to spill over the lip of the bath, took a big metal thing from the box. He fastened it around the tap and gave it a sharp yank. The metal screeched, but the water came to a stop.

"There," he said, picking up his toolbox. "Old taps, those.

Swell up when they get hot. Best not to leave them running unattended."

"I didn't," Poppy replied, too quickly. The plumber raised his eyebrows. "I really didn't," she repeated.

He made a noncommittal noise and started to go downstairs. "Do you want a glass of water or something?" she said to his turned back. "Cup of tea? While you write me an invoice?"

He shook his head, and pulled a pad from his pocket, scribbling numbers on it.

"Has this happened before?" she asked. "With the previous owners?"

The man fixed her with an expression of pure loathing, and then tore the paper from the pad. He held it between two shaking fingers. As soon as she touched it, he drew his hand away. She looked down. In wobbly blue writing the total at the end read "£800."

"Eight hundred?" she asked, horrified.

He nodded. "I want it paid by the end of the week." And with that he turned, yanked the front door open, turned his van around in a spray of gravel and was gone.

CHAPTER 18

Poppy dropped down onto the stairs and pulled her knees up to her chest. She pressed the screen of her phone. "Hey," she said.

"Are you all right?" came Drew's calm voice. "Do I need to bring scuba gear home with me?"

She couldn't bring herself to laugh. "I'm OK."

"Sorry, terrible joke," he said. "Are you OK? You sound frightened."

"I turned the taps off."

"What?"

"I didn't leave the taps on. I definitely turned them off before I went downstairs."

Drew's voice was low and gentle. "It's an ancient bath. You probably thought you had, or very nearly did, or something like that. It's not your fault."

"I turned them off," she repeated.

"Was the plumber OK?" Drew asked, clearly trying to change the subject. He didn't believe her. He thought she was lying; he thought she was trying to cover her own back.

"He stopped the bath," she said. "He massively overcharged us, though."

"I wouldn't worry about that."

"Eight hundred quid, Drew."

"Well, he did come really pretty quickly. Andrea probably had to offer that to get him to leave a job. Anyway, darling, I am so sorry but I've got to go into a meeting. You're all right, aren't you?"

"Yes."

"Promise?"

"Yes."

"I'll take you out for supper tonight. Cheer you up. You've not had the best week, I know that."

Poppy didn't reply.

"I love you," he said, as he hung up.

"I turned the taps off," she said as his voice turned into a beep, telling her he was gone.

Later that afternoon Poppy's phone buzzed.

"Gina? What's up?"

"Nothing," she said, clearly lying.

"Are you crying?"

"No," she said with a little sob.

"What's going on?"

There was another little whining noise. "Gina, talk to me. What's wrong?"

"Bella found stuff in my room."

"What?" Bella was the littlest of the Winterson family. She was four and she adored Gina, who had worked there since Bella was a month old. "What did she find?"

"Weed," sobbed Gina. "It was in my drawer."

"Why was she in your room?" asked Poppy. It was a stupid question—it was obvious what was coming.

"She wanted to play." Gina's voice had calmed a little. "She took it to show her mum." Now her voice was strangled, as though she couldn't get enough air.

"Shit," said Poppy.

"Yep." Gina half laughed, half cried.

"Are you fired?"

She heard Gina breathe deeply; she would be nodding into the phone.

"Notice period?"

"Nope."

"When do you have to leave?"

"She said I could have until tomorrow to find somewhere to stay. Poppy, she was so nice about it, I thought she was going to cry too. She just kept saying that if Bella had got hold of it or eaten it or if it had been harder stuff, which is mad because you know I don't do anything harder—"

"Gina," Poppy said, forgetting to sound sympathetic, overwhelmed by the genius of what she had just realized, "I have such a brilliant idea."

"What?"

"Drew keeps nagging me to hire someone to come help me here, and I'm on my own a lot—why don't you come down here for a bit?"

It was perfect. Gina needed somewhere to go, and Poppy wouldn't have to be alone if Gina were here.

The other end of the line was quiet. "Gee?"

"I don't know," said Gina. "Wouldn't that be weird, me working for you?"

"No!" said Poppy, getting to her feet. "It'll be amazing. You can help me with the house and we'll pay you whatever they were paying you and you can crash here until you find another job. We've got all of Drew's mates coming to stay soon and I've got no idea where to start with getting the house ready or planning the weekend."

They could take on the house together. A strange feeling inside told her that the house wouldn't dare fuck with Gina the way it did with her. No one ever did.

"Are you sure?" Gina sounded a little bit happier.

"A million percent," said Poppy. She needed to sort Gina's room out—and get her some keys cut. Her mind was racing with all the little things she could do.

"If you're sure you're sure?"

"Pack your stuff!" said Poppy. "Get a taxi from the station, on me."

"OK," said Gina. "See you tomorrow."

"Darling?" Drew's voice called out.

"I'm out here."

Poppy was sitting on the terrace, wrapped in a blanket and watching the sun go down. Drew kissed Poppy's forehead and pulled out a chair.

"Do you want a glass of wine?" she asked.

Drew nodded and pulled the bottle from the ice bucket. "Are you OK?"

"Fine," she said. The bath incident seemed like a long time ago. "Fully recovered. How was your day?"

"Busy."

"Good busy?"

"I suppose so, yes. I reckon next month I should be able to work mostly from here, maybe just go into the office a couple of times a week. Did you have a good day, apart from the obvious?"

"Yes," she said. "Productive."

"You seem happier this evening?" he said.

"That's because I am," she replied. "I have a surprise for you."

"A surprise? I thought you weren't sure about surprises?"

"That's getting surprises. Giving them, however, I am a big fan of."

"I'm a big fan of this dress." He smiled, leaning forward to kiss her. "So, what's the surprise?"

"I hired someone!"

Drew looked confused. "I know? The girl from Bath—she did a brilliant job with the kitchen."

"Well, actually I hired someone else."

"I thought you liked the Bath girl?"

"Well, I did. But then the absolute perfect person became available."

"Who?"

"My friend Gina!"

Drew's shoulders rose a couple of centimeters. "Your friend?"

"Her family . . ." She paused. ". . . don't need her anymore, she's looking for work and I thought she could come and stay with us for a bit and help out."

"So, she's staying as a guest?"

"No, she'll be helping out too."

"She's going to work here?"

Poppy could feel her happy glow fading away. "What's wrong? I thought this was perfect? Gina can keep me company, and help me keep everything working properly, and it's only temporary until she finds another job." *And I won't have to be alone in this house anymore*, she didn't say.

Drew still didn't look convinced.

"What's the problem?" she asked.

"It's just . . ." He seemed to be struggling to find the words. He had the same expression that Rafe used to get when he wanted to be comforted but he thought he was too old for it. "I don't want you to hate me for saying this . . ."

"But?"

"But having a friend work for you can be difficult. Uncomfortable even. Is this about . . . what happened earlier? Because I know you're shaken, and it's been a difficult week, but I'm really not sure this is a great move."

Poppy squeezed her eyebrows together. "What? How?"

Drew looked worried. "I understand you were frightened earlier, you don't like being alone, you need a friend. But to be honest, Poppy, I had imagined hiring someone who'd come in during the day and then bugger off in the evenings and on the weekends so that we could have time together. Having your friend here 24/7, it just—"

"Oh God, don't worry about that," interrupted Poppy. "Gina will have about fifteen million friends after she's been here for a week. She picks people up wherever she goes. She adopted me on my first day at the playground. Rafe pushed another child and she lied to the other child's nanny, said he fell. She's the best."

"Unless you're a recently pushed child," said Drew.

Poppy laughed. "You're going to love having her here, I promise. She's my urban family—like a sister I chose. I want you to get to know her."

Drew didn't look convinced, but that didn't matter. He

155

would only have to meet Gina and he'd adore her. Everyone did. It was one of the many wonderful things about her. She was too loud and too tall and far too much, but just when you started to think she was a little bit annoying, she'd do something so ridiculously funny or generous or kind that you'd fall irrevocably in love with her.

CHAPTER 19

Saturday was drizzly and gray, the first day of bad weather since they had moved in. Soon the leaves on the trees across the garden and into the valley would be crisp and orange. The swimming pool would need to be closed up. She'd have to find out how the central heating worked. If it worked.

Poppy pulled on a pair of jeans, stiff and new, and one of Drew's sweaters. Her winter clothes, the ones that Ralph had arranged to have rescued from the Hendersons' house, were in three neat boxes in the wardrobe, taped and labeled. Out of interest, she pulled the tape off the top of one of the boxes. They were perfectly folded. Would she ever feel normal about being someone who had their clothes folded for them, rather than the person who did the folding? She pulled a sweater, pale pink and acrylic, from the box. It smelled different. A mixture of the Hendersons' preferred brand of fabric softener, a perfume she had left behind in Ibiza and a very faint note of damp from her old bedroom.

Maybe she should have left Mrs. Henderson to throw them away, or more likely whoever Mrs. Henderson had replaced her with. But she hadn't wanted to seem profligate. She couldn't bring herself to unpack them; they were a reminder of a world she had left behind. But nor could she get rid of them; she was still that person even if her surroundings had changed. She kicked the box back under the bed.

"Have you eaten?" she asked Drew, who was sitting at the kitchen table reading the paper.

"Yes," he said, looking up. "Do you want coffee?"

Just another tiny way that Drew didn't realize how gilded his life was. Coffee was never granules that foamed as you added hot water, always espresso from a fancy machine. She poured herself a cup and then slid down onto the cracked leather kitchen sofa. "Let's go for a walk after breakfast," she said.

"It's raining?"

"You're quite right." She smiled. "It is indeed raining."

"You don't want to wait until it cheers up outside?"

She shook her head. "I like rainy walks. And anyway, Gina is coming later. Let's go out together before she gets here."

He kissed the top of her head. "Anything you want, my darling. God, you look beautiful."

Poppy squirmed away, uncomfortable. "Stop it," she said.

Drew gave his little half smile. "Oh, I'm sorry," he said, "am I not supposed to tell you that?" He wrapped his arms around her and lifted her off the floor, kissing her neck and laughing. "It's your own fault. You shouldn't be so bloody gorgeous."

An hour later, they pulled their wellies on and started through the garden into the field. Poppy's borrowed boots from the back door were a size too big, even with the thick socks she had nicked from Drew's sock drawer.

"Those look familiar," he had said as she pulled the boots on.

"What's yours is mine now, remember?" she'd told him.

Drew walked quickly, taking long confident strides. "I think we can go up there," he said, pointing across the garden and into one of the fields, "and down into the woods, then if we follow the footpath it'll loop back around."

Poppy had no idea if any of what he said made sense, but he said it with such confidence that it didn't occur to her not to follow him.

"Maybe we should get a dog," she said to Drew, whose gaze was locked on the treetops.

He seemed surprised to find her next to him. "What?"

"A dog. We should get a dog."

He smiled. "That's an idea. What makes you say that?"

"Look at all this." She held her arms out, palms facing up to the rain. The sky was still gray but the green of the grass and the trees and everything around was so lush and aggressively alive. "Perfect for a dog."

"What sort? Not one of those silly little lapdogs. I'm always worried I'm going to step on one." He made a face, with his tongue sticking out of his mouth. Drew wasn't silly often. There was something magical about it when it happened.

"Definitely not." She laughed. "A proper dog. A black Lab or something like that."

"You're becoming more and more *Country Life* with every week you spend here."

"You'll come home one night and find me in tweed and pearls."

Drew made a face. "And a velvet headband holding your hair back?"

"A sensible bob."

"Comfortable shoes, bought from a catalog?"

"And elastic-waist pants that don't need to be ironed for the weekend."

"Stop." He pulled Poppy into his arms. "It's too sexy, I can't resist."

They trudged up the hill arm in arm, the grass slippery, and stood on the crest of it, looking back at the house. It looked so little, nestled in between the hills, safe and warm. "That's our house," she said. It was a silly thing to say, really. Not as if Drew didn't know that. But the words felt nice in her mouth, and from Drew's expression it seemed as though he shared her sentimentality. They would do this walk again, she decided. With friends, after a Sunday lunch. With a baby strapped to her front, smiling at the patterns of leaves overhead. With toddlers padding fat-footed through the grass. With sulking, moody teens who didn't want to go on a walk. Together just the two of them again, when Drew couldn't take the hill at double time and they had to check that it wasn't too slippery before they left. This would be their life, now and for as long as she could imagine.

What kind of a father would Drew be? What had his own father been like? Would he want to be like him? Surely it was fair to want to know something about the people who would have been grandparents to her children?

"Drew?" she asked. There was a little gap in the fence around the field. They slipped through it, into the woods. It was quiet here, a comforting sort of quietness which came from being under the canopy of green leaves. "Can I ask you something?"

"What is it?"

Her nerve failed. Today was too lovely to spoil.

She took a breath and erased the question from her lips. "Don't think I'm stupid," she said instead, "but what do you do?"

He slowed down, walking in step with her along the soft earthen path. To their left a river—river was probably too grand a word—a stream wiggled its way through the wood, splitting it in two. "You know what I do."

"Venture capital," she said. "But I don't understand what you actually do, do. Like, when you get into the office. What happens?"

"I invest money. And when that money makes money, I get a cut."

"And you're good at it?"

"I suppose so."

"Have you always done that?"

His gaze dropped to the ground. "I invested my inheritance, when I came into it."

"That must have been such an awful time."

Drew stopped. She realized, seeing the lines—two parallel ones, like an eleven between his eyebrows—that she had said the wrong thing. "Sorry," she said. She kept walking. If they kept moving and kept talking, there was no reason to dwell on her asking about the past.

"I'm not much good at talking about it," he said after they had walked for a few minutes in silence.

"You don't have to," she replied, reaching for his hand, wrapping it with her own, trying to tell him that she was sorry, that she knew she had upset him and that she hadn't meant to.

His hands were smooth against hers. Sweat was prickling

along her spine, under her sweater. "Nearly home," she said as they came out of the woods and back onto the grass. The sky felt bright by comparison. She blinked.

"There's a car on the drive," said Drew.

"Gina!" said Poppy. "She must be early!"

"Very early," said Drew. He didn't sound pleased.

"You're going to love her," she said. There was no point asking why he was annoyed. He wouldn't tell her the truth anyway. She picked up her heavy rubber feet and started to run—as much as she was able to—across the field. "Come on!" she called back to Drew. "Or can't you keep up with your *much* younger wife?"

Drew laughed and charged up behind her, catching her around the waist and kissing her neck, pushing her backward into the grass. She squealed at the wetness of it on the back of her bare neck, but returned his kisses.

It was like a film, or a photograph. If she had seen them together she would have been swollen with jealousy. She would have been heart-rippingly jealous of the girl in the wellies with the smile, the enormous engagement ring and the gorgeous husband. But she didn't have to be jealous. It was real. It was hers.

CHAPTER 20

Gina was dragging her fourth suitcase out of the back of the taxi when they arrived back at the house.

"Poppy!" she screamed the moment she saw her friend coming across the drive. Gina ran over, sneakers crunching on the gravel. Both girls wrapped their arms around each other and Gina dragged Poppy off her feet, spinning her around.

"This is Drew," Poppy said, proudly presenting her husband as if she had created him.

"I know," she said, as Drew held his hand out.

"The famous Gina. I've heard a lot about you." His voice wasn't warm as it had been on their walk, it was formal. Sort of like when he ordered in restaurants or spoke to someone on the phone.

"Nice to meet you," Gina returned.

A silence filled the air around them. "How much did you pack!" Poppy asked, fumbling for something to say.

"I didn't know how many ball gowns I'd need. Fuck me, Pops, this place is amazing."

For the first time, Poppy felt as if she wasn't the person

who belonged here the least. "Thank you!" she squealed. "Let's take your stuff upstairs."

"Yes! Oh, and we need to pay Greg."

"Greg?"

"The cabbie. I didn't have any cash." She gestured toward the van sitting on the drive. "I think it's two hundred."

"Two hundred quid?"

"Yeah. You said to get a cab."

Poppy had meant from the station. Not from London.

"Of course," said Drew. He put his hand on Poppy's waist. "Darling, why don't you settle Gina in and I'll sort the cabbie out." He pulled his wallet from inside his padded jacket and strode over to the car. Gina gave a low whistle.

"Where can I get me one of those?"

"A husband? You get asked out about fifty times a day."

"A sugar daddy." Gina smiled, her teeth bright white against her lips.

"He's only fifteen years older than me! He's not a sugar daddy!"

"Course not, babe. Course not."

Poppy pushed the kitchen door open and pulled off her wellies. "Let me give you the tour!" she said, excited to show Gina the house. Gina dropped her bag on the kitchen sofa and went to the fridge.

"First things first," she said, taking out a bottle of wine. "That was a fucker of a drive. Not sure I've got the stamina to walk around the whole of this place straight away."

"Of course," Poppy said. "I'll start making lunch then."

"Luncheon," said Gina, doing an affected accent.

"Oh piss off," Poppy replied, meaning to sound amused.

The words came out harder than she had anticipated. Gina raised her eyebrows. "Sorry," Poppy said. "I'm so glad you're here."

"Me too, babe," said Gina as she poured herself a glass of wine, slopping the pale yellow liquid into a glass. "It's incredible."

"I know," Poppy said, looking around. "We're so lucky."

She had been telling herself that a lot lately. It had become like a little mantra. Every time she heard a noise from upstairs and felt her skin prickle, every time she woke up and found Drew gone. So lucky. So, so lucky.

And anyway, Gina was here now. She wasn't going to be alone anymore.

"This is your room," said Poppy, opening the door to the little square room. It was on a long corridor of little storage rooms on the very top floor; apparently it was originally where the servants would have lived.

"Very funny," Gina said. "Up in the servants' quarters because I'm your skiv. Where's my real room?"

Poppy blushed from her forehead to her chest, her skin blotching as she tried to explain. It had been Drew's idea for Gina to be up here, leaving them the entire middle floor to themselves. "The guest bedrooms are all so close together. Drew thought you might prefer some privacy. You've got your own bathroom up here, and you could have one of the other rooms as a living room, like having an apartment," she faltered. "But if you want to move down to one of the guest rooms, you can? But I think Drew wanted to put his friends in there when they come to stay . . ."

"No, it's fine. It's only for a few weeks. Drew probably wants to be able to bang you senseless without me hearing," said Gina, digging through the huge canvas tote she used as a handbag. "I brought you something." She held out a little blue box, tied with a creamy white ribbon. Poppy raised one eyebrow. She and Gina didn't do presents. It wasn't their thing. Not even Christmas and birthdays: they both knew they were on shit money and even shittier levels of free time; the gift of not having to buy a gift was what they both really wanted.

"What is it?" Poppy asked, taking the box.

"You know how a present works, right?" Gina laughed.

Poppy pulled the bow and lifted the lid. In the box was another box, square and suede. "Is there going to be another box inside this as well?" asked Poppy.

"You are so suspicious!"

Inside the suede box, sitting on a little cushion, was a gold bracelet. A thin, almost invisible gold chain, with a round disc in the middle. On the disc were the letters P and G. Poppy's eyes filled with tears. "Gina," she said, her voice a little rough. "Why?"

"Don't you like it?"

"I love it, you idiot, but you didn't have to." Gina never had any money; she was the kind of person who bought the whole bar a shot once she had a couple of drinks inside her. How had she managed this?

Gina looked uncomfortable, her eyes on the floor. "I just wanted to say thank you and stuff."

Poppy held her wrist out, getting Gina to do the fiddly clasp.

"Let's go down and have a drink. I can't wait for you to get to know Drew. You'll love him."

"Look what Gina gave me!" Poppy said, thrusting her wrist at Drew when they reached the kitchen.

Drew smiled. "Beautiful."

"It's no big deal," said Gina, refilling her wine glass. "Just wanted to say thanks and stuff."

"Very sweet of you, Gina," Drew said, holding her gaze.

Poppy looked up at them both and felt her body unfurl. The two people she loved most in the world were here, in her home. This, she decided, must be what it felt like to have a family.

BEFORE

Caroline and Jim had been nervous to ask Poppy about coming on holiday with them.

It had been Jack's idea, to start with. Jack who, since Poppy's arrival, had started joining in with the family again rather than hiding in his room with his laptop.

"Why isn't Poppy coming to France?" he had asked that weekend. Poppy had been staying with a university friend and the family had gone for a walk and a pub lunch in the country. When they had reached the pub, Caroline had asked for a table for six, and then had to correct herself.

"Because it's a family holiday," Jim had said, putting Grace into the high chair she'd outgrown. "And it would be boring for her."

"Why?" asked Ella.

"Because there's not much for a twenty-one-year-old to do in Côte Rouge," Caroline had replied, pretending she wasn't wondering the same thing.

Would Poppy want to come? Would it be wrong to ask—put her in an awkward position?

"Did you ask her, though?" Jack had insisted, tearing into the bread. Caroline couldn't bring herself to tell him to slow down. Yes, he would eat half a free baguette and then leave his main course, but she didn't want to start a row.

"No," she said. "Jim, can you try and catch the waitress's eye and order some wine?"

"Who's driving?"

She rolled her eyes. "Me, apparently. But I can still have one glass."

"You should ask her," announced Ella. "She might feel left out otherwise. You wouldn't like it if we all went on holiday without you, would you, Mummy?"

Caroline decided that, while she didn't approve of sugar-coating things for the children, it probably wouldn't be fair to tell her daughter that she would be absolutely fine with them all going off on holiday without her if it meant two weeks alone in a nice quiet house. Her only concern would be how long Jim could cope with all three of them without losing it. Nevertheless, the thought had stuck with her. Was it cruel to leave Poppy all alone at the house? They'd agreed that they'd pay her half her usual weekly salary, she'd have the house to herself and be able to do babysitting for other people. That was a good deal, wasn't it?

"Do you think they were right?" she asked Jim on the drive home, the two younger children crashed out in the back of the car, Jack plugged into an iPad.

"About what?"

"Poppy. France." She pulled off the roundabout. Jim gripped irritatingly at the handle above the window and took a sharp intake of breath. "What?" she asked.

"You didn't signal."

"I did!"

"It doesn't count if you do it as you're pulling out."

She sighed and focused on the road. The asphalt slid beneath their wheels and the greenness of the country turned to gray as they came back into London.

"There wouldn't be any harm in asking, would there?"

"What if she felt obliged?" Caroline checked the children's faces in her mirror.

"She's not like that."

"You're sure?"

"She loves them. Really loves them. And I think she likes being around us. It sounds like her mother is a right cow, and her dad left for another woman. He's got a second family and he doesn't bother with her anymore."

"Really?" Caroline was surprised. Poppy hadn't gone into detail about her father whenever they'd spoken. It stung a little bit. "How do you know that?"

"I asked."

"Nosy." She was more than a little pleased to know that Jim had asked, that Poppy hadn't volunteered it because she trusted him more.

"I was giving her a lift to the station, and it came up. Her mum left her sister's dad for her dad, and then he fucked off."

Caroline sighed. "What a mess. No wonder she doesn't ever want to go home."

"So we'll ask her?"

The prospect of Poppy coming with them lightened the worry that had been sitting all along Caroline's spine, tightening her back. She wanted to be good at family holidays, truly she did. She wanted to be able to leave home and work and everything "London" in London. But she couldn't. For her, the annual French holiday was another fortnight of cooking meals and clearing them up—just like home life.

Maybe with Poppy there she would be able to steal half an hour by the pool to read a book.

Was it wrong, she wondered idly, that she was so happy to outsource so much to Poppy? She should probably resent Poppy for being so good at it all. But she couldn't. Something about Poppy's gratitude at being included made her impossible to dislike. She still seemed to assume that Caroline knew best, that the kids would rather be with their mother than with her. She was genuinely, unquestionably kind.

Caroline smiled. "Let's ask her."

"You're sure?" Jim sounded surprised.

"Yes," she said. "Absolutely sure. We just have to make sure that she doesn't feel like she has to."

Poppy's face was like a sunrise when they asked her. "I thought you were going to fire me!" she yelped as she jumped up from the kitchen stool and threw her arms around Caroline. "You're absolutely sure you want me to come? I won't spoil the family time? I can go off and give you space whenever you want it."

Caroline's face split into a grin. How could anyone be so excited about the prospect of two weeks in France?

"You might live to regret it!" Jim laughed as Poppy hugged him. "If it's pissing it down for two whole weeks and we have to go to the Museum of French Country Life every day."

Caroline watched as Poppy wrapped her arms around Jim's shoulder and brushed her cheek against his chest. There was something so hungry there. But then Poppy had grown up without a father. Caroline smiled at them. She wouldn't give in to the nasty little whispers at the back of her mind.

CHAPTER 21

"Would you have believed it?" Poppy called up the stairs. "If someone had told us this time last year that we'd be doing this right now? Being here?"

"Not a chance," said Gina as she came down the stairs from her room. "I feel like I should be singing that 'I Think I'm Gonna Like It Here' song from *Annie*." She jumped down the final steps, her legs impossibly long and thin. She'd only been here a week, but somehow seemed far more at ease with the house than Poppy did.

"I still feel like that too," said Poppy. "All the time. I keep seeing myself in windows and trying to work out who that grown-up woman is."

"Gotta get over that, babe. It's your house."

Poppy snorted as they wandered toward the kitchen, shoulder to shoulder. "Technically yeah, but come on. It's not like I put anything into buying it, is it? It's not, y'know, *mine* mine."

"I thought Drew kept telling you it's equally yours and all that?"

"He does. He's the same way about the money. Gave me all these credit cards, keeps trying to encourage me to

172

buy stuff. But it doesn't feel right; every time I use that card I feel like I'm taking advantage."

Gina rolled her eyes. "You have such problems. So, what's the plan for today? Walk? Shopping? *Pub?*"

Poppy took a glass down from the shelf at the end of the kitchen and filled it with water. "I know, I know. My diamond shoes are too tight. What do you feel like doing?"

"Where are the real drinks?" asked Gina.

"Booze?"

Gina nodded her head and pretended to pant like a puppy. "I'm parched."

"Um," Poppy said, thinking of all the perfectly chosen bottles of white wine in the wine fridge. It was only just midday. "There's some vodka in the larder. And rum, I think." There was in fact an entire tray of bottles in the dining room.

"What are you having?" Gina asked.

"Probably just this," said Poppy, pointing at the jug of water.

"Really?"

How was she supposed to tell Gina that the idea of Drew coming back to find her and her friend pissed on the expensive wine he'd bought made her feel intensely guilty? "Why don't we go for a walk?"

"He's got you on a short leash."

The comment stung. "It's not that," Poppy said. "You're super welcome to drink; I'm just not really in the mood."

Gina was smiling now. "Oh my God . . . are you?"

"No! God no. Absolutely not. I'm on my period right now."

She had run out of pills just after they'd arrived back in

England, and when she told Drew he had offered to get a concierge doctor to prescribe some. "Or," he had said, "if you're ready, you could stop taking them. No pressure. Just a thought." So she had stopped. But nothing had happened yet, and when her period arrived a couple of days ago it had brought a gentle sort of sadness where once upon a time it had brought relief.

"Oh. Sorry." Gina picked up the jug. "It wouldn't be the end of the world if you were, though. You've got enough bedrooms. Come and sit outside so I can have a cigarette."

Poppy followed Gina out onto the terrace, down the stone steps and along the path. "I know it wouldn't," she said. "I just don't know if I'm ready."

"Have you talked about it?"

Poppy shook her head, wanting to keep the little fantasy world full of children between her and Drew.

Gina had rolled a cigarette and put her legs up on the wooden table. Long streams of smoke came from her lips. Poppy picked her way over to sit with her. Her skin pimpled in the cool air. It would be too cold to sit out here before long.

She could feel the silence between her and Gina stretching thin.

"I'm sorry, Gee. I don't mean to be boring. I'm just kind of still on best behavior."

"Does he know about what happened?"

She shook her head again.

"Are you going to tell him?"

"We're not really like that," she said.

"Like what?"

As the words left Gina's lips, Poppy regretted what she

had said. This was not the kind of arrangement that Gina would agree with.

"We have this thing: we agreed we weren't going to talk about stuff that happened before we met."

Gina sat up. "What?"

"Basically, we've both dated people where it's been all about the past, and we didn't want that. So we thought we'd skip over all the stuff that happened before and just be in the now."

Gina looked horrified. "And you don't want to know what he's hiding?"

"Hiding?"

"Why else would he agree to that?"

"I agreed to it."

"Exactly."

"Gina!" Poppy got to her feet. "Low fucking blow."

Gina stood up. Poppy resented how long she was, how her height lent her an unquestionable sense of authority. "Oh come on. You know exactly why you went for this 'deal.' You know what you're hiding. You don't think he's got his reasons too? Normal people don't do this. Normal people don't make bargains—"

"I'm going to go inside. It's cold."

"Poppy," Gina called after her. Poppy didn't turn around. Her chest was tight and her head even tighter and all she wanted to do was get back to the house, away from Gina's words.

Poppy knew that what Gina was saying was true. There must be a reason that Drew didn't want to talk. There must be something lurking in his past. She had known the very moment he had suggested it, and that feeling had gotten worse ever since they came back to England. It was there constantly, a little tension in the back of her neck, a little weight at the back of her stomach. She managed to ignore it most of the time but Gina had turned the volume up on it, made all the little worry-whispers into screams.

Didn't Gina realize? How could she fail to understand how precarious this all was? Poppy didn't deserve Drew; she knew that. She didn't deserve Drew's love or his money or his kindness. So it didn't matter what the secrets were. One day he would find out. He would know who Poppy was and what she had done and then it would all be gone.

It was easy for Gina. She had a huge, loving, loud family in south London who took the piss out of her for working in Chelsea and having famous employers. They were proud of her, even though they'd never say it to her face. Gina had tried to bond with her over it once, misunderstanding about Poppy's family, thinking they were the same. "I know what it's like," she'd said. "But the second I walk out that door, it's all 'Gina's done so well.' They just won't say it to your face." Poppy had nodded and agreed and pretended that the advice had made her feel better because she didn't want to be rude or hurt Gina's feelings. But it wasn't like that.

Loving Drew, being so desperate to keep him—she knew it was a cliché. Predictable. Daddy issues. She knew all of that. But she also couldn't remember the last person who had held her for any length of time, or caught her arm as she walked past and pulled her in for a kiss. When was the last time she'd had sober sex? She couldn't take another night of someone's teeth clashing against hers, their fingers pushing inside the dry folds of her vagina and asking, moments later, "Did you come?" She never wanted to wake up in a stranger's house with furry teeth and a dead phone battery and start walking in a random direction out of the front door in the hope that she'd reach a tube station, because she was too ashamed to admit that she didn't know where she was.

Everything in Drew's world was clean and pure and right. Someone came to pick up their laundry and then brought it back folded and ironed and neat. Nothing ever smelled of damp. Nothing was plastic or broken or shit. She never had to wonder if twenty quid was too much to pay for a white T-shirt. Drew cared if she came. He listened when she spoke. He noticed if her mood was low. Once he'd seen her crying at a stupid program on TV while he was reading his book and he'd put the book down and wrapped his arms around her. Never in her life had she been touched so often or so kindly. And so Gina might not get it, she might think that Poppy was stupid and naïve to let Drew keep his secret, but she had no idea what it was like to be alone in the world.

CHAPTER 22

Drew had given Poppy plenty of notice that he would be going to Frankfurt for a week, but as his departure drew nearer she found herself dreading it. She was surprised at how dependent she had become on his presence. It had been frighteningly easy to get used to.

"Do you really have to go?" she asked, sitting on their bed.

"I do," Drew replied, taking a shirt from the wardrobe. "But it's only a week. I'll be back by the weekend, and I'll call you every night."

"I suppose."

"It won't always be like this. I promise. Once I've finished setting up this project I'll be able to work from home, and I won't need to work every day. It's a means to an end."

"I know," she said, her voice small.

He brushed some dust from the shirt's left shoulder. "That wardrobe is filthy."

"I'll clean it while you're away."

"That wasn't what I meant."

"I don't mind. I'll be bored anyway."

"You've got Gina?"

"True."

Things between Poppy and Gina had been strained since their row. In fact, she'd barely seen her. Drew had seemed pleased by her absence. He'd come home the night of the row and asked where Gina was. Poppy had guessed she was at the pub quiz, making friends in the village, and told Drew so. He had seemed mollified by it, as though his concerns that Gina was going to follow them around the house interrupting their couple time had proved unfounded. Poppy had toyed with telling Drew about the argument, about how hurt she was that Gina seemed to disapprove of their relationship. But she knew better than that.

Since Poppy had told her about the deal, Gina had avoided Drew. If he was in the kitchen, Gina would take her drink outside, ostensibly because she wanted to smoke. If he was reading in the sitting room she would pretend she'd gone in to get a magazine and then retreat upstairs. It wasn't just Gina either. While Drew was always pleasant and polite toward Gina, he didn't seem able to fake warmth toward her.

"Darling," said Drew, putting socks in his suitcase. "You look miserable. It's only five days. Please try to cheer up."

He doesn't know about Gina, she tried to remind herself. "It's fine," she said, getting up. "I'm going in the shower."

Drew caught her arm and gently tugged her back. "Hey— what's going on? You seem upset. It's only four nights, I'll be back late on Friday. You're not annoyed, are you?"

It was simpler to pretend that she was angry at him for leaving than it was to explain that Gina's comments had wedged themselves in her brain and played on repeat for the last week, that she was scared everything they had built was on a shifting foundation and that she was going to end up right back where she had started—alone. "I just didn't realize you'd be away so much. It's not fair."

Drew looked hurt. "I'm sorry. You've got the car and you have Gina here. You've got the cards—is there anything I can . . ." He seemed to be struggling for words. Or rather, for a solution. Poppy remembered Gina explaining something she'd read in a book once, while they sat in the garden watching the boys ignore the wooden learning toys and play with sticks they'd found: that men needed to fix things. "It's so easy to keep them happy. You have to give them a small challenge that they can overcome," she had said. Poppy had rolled her eyes at the time and said that men weren't all the same and that you couldn't learn to date one from a book. But now Poppy wondered if there might have been some truth to it. There was no problem that Drew didn't want to fix.

"It's not that," she said, wishing she hadn't started the conversation at all. "I just need something to do."

"Why not find something?" asked Drew. "Have you seen my brown shoes?"

"In the wardrobe," she said, reveling at how married they had become in only a couple of months. She'd only ever seen it happen the other way around. Another person's tongue in her mouth, hands in her underwear, breath on her skin and then the next day, nothing. Intimacy undone entirely. Sometimes she'd go to a party with Gina and see someone across the room whom she'd slept with and marvel at how it was possible to give your body over to someone for a few hours, sleep next to them with a naked face and naked body, and then not even smile at each other across a crowded room.

"I am trying to find something. I'm not just sitting on my arse all day."

"No one said you were."

Drew stood behind her, looking at her face in the mirror. His chin was the exact same height as the top of her head. "You can do anything you want. Maybe my going away will give you some space to think about what it is you want to do?"

Poppy wrapped herself in a towel. "We need new towels," she said. "The ones Ralph bought are scratchy."

"Order new ones," said Drew.

"That's not the point."

"You just said you dislike the towels?"

"It's not about the towels."

"Then what is it about?"

Poppy made a long, exasperated noise. "It's about living here; it's about not having anything to do. I feel like I belong in some Victorian novel. None of this stuff is mine. I didn't choose any of it. When your friends come they're going to take one look at this place and know I don't know what to do with it."

Drew's face clouded with hurt. "I thought you were happy here."

"I am!" she protested. She'd spent the last three weeks fighting her reservations about the house because she didn't want to disappoint Drew, who clearly felt like he had come home. "But it's like a museum of someone else's life," she said gently. "The drawers are still lined with old newspapers. The plants in the garden were chosen by someone else. Every day I find things in cupboards that don't belong to us."

"I could have someone come in and clear the house? I just thought that it would be best; we didn't have any of our own things . . ." He trailed off. "I can have Ralph send someone to get rid of it all."

Poppy shook her head. "I don't want Ralph to do anything. I'll sort it out—I'll fix it, I just . . . It's a lot. Moving here, being here. It's a big adjustment. That's all."

Drew nodded. "I know. I'm sorry."

"Don't be sorry."

"I just want you to be happy."

"I am happy."

"You don't seem it."

"I'm just starting a row because you're going away. You should ignore me. It was just that Gina said—" She stopped immediately before she said too much.

Drew didn't look impressed. "I didn't realize we were living in a harem."

"We're not."

"So I'm not accountable to Gina. And neither are you."

"I'm sorry."

Drew sat down on the bed next to her. "Don't be sorry. But, my love, Gina doesn't always know best. You're clever and brilliant and bright. You can think for yourself."

She leaned into his chest, feeling the warmth of his torso. She could hardly remember what her point had been in the first place.

"I really have to go," Drew said to her back. "Unless you want me to book another flight? I can go later . . ."

He meant it. She knew that. If she told him to miss his flight for the sake of fifteen minutes with her, he would. "It's OK," she said. "Go. Just promise you'll come back safe."

She closed the door behind her and stood under the spluttering hot water from the ancient shower, thinking about the expression of hurt on Drew's face when she had tried to explain how she felt. He loved this house. It was everything he had ever wanted. She was the problem. She was the one the house didn't like—the one who didn't belong.

"Gina?" she called up the little staircase to Gina's room. She waited a moment. Nothing. Then, footsteps, light quick ones, coming down the stairs.

"Do you need something?" she asked, appearing through the little wooden door. She was too long for it really, all limbs and neck. When they had walked in the park back in London, each holding a pram, Poppy had enjoyed the feeling of being comparatively petite. It didn't happen often, at five foot seven.

"I hate things being like this," she said, looking determinedly between Gina's eyes. "With us."

Gina made a noncommittal noise.

"I know Drew and I haven't had the most normal start," she said. "But you were all up for this back when I was in Ibiza. What happened to 'when you know, you know'?"

Gina made the same noise. Poppy steadied herself. She was going to be like Drew, or at least how she imagined Drew would be in a meeting. Assertive. Firm. She wasn't going to raise her voice or, even worse, cry. "Don't you like him?" she asked.

"It's not that," Gina replied. "It's just—" She stopped, seeming to struggle for words, which was desperately unlike her. "I don't know. I think something's off."

"You're right," said Poppy.

"Really?"

"Yep. Something is off. I think it's the house."

"The house?"

"It's like living in someone else's house. I feel like it's a really fancy holiday rental. It's all so temporary and none of it is ours. Every time I pick up a book or make coffee I feel like I'm on the set of a play and I should be wearing a costume and pretending to answer to Mrs. Spencer."

Gina didn't look convinced. "You think it's the house? Not the fact that you're not allowed to talk about anything that happened before you and Drew met each other?"

"I'm not saying it's the only problem. I know Drew and I got married fast and I know we still need to get to know each other, but that's between us. And it's not that I'm 'not allowed' to talk about it. I can talk about anything that I want. We just agreed not to quiz each other about everything." It wasn't entirely true, but Gina seemed determined to disapprove and Poppy couldn't face giving her any more ammunition.

"I know you're scared to tell him about everything that happened. But you should do it. It made us closer when you told me. Right?"

Poppy pulled herself up to her full height and steadied herself. "Gee, this isn't a negotiation. You know I want all of that stuff left in the past. I'm not talking to him about it. And much as I love you, we don't have to prove our relationship to you."

"Look, babe, I'm just saying that whole deal thing is fucked up, it's not *normal* . . ."

"I know it's not normal. But we're not pretending to be

normal. We're doing things differently and if that makes us happy then that's our business. OK?"

"But—"

Poppy forced the words out of her mouth. "Gina, I'm not asking. I need you to drop this. I love you and I want you to stay, but if you think this is a car crash or you don't like Drew then there's no point in you being here." She wanted to keep talking, to say that Gina was her best friend, that she needed her now more than ever. She wanted to remind her that she'd seen Gina through a dozen horrific relationships. There was the time that Gina had been dating her dealer and he'd locked both Poppy and Gina in his car outside his apartment building for three hours because Gina had pissed him off. She hadn't even broken up with him for that. Poppy had gone to the clinic with Gina after the same boyfriend had given her chlamydia three different times. She'd once taken all of the Winterson kids as well as the Henderson children to the park in the pouring rain for four hours, just so that Gina could spend a morning in bed with the Italian guy from Pret she'd fallen in love with, before he went back to Naples.

Poppy wanted to throw every stupid choice and poorly thought through plan back in Gina's face, to rub it in that she was a million miles from healthy herself. But that wasn't the deal. That wasn't how friends treated each other, and with Drew gone, all alone in this place, she needed Gina. "I want you to stay," she said instead. "But you have to stop bringing up the past and you have to get on board with me and Drew."

Gina nodded. "OK." Maybe Gina had gotten there by herself. "So, what's the plan?"

"Plan?"

"You've got that face on that you get when you're about to try to get kids enthusiastic about baking."

Poppy smiled. "I was wondering whether you'd be up for a bit of a project."

"Project?"

"You know how I said I thought the house was the problem? I thought maybe we could do it up while Drew is away. Before all his friends come to stay."

Gina smiled. "You're not seriously saying you think we can do this in five days?"

"Oh come on."

"Five days? Have you seen the size of this place?"

"I know, I know," Poppy said. "But think how fun it'll be. Like *Changing Rooms*."

"All right," said Gina, with a half sigh, half laugh. "I'll go put my cute but wholesome painting outfit on and you go get the car keys. We need to shop."

BEFORE

Arriving at Côte Rouge was always the same. Just when whoever was driving felt like their ankle was going to split, and it was getting dark, and it wasn't possible to keep going for another moment, the tiny drive opened up in the hedge, and everything sounded different. The wheels of the car were gentle and soft on the grass, and sitting there on the cliff, all white and higgledy and perfect, was the house. Just as it had been when they had left it the year before. The sun would be slipping down behind the hills, the stones hot from the day, and the air scented with flowers and sun. The children would struggle out of the car, rubbing their eyes and whining about being tired and hungry, their legs funny after sitting down for so long. But underneath all of it was a sense of relief. Of coming home.

Caroline and Jim had first come here almost two decades ago, before they were married. It belonged to a friend of a friend's grandparents, who rented it to them for a fraction of the market price because they left it tidy and recommended it to everyone they knew. The first time they had come here, they'd made love in every single room, on the itchy carpet of the living room, on the rickety hob in the

187

kitchen, and dozens of times by the pool. They had come back on their honeymoon. They had conceived Jack here, and Caroline was almost sure Grace too.

Dragging a suitcase from the trunk of the car, she looked over to see Poppy's face. The pink-orange light clashed with her hair a little, and she looked tired from the drive, a mark from where she had been resting her head on the window indented on her cheek.

"Are you OK?" she called over.

Poppy gave her an enormous smile. "I can't believe it," she said. "It's incredible."

Her enthusiasm was contagious. "I know," Caroline replied. "Every time we come, I can't quite believe my luck."

The children had followed Jim inside. Lights were flickering on, illuminating the stone windowsills. "I should go and put Grace down," said Poppy.

"I'll do it," offered Caroline. "You're on holiday."

Poppy laughed. "I'm here to help."

"If I don't see you lying by that pool at least four hours a day, I'm going to be extremely disappointed."

"I want to help. It's easier with more of you."

"It certainly is," said Caroline. Poppy had no idea how much easier. She clearly didn't know the effect that she'd had. The countertops weren't sticky and they didn't constantly run out of milk or juice. But it was more than that. Anyone could have done that. It was like the three of them were a team, taking it in turns to do the hard parts, and getting to enjoy the fun bits. Caroline had found herself playing a lengthy game of Operation with Jack, all on his own. How long had it been since she had just spent time with her son? It felt as if the previous fourteen years had consisted exclusively of trying to get Jack either to do something, or to stop doing something. But Poppy had changed that. The children didn't feel shortchanged hanging out with her; they didn't feel fobbed off.

Caroline stretched upward. Her jeans had dug into her waist, making red grooves in her skin, and her feet felt caged in her Converse, sweaty and trapped.

"Let's go in," she said, taking a last sweep of the view.

"It's hard to stop looking," said Poppy.

"Yes," said Caroline. "It really is."

CHAPTER 23

"OK, thaaanks," said Gina, hanging up the phone. "They're sending two painters, a tiler and a carpenter tomorrow."

"Amazing! You are literally the most persuasive person who has ever lived."

"What can I say?" Gina laughed, clearly feeling pleased with her achievements. She swiped at the display on the car, a little screen where a radio would have been on a normal car. "This thing is smarter than I am," she muttered, but after a minute she managed it, and music sprang from the speakers all around them. Poppy signaled and pulled out onto the main road, a long clear sweep of pavement slicing through the green hills. She pushed her foot toward the floor, feeling the acceleration and the music and the sunshine through the windows. "Fuck yes," shouted Gina as their speed climbed.

It was just like it used to be, when Poppy and her friends would pile into the back of someone's borrowed Nova and speed down the roads by the sea, going faster and faster with music as loud as it would go, warping the speaker. Someone would always have a cigarette on the go, ash flying everywhere in the wind. It would be impossible to hear

anyone, so it didn't matter how badly you sang or if you
didn't know the right words.

She was older now. And she did know the words. The
car was worth twenty times what the Nova had been, and
she was old enough to think that driving after three cans of
White Strike was madness. But still, it was the same feeling
of euphoria.

The back of the car was full, a tangle of stuff. They'd
started at John Lewis, working from the ground up. New
pots, pans, cutlery, glasses, everything really. Then towels.
Tablecloths. Bed linen. Everything anyone could need for a
bathroom. New bins, coat hangers, laundry baskets. They'd
loaded everything that would fit into the car, and the rest
was being delivered tomorrow because Gina had sweet-
talked the man behind the counter and Poppy had agreed
to take out a store card. Tomorrow would bring new bed
frames: a huge pale blue wooden one for their bedroom, a
sleigh bed for the Green Room and a bright yellow metal-
framed one for the Blue Room, which Gina had talked
her into. They had chosen a beautiful wooden table with
benches for the kitchen, and an enormous round dining
table and chairs for the dining room. "It can be extended
to seat up to fourteen," the saleswoman had said sweetly.
Poppy had tried to ignore the thought that she didn't have
fourteen people to invite to dinner.

A small part of her was worried about how much she had
spent. She'd used the credit card for most of it, putting a
few bits on the newly minted store card. The first time she
had run the card through the reader she had expected some
kind of alarm to go off, for someone to realize that she was
an imposter. But all that happened was a smiling woman

saying, "Thank you for your patronage, Mrs. Spencer," as Poppy looked down at the receipt. She had never spent an amount of money with a comma in it before.

"Are you OK?" Gina had asked her. "You look like you've been smacked in the back of the head with one of the new Le Creuset pots."

"Fine," Poppy had said. "Just . . . fucking hell, that was a lot of money."

Gina had laughed. "You're rich now. Embrace it. I know I would."

Maybe she'd followed the advice, or maybe the guilt had worn off, but as she changed lanes, flicking her eyes back to check the road behind her, she felt a warm glow. In the trunk of the car was a whole new world. Things that were going to transform the house from a museum to someone else's family to her own. Hers and Drew's. He would be pleased, she told herself. How could he not be?

CHAPTER 24

After five days of decorating, Poppy ached in places she'd never been aware of having before, and the skin on her hands was so dry that they rasped when she rubbed them together. But the house had become beautiful. It was like one of those makeover films, the ones where they picked someone quite attractive with some easily fixed flaws and then made them perfect. Thursday House was the architectural equivalent of a stunning girl with glasses and frizzy hair. Everything Gina and Poppy did made the house more and more gorgeous.

They had started in the hall. That was where the house started, they reasoned, so that was the place to begin. On a complete hunch, egged on by Gina and encouraged by what she had read online about the house and the period it was built, Poppy had pulled up a floorboard. Lo and behold, underneath them was the most incredible floor she had ever seen. Cerulean blue tiles, studded with gold painted stars. She had summoned a nice floor specialist from the internet, who turned up with his enormous teenage son and pulled the rest of the boards up. "They're odd boards," he had said as he wrenched them up. "Most of 'em come up easy, but it's like these ones are fighting back!"

The words had sent a shiver of fear through Poppy, but she had ignored it. The new floor was beautiful, and seeing the crumbling brown floorboards sitting in the dumpster outside gave her a feeling of triumph.

The floor was so beautiful that the walls shouldn't be over the top, they had agreed. So they had been painted the most delicate (expensive—Gina insisted paint should be expensive) shade of pale gray. Then, flush from their success with the floor, they pulled the carpet off the huge staircase and found that underneath it was a beautiful yellow stone, just like the outside of the house. "That'll be a fucking nightmare when you have kids," Gina had said.

The drawing room was repainted, the ancient furniture steam-cleaned and anything ugly or uncomfortable swapped for something soft and luxurious.

Gina had taken to the redecoration like nothing Poppy had ever seen before. She'd be up by seven, dressed in a tiny T-shirt that the team of workmen seemed to appreciate and pulling wallpaper off the walls or chucking almost anything that came with the house in the trash. "Don't you think we should keep that?" Poppy asked as Gina carried a rolled-up rug to the dumpster.

"Why, do you like it?"

"Well, no."

"Then why would we keep it?"

"It might be valuable."

"What, like you don't have enough money?" Gina laughed.

"It's not that . . ." Poppy trailed off.

"I'd have been so good at being rich," said Gina, throwing the rug into the dumpster. "Maybe it should have been me."

The kitchen was the most exciting part. Poppy had the stone floors sandblasted, the cabinets stripped and painted the palest butter yellow, and the overhead beams white-washed. The Aga stayed put, in pride of place, but she indulged in a microwave, an enormous eight-slice toaster "for when we have guests" and an American fridge the size of a wardrobe. She put a new sofa under the window, covered in cushions and blankets, and the beautiful new table sat at the far end, by the French windows, which led out onto the terrace.

Upstairs, aware that time wasn't on their side, they prioritized the main guest bedrooms and the bathroom. "I promise we'll do your room next," Poppy had said to Gina. If Gina was annoyed about her room being left untouched, she hadn't said anything. But then they'd both been too busy to do much other than sing along to the Hits of the Noughties on the iPod speaker and labor on any part of the project that didn't need the skills of the army of professionals. Poppy was nervous of trying anything, remembering her experience with the lampshade. But Gina had tied her hair back, picked up a brush and slapped a bold shade of mustard on the walls of the Yellow Room. And while pots of paint seemed to tip over more often than felt normal, and doors tended to slam without any explanation, it was working. Gina was winning.

Watching Gina attack the house emboldened Poppy, so after a couple of days of standing on the sidelines watching the others, she braced herself to pull the wallpaper off the dining-room wall. She peeled back the sheets and smiled to see wobbly childish writing on the wall. *Simon & William were here*, it read.

Who had Simon and William been, and how long ago had they been allowed to pencil on the walls before the paper went on? She had no idea how old the wallpaper was. It could have been decades ago, centuries even. Perhaps there were documents that came with the house that told its story? She made a mental note to ask Drew when he came home.

Knowing her limitations, Poppy had hired someone to do the Blue Room in a graphic blue and copper paper that cost more than a day's pay as a nanny for just one roll. She did, however, paint her and Drew's room. All of the rest of the house had been decorated for other people. She wanted to do something just for them, something physical. So she put out dust sheets, opened the windows and started painting, determinedly covering the walls with the palest of rose pinks. It was her house. Her bedroom. She was going to make it feel like her home.

CHAPTER 25

Poppy tried to sit up, but her bones seemed ten times their usual weight. She blinked, trying to unstick her eyelids, and slowly dragged herself up. She was on the floor, the carpet underneath her fingers. She looked around, trying to work out what time it was, and how she had ended up on the floor. Gina was standing over her, fanning her with a magazine. "You passed out, you tit," said Gina, offering a hand to pull Poppy up. "Lucky you didn't fall off the ladder. Looks like you got dizzy and lay down before it really hit you. Why didn't you open the windows?"

"I did."

Gina arched an eyebrow. "You didn't. They're all closed."

"I had them open," Poppy said. Her head was heavy and her neck ached. "How could they have closed?"

"They must have blown shut."

"My head hurts."

"Yeah, no wonder, you've inhaled more paint fumes than my brothers did when we were teenagers. Do you want me to help you finish?"

Poppy staggered to her feet and headed toward the stairs.

"Where are you going?" came Gina's voice from behind her.

"I don't want to be here."

"Here? What the fuck are you talking about?"

"This house. Gina, I had the windows open. I did. Look, I know this sounds mental but I think they closed themselves."

Gina calmly led Poppy into the kitchen where she put the kettle on and made two large cups of tea. Every time Poppy tried to start talking again, Gina hushed her. Eventually, once the tea was gone, Gina took both of Poppy's hands and looked her in the eyes.

"You think those windows closed themselves?"

Poppy nodded. "It's not just that. It's loads of stuff. Like when I tried to change that lightbulb. And the bath over-flowing when I know I turned the taps off. The first day we arrived here a mirror fell off the wall. You don't think that's weird?"

"So, what, the house is haunted?"

Poppy shook her head.

"Then what?"

"Not haunted. It's not like that. It's like . . ." She trailed off. "It's like it doesn't want me here."

To her surprise, Gina didn't laugh in her face or tell her that she was going mad. "OK," she said. "Why not?"

Poppy couldn't meet Gina's eyes. "I don't know. Because I'm not good enough? Not that type of person? It's all so weird. The family who lived here before just disappearing and leaving all their stuff . . ." She paused. "I don't think it's a happy place. And I don't think it wants me here."

"Well, maybe you have to show it who's boss."

"I don't think I can."

"Of course you can. You're not seriously going to let a load of stone and wood tell you what you can and can't do?" Gina got up, pulling herself to full height. "Tell the house it's not the boss of you."

Poppy shook her head. "There are people working in every bloody room; they'll hear me."

"They don't care what you do as long as you pay on time. Come on."

"You're not the boss of me," said Poppy, mostly to get Gina to leave her alone.

"Louder. Aim it at the wall."

Poppy repeated herself, feeling ridiculous as she aimed her words at the wall.

"And once more with feeling," Gina instructed.

"You're not the boss of me," Poppy yelled at the wall.

"Right," said Gina. "Now we prove it. We're going to finish the painting. Come on."

And so they painted the rest of the bedroom, singing along to Hits of the Nineties. Occasionally, while smiling at Gina's Backstreet Boys descant, fear would niggle at her. But then Gina would say something about whether Ronan Keating had a massive penis or not, and she'd laugh. Gina's presence made it difficult to feel afraid.

When they finally sat down at the end of the day, the room was perfect. It was the prettiest color she had ever seen, and next to the newly painted white floorboards it was better than she'd even dreamed. The bed had been delivered the day before, beautiful and enormous and dominating the room. A long white chest sat at the end of it, with a dusky pink velvet cushion on top. The carpenter, whom she'd had to find from five villages over because no one in

Linfield would agree to come, had built a matching window seat under the enormous picture window and by blissful good fortune she had found a pair of heavy silk curtains online that matched everything else.

"Shall we walk it?" Poppy said to Gina, who was lying next to her on the newly comfortable sofa in the sitting room, where they had replaced the too-big lampshade and painted the walls dark red.

"Go on then," she said, "but only if you get me a drink."

Poppy came back with a double vodka and tonic for Gina, who had called redecorating "thirsty" work and gone through two bottles of Grey Goose in a week. "It's amazing," she said. "I can't believe we did it."

Gina took a slug of her drink. "Would you think I was mental if I said that I actually had fun?"

Poppy shook her head. "I've had so much fun. It's like a different house."

"Nah." Gina got up, her glass already half-empty. "It was always an amazing house. We just made it look like it should have looked. I've had some trippy dreams since we've been doing it, though. Probably all the paint fumes."

"Me too! Like what?"

"Oh, weird shit, like the house kept going back to how it was before we started, or falling down. Loads of dreams that I'm falling."

Poppy opened her mouth.

"No," Gina interrupted, "don't give me that face. It's not haunted, it's not possessed, it's paint fumes. What time does his lordship get back?"

In answer to the question, the noise of crunching

gravel sounded outside. "Right now!" said Poppy, her face lighting up.

"Cool," said Gina, setting the glass down on the side table. "I'm heading off."

"What? Why?"

"I told you, I'm going to London this weekend."

"Do you have to go now?"

Gina looked at the clock. Poppy watched as her lips moved, almost imperceptibly. She was working out what fake train to claim to get so that she wouldn't be able to stay. "Gee, why are you in such a rush?"

"I'm not," she said, heading into the corridor. "I just want you and Drew to have the place to yourself. He'll probably want to shag you in every room seeing as you've made it look so amazing."

"Darling?" Drew's voice came from the front door. Poppy ran along the corridor, up the little stairs that connected the front and the back of the house and into Drew's arms.

"The floor . . ." he said.

"Do you like it?"

"It's . . ." He paused, kneeling down to have a look at it. "How did you manage it?"

"It was already there! We pulled up the floorboards."

Drew's face was a picture of marvel. "Bloody hell, Poppy, this is extraordinary."

"Come with me and see the kitchen."

Gina was shoving things into her handbag when they walked in.

Drew opened his arms, offering her a hug. "Gina, it's incredible. I can't thank you enough."

"Oh, no, it was all Poppy, really. I just helped. Her vision."

She shoved her feet into her sneakers, treading the backs down. "I'm going to the station, OK? I can borrow your car, right?" She directed her question toward Poppy.

Poppy nodded.

"I'll be back on Sunday, all right? Jesus, lose the long face or your husband'll take one look at you and top himself." Gina stopped, looking guilty.

"Are you all right to drive?" said Poppy, ignoring the comment. She slipped her hand into Drew's.

"Yes, Mum." She dropped a kiss on the top of Poppy's head, as if she were twenty years younger than her rather than two, and gave Drew an awkward sort of wave.

"That was really weird," said Poppy as she listened to the car drive away. "It was like she wanted to get away from you."

Drew shrugged. "Maybe she's just being respectful of us needing some time together. She's good like that."

"Yeah. Maybe."

"So, are you going to show me the rest of your miracle works?"

"Yes!"

Drew seemed to want to stop and wonder at every tiny thing, each new bookshelf or lamp or lampshade, while Poppy wanted to run around the house pointing at things. She couldn't remember the last time she was this excited. When they reached the dining room Drew looked gobsmacked.

"It was amazing," Poppy said, running her hands over the new wallpaper. "When I pulled the paper off the walls

I found kids' writing. Do you know who Simon and Wil-liam were?"

Drew shook his head. "Not sure. Maybe the kids of the family who lived here before? You really are astonishing," he said, wandering back into the hall. "It's like a different house. Those are all my books!" He pointed to the new wall of books on the landing.

"I called Ralph," she said. "He had them sent up from storage. You do like it, don't you?"

Drew wrapped his arms around her and squeezed. "I love it. It feels like you've given it what it wanted."

Quietly Poppy thought that it was quite the opposite, more that she and Gina had bullied the house into submission, but she didn't say that. Instead she melted her body into Drew's and focused on the perfect floor beneath her feet.

BEFORE

"I like this music," said Poppy, rinsing lettuce leaves in the ancient colander. She gestured toward the little speaker Caroline and Jim had bought on their second trip to the house and left here, so that they could always have music when they visited. "What is it?"

"She's called Dory Previn," Caroline replied. "She's great, isn't she? Jim was obsessed with her when we were at university. It still reminds me of sharing a single bed in his room." She looked up, through the window, and saw that the children were sitting outside on the grass with Jim, attacking enormous ice creams. "They're never going to sleep after that much sugar. I suppose that's the point of being on holiday."

"They're going to have the best memories of this place when they grow up."

"What were holidays like when you were growing up?" Caroline asked. It wasn't a fair question, not really. She knew Poppy wasn't close to her family. But she wanted to know why. Poppy was so reliable, so helpful. So funny and sweet and so very much a part of family life. How could her mother have turned against her?

"We didn't go away much."

"Why not?"

"Money. But even if we'd had any, my mum doesn't like going far from home. She doesn't drive or anything."

"Didn't she drop you off at university?"

"Nope," Poppy replied casually as she put a glass in the dishwasher.

"Then how did you get there?"

"Train." Poppy grinned. "The girl handing out room keys looked so upset when I told her I was on my own, I'm pretty sure she swapped me into a bigger room."

The vision of Poppy, even younger than she was now, standing on the platform at Durham train station on her own with everything she owned in one suitcase tore at Caroline's chest. A little part of her liked hearing about Poppy's mother. Whatever her own failings were—however late she stayed at the office sometimes—she was nothing like Mrs. Grant.

"We can drop you back in October," she heard herself say.

Poppy's chest flushed pink. She seemed to be concentrating rather harder than she needed to on chopping an onion. "Oh, you don't need to do that. Really."

"We'd like to," said Caroline firmly. Poppy looked embarrassed, so Caroline decided to shift the focus of the conversation. "So where was the first place you ever went away to?"

"Away like abroad?"

Caroline nodded.

"Here."

"This is your first ever trip abroad?" She tried to keep her voice light, as though she wasn't surprised. But how was that possible in an age of twenty-quid flights and package deals? How could Poppy have spent twenty-one years living in the UK and never gone anywhere?

"We lived by the sea," Poppy volunteered. "So it never seemed to make much sense going away to a holiday place. That's why I was so worried about the passport thing."

"What passport thing?"

"About not having one. Didn't Jim tell you?"

Caroline caught her face before it changed. "Of course he did. Anyway, all that matters is that we've got you here now. And it's going to be great. I promise. Shall we take this lot outside? Not that there's any chance of those little monsters eating a single savory bite after those ice creams."

Caroline picked up the bowl of salad and the plate of cheese and meat. There was no point cooking proper meals here; they'd just bought all sorts of bits from the supermarket. The kids loved French shops. In London they'd whine and moan about trailing around Waitrose, but here everything was foreign and exciting and they loved running up and down the aisles guessing what things were and trying to sneak things into the cart. Caroline didn't much care what they ate on holiday, but she knew that her job was to play the straight man, to make it look like they were getting away with something. Being boring was what they wanted from her, so it was what she did. Wasn't that the thing about parenting?

"This all looks amazing!" said Jim, sitting down at the little wooden table. The chairs were all just a little bit wobbly, and would give you a splinter in the back of your thigh if you fidgeted too much. Would the shabbiness here always be charming? Or would they come to a point in their life where they wanted luxury? Would they be willing to trade off the total privacy and silence of Côte Rouge for convenience? Activities. TVs that always worked, electricity that didn't fuse if too many people tried to use a plug at the same time.

"What's that?" asked Poppy, pointing at one of the cheeses.

"Pont l'Évêque," said Jim, before Caroline answered. "It's a bit stronger than Brie, but not much. You'll probably like it."

He clearly loved this role, educating her. Telling her what various foods were, getting her to drink wine. "I drink wine," she had insisted earlier in the holidays. "But only on nights out."

"You don't have to drink it to get slaughtered," Jim had insisted. He'd poured her a New Zealand Sauvignon and made her try it. Either she had liked it very much, or she'd committed to being polite and pretended with utter conviction. She'd mentioned school plays to Caroline, offhand. Something about being in a show at Durham. So clearly she had it in her to pretend.

Caroline was quite sure that Poppy would never reject anything she or Jim suggested, in case it offended them.

As Caroline sat down to join her family at the table, she couldn't stop the voice in her head. What was the "passport thing"?

Why had Jim kept it from her?

CHAPTER 26

Drew and Poppy had, as Gina predicted, taken it upon themselves to christen every room in the house. Forty-eight hours had skipped by in a blur of tangled limbs, laughter, red wine and delicious food. Poppy had cooked every meal in her knickers and one of Drew's shirts, a cliché he loved. Time had evaporated and Monday morning had arrived, dark and unwelcome. Poppy had woken up from a bone-meltingly deep sleep to find that Drew had already gone and Gina was yet to return, despite having said she would be back on Sunday. Yet again, she was alone here.

Poppy lay on her bed, staring at the ceiling. She and Gina had painted the walls, but hadn't had the right shade of white to do the ceiling. It had a small yellow patch that needed extra attention. Perhaps it would need plastering. She added it to the list of things she kept in her head, things that still needed doing. The taps in the downstairs loo. The back door at the side of the house. These little things were like life rafts. The week with Gina, so busy and productive, had been perfect. Finding other things to do and adding them to her list, knowing that her work wasn't all over, would keep her sane. A little bit of her wondered if she'd been too quick to finish the job, rushing to get it done before Drew got back from his trip, before his friends descended. Should she have saved something, made the whole thing last longer?

What a cliché. Younger wife, wanting to make everything look perfect, as if that would change anything. As if that would earn her place in this house. Poppy had found a book in the school library, years ago. *Rebecca*. It was the story of a young woman who married a much older man and moved to his huge house in the country. She hadn't finished it. She'd found the heroine, who walked around the house intimidated by it, wishing she belonged, too irritating. *Just fucking do something*, she had thought, and she had shoved the paperback back onto the shelf, the plastic covering bending backward as it caught on a next-door book. She smiled to herself, remembering it. If only she could be eighteen and know everything again.

The doorbell punctured her thoughts. Who could that be? She got up and pulled a pair of shorts from the chair in the corner of the room, finding a T-shirt to cover her nakedness and twisting her hair into a bun. Not that it would be anyone important. If Gina was back she would have used her keys. Drew the same. And no one had visited since they had arrived; no neighbors had dropped by to see them. It had surprised Poppy, to start with. She had thought that village life would mean fetes and bake sales and people popping over to introduce themselves. "Maybe if we lived in the village itself?" Drew had explained. "But if you live on one of the lanes, it's not really like that."

Poppy pulled the door open and saw the postman

standing there, a heavyset man in a short-sleeved shirt and knee-length shorts.

"Parcel for you," he said, holding out a large Jiffy bag.

"Thanks," said Poppy, squinting into the sunlight. She took the little screen from him and slowly wrote her name with the plastic pencil.

"Doesn't need to be accurate," he told her as he realized what she was doing. But Poppy had had so few chances to write her married name, she could hardly resist.

"Beautiful day," she said, handing it back.

Mrs. Drew Spencer, read the label. Which meant it was for both of them—the sort of confusing law of etiquette she'd never have known about if it weren't for her years with the Hendersons. Did she have to wait for Drew to come home to open it? She looked up at the clock. He wouldn't be home for hours and hours. He wouldn't mind. A little guiltily, she pulled at the tab and tipped a cream box, tied with a blue ribbon, onto the table. There was a card. *Congratulations on your wedding, much love, Dilly & Mac.*

They were Drew's friends. Mac had been at school with Drew, and they'd shared an apartment in New York for a couple of years. Drew had told her that during one of his rare bouts of sharing. They were one of the couples coming to stay next weekend. God, it was next weekend. Poppy counted on her fingers to make sure that she had the date right. Yes, it was next weekend. That had come around terrifyingly quickly.

Poppy ran a finger over the heavy card. The writing was cramped, but neat. A blue fountain pen. She could just imagine what Dilly would be like, the kind of precise person who wanted to send a wedding present now rather than bring it with her when she visited. She would be embarrassed if she had to watch them open it. Poppy had been shocked when she'd discovered that children like the Hendersons' kids weren't allowed to open birthday presents at their party, but instead had to wait until everyone had gone home.

Poppy decided that Dilly, whoever she was, would have told Mac one evening when he came home from work that she'd sent Drew and his new wife a present for their wedding. Then they'd speculate about her—guess how old she was and what she looked like. One of their children would probably offer to look her up online and then be surprised not to find anything. "Are you sure that's her name, Mummy?" she imagined a lanky teenager asking.

Poppy tugged at the ribbon and lifted the lid of the box. The tissue paper was sealed by a sticker. She slid her finger underneath it and then lifted the paper. Inside was a silver photo frame. She picked it up. Expensive. Classic. Not, if she was going to be honest, very exciting. It was intensely plain. The kind of thing she would never have bought for herself, especially as it probably cost several hundred pounds. But the kind of thing that would be nice to have. She picked it up. She would put a photo from their wedding in it, and put it in the drawing room, so that when Dilly and Mac came to stay they would be able to see that she and Drew liked it. And that way they'd have to approve of at least one aspect of her decoration.

The only hard copy of their wedding photo was in a brown leather frame in Drew's office. She pushed the door open and breathed in the strangely male scent of the room. Drew had never said that she couldn't use the study, nor had he ever claimed it for himself. But something about all the leather and books, the way that sound went dead as soon as you made any, meant Poppy didn't feel at ease in here. She picked up the photo frame. "Do you realize," she had asked Drew on their wedding day, "that was the first photo anyone's ever taken of us?" They'd laughed at the ridiculousness of it. Poppy had printed the photo out at a little shop in the town center, determined to have a copy of it to take home. There were a few others on his phone, snapped by the witnesses they'd dragged in off the street, by the waiter at the restaurant. She should get those printed too. Make them a little wedding album.

She pried the back off the frame, turning the little fobs that held it on, and then pulling at the strut that supported it. It was surprisingly difficult. Putting her hand flat on the frame and yanking at the back, it finally came loose. And with it came a photo. Not the picture of her and Drew, laughing outside the town hall in a shower of white rose petals. Another photo, hidden between their wedding picture and the back of the frame.

It was an image of two little boys. One of whom looked unmistakably like Drew. Curly dark hair, worried eyes, he couldn't have been more than four or five. And they were standing in front of the house. This house. Thursday House. His skinny little legs in navy-blue shorts, and the other boy, three or four inches taller, standing next to him. Was it Drew as a child? Or could it be something else? She tried to dismiss the thought. There was no way. He couldn't have a child. He would have mentioned it. He would have told her.

Would he? the nasty voice in the back of her head piped

up. *He was the one who didn't want to talk about the past. There would have been someone before you. Multiple someones. Perhaps a whole little family.*

She tried to block the voice out, clamping her hands over her ears as if it was playing outside her mind rather than inside it. *Shut up shut up shut up,* she repeated over and over again.

She blinked hard, as if she was trying to reset the image, as if by closing her eyes tight enough she'd be able to see something else, something that wiped the picture away. But no matter how tightly she squeezed her lids shut, the image didn't change. It looked so, so much like Drew. And they were unquestionably standing outside Thursday House, on the steps that led up to the front door. She ran her eyes over the boys' clothes, trying to work out when they belonged. Shorts, a T-shirt, sandals. It could have been taken a few years ago or a few decades ago.

It must mean something to him, otherwise he wouldn't have it. Why would he have a photo of himself here? But if it was his child, or some relative, why hide it? Maybe it could be a nephew or a cousin or something? But even as she told herself the comforting lie she knew it wasn't true. If it were that innocent he could have put it up on the wall. Poppy had assumed that there were hardly any photos of Drew or his family because of the accident, because seeing images of his parents and his brother must be too painful for him. The horrible little voice was louder now. *Why wouldn't he want to talk about the past? He suggested it for the same reason you agreed to it. He's got something to hide.* This time the voice didn't sound like her mother, it sounded like Gina.

She peeled the wedding photo off the glass and placed the

photo of the little boys back into the frame, securing the back and putting it exactly where Drew had had it. Then she took the wedding photo and the shiny new frame to the drawing room.

"Hey, it's me," Poppy said into the phone. Her voice was low, even though there was no one at home, no one for almost a square mile around her. "Are you coming back today?"

"Poppy? Jesus, what time is it?"

She looked at the display on the oven. "Nearly twelve."

Gina groaned. "Yeah, yeah, I'm coming back. I'll get moving. Just need to work out where I am." She laughed, but Poppy couldn't summon the energy to join in.

"Are you OK, babe?" Gina sounded more sober.

"I think so."

"What's going on?"

"It's nothing, it's just . . ." She paused. The instinct that had warned her not to complain about Gina to Drew was telling her the same thing in reverse. What would she really gain by telling Gina any of this, before she'd given Drew a chance to explain? "It's fine. I'll see you tonight? Let me know if you need me to get you a taxi from the station. Don't drive the car if you're over the limit, OK? The roads round here are mental."

"Yes, Mum," said Gina. She heard a man's voice in the background and the little giggle Gina did when she liked a boy. The line went dead. Poppy looked at the blank screen of the phone and sighed, trying to slow her heartbeat, trying to convince herself that there was probably a rational explanation, that it was going to be all right. Poppy was an expert in shoving feelings down, in sending panic to the back of her mind and carrying on regardless. But however hard she tried, it just didn't seem to work. Every instinct she had was screaming inside her head. Something wasn't right.

CHAPTER 27

Hours later, the light in the study was blue and the book Poppy had been trying to read lay abandoned at her feet. She had sat, motionless, waiting for Drew to get home for what must have been hours.

"Darling?" a voice called from somewhere in the house. Drew's voice.

"I'm in the study," she called back. Her voice sounded weird; even she could hear that.

She heard Drew's feet, light on the hall floor, three quick taps up the steps from the hall and there he was, smiling in the doorway. "Hello, darling. What are you doing in here?"

"Hi," she tried again, but her voice sounded just as odd as ever.

Drew's face fell. "What's wrong?"

"Nothing," she said, unsure why she was lying. What would be so wrong with asking about the photo? What could possibly happen?

"You look utterly miserable," he said. "You're not dressed?"

Poppy looked down at her clothes; she had no idea she hadn't got dressed. The pajama shorts. The T-shirt. "I'm not feeling great," she said. Which was true. Acid was burning the back of her throat.

"Oh darling. Do you think it's something you ate?" he asked. He sat down next to her, leaning forward to push a strand of hair out of her face. "Or could it be . . ." He trailed off, leaving her in no doubt about his meaning.

"No, no. I think it's just a bug."

Did he look disappointed? "You're home early," she said.

"I finished everything I needed to do; Andrea is running things amazingly so I didn't need to be there. I thought I'd come home and surprise you, maybe take you out. But if you're not feeling well you might just want to go back to bed?"

Poppy opened her mouth to say yes, to say that she wanted some sleep. Her sickness would buy her at least twenty-four hours to think about it, to construct a plan. But the thought didn't feel right. It sat uneasy inside her—an odd, awkward sensation. She didn't want to plot and plan. She didn't want to wait until Gina got back and then have a whispered conversation about strategy in her bedroom. She wanted to talk to her husband.

"I found a photo," she said, hoping that Drew would finish the conversation for her.

"A photo? What photo?"

She got to her feet. Words were too slippery, too hard to twist into the right order. She walked across the room, picked up the frame and held it out to him.

"That photo."

Drew's eyebrows drew closer together and he put his hands to his head. "I see."

The carriage clock on the desk ticked. The click, click, click of the second hand seemed to fill the room, a noise that would usually be so easy to ignore drowning Poppy's ears.

"Sit down," said Drew.

"I don't want to sit down."

"Please," he said. "Please sit down."

Poppy sat on the arm of the leather sofa, both feet on the floor. A compromise. Drew sat at the other end, his back against the corner. "What would you like to know?" he asked.

"The truth," said Poppy. "About what the hell is going on?"

He was going to tell her that he had a child. She knew it. And a wife, probably. Would they even be separated? Was this just some bizarre affair—had he brought her back here to play lady of the manor in some strange game? She could feel it all falling away, the house and the cars and the security. But more than that. Him. The warmth of his body on hers when they got into bed at night, his voice in the morning offering her coffee. His calm, sweet, reassuring presence that had made her feel safe for the first time in her life, his solid, reassuring love that had said, without saying it out loud, that she could finally stop running.

"Who is it?" she asked eventually, needing to hear something other than the clock. *Please*, she thought, *tell me something good. Tell me something that makes me believe all of this won't go away, something that means I can stay here and keep loving you.*

"It's me," he said quietly.

This wasn't how Poppy expected it to work. She was supposed to ask him and he was supposed to offer a lengthy explanation. His silence, his enduring commitment to telling her absolutely nothing: that wasn't what was supposed to happen. There were too many questions. Poppy couldn't decide which one to ask first.

Drew pinched the bridge of his nose, closing his eyes. He looked as if he was in pain. "I thought we weren't going to do this."

For the first time since she saw the photo, frustration and anger overtook Poppy's confusion. "You can't expect me to just ignore this."

Drew remained silent.

"Anyway, if you didn't want to 'do this' then why do you have a secret photo hidden in your study? It was only a matter of time until I found it."

"It's not a secret photo."

"It's hidden behind another photo in a frame. That sounds pretty fucking secret to me."

Drew blinked. It was the first time Poppy had ever sworn at him.

"Just tell me the truth."

"It's a picture of me," he said after a little while.

"Go on?"

"It's me as a child."

"So why would you hide it?"

"I thought you might find it strange," he said quietly.

"Find what strange?"

"Moving here."

"Why?"

"Because it was my house."

"I'm sorry?"

"This place. When I was a child. It's where we lived before the accident."

"We?"

"My family."

"You lived at Thursday House?"

"Yes. Though it wasn't called that then. It didn't have a name when we lived here, just a number. I changed it when I bought it for us."

"Until the accident?"

He nodded. "Then it was sold to give me a lump sum, for school and university—" He stopped. "Please don't think I'm being indulgent, but I didn't get a chance to come back, after the accident. When we got back from Ibiza that was the first time that I had been back in thirty-five years."

Drew's face was serious, pale underneath its olive tone. Poppy's stomach was twisting; she wanted to put her arms around him, to expunge the guilt he was so clearly racked with.

"I know I did a terrible thing, lying to you. But I had always promised myself I'd come back here eventually, and I so badly wanted to do it with you. I thought you might find it strange, or might not want to live here because of the history. I was worried you'd never feel like it was your home. I should have told you. I'm sorry, Poppy. I—"

She couldn't believe the relief that came with hearing his explanation. This was it. This was why she had felt something was off, why she'd worried and wondered and not been able to relax into living here.

Poppy covered his mouth with hers, kneeling on the worn brown leather of the sofa. She straddled his body, grabbing at his arms, his chest, running her hands over his head and down his back. It was just like the first time they had sex, rushed and desperate and almost angry. She understood now. All the little niggles, the heavy feeling at the back of her head that told her something was up. This was it. His secret. She felt light. Giddy even. She could handle this.

Drew pulled away from her, his hands either side of her body, literally pushing her away. "What are you doing?"

"It's OK," she said as she undid his belt. "I get it."

"You understand?"

"I understand why you did it."

Drew put his hands into her hair and pulled her lips to his, tender where she had been aggressive. "You're sure?" he murmured.

"Sure," she said.

"I know what we agreed, but if you want to know anything, if there's anything you need to ask me—"

"I don't," she said, her lips on his neck. She unzipped his jeans. He sprang free of the fabric. He hissed as she felt for him, and grabbed her hips, pulling her down onto him. He gave a low groan as she straddled him. He was usually so patient when they had sex, so led by what she wanted, but now it seemed as if what she wanted didn't matter. Despite the fact she was on top, he was moving her, manipulating her body, setting the rhythm of her movement. He reached between her legs and placed his knuckles against her clitoris. As she moved back and forward she pressed against his hand, each movement bringing her pleasure and then taking it away. "Stop it," she whispered, "that's mean."

In response, he ground his hand against her harder,

bringing her to an almost painful climax while he gave a long, low groan into her ear.

"I love you," she said, scraping the hair away from her face where it had matted with sweat.

"I love you too," he replied. "That was something of a surprise."

She got to her feet, odd but familiar wetness seeping into the gusset of her knickers. "I don't mind," she said. "All the stuff, about the house. I wanted you to get that I don't mind." Something about his lie had eased her guilt. The pendulum inside her, nagging at her, making her feel guilty, was a little lighter.

Drew pulled her back toward him, lying back on the leather sofa. His heart was thudding through his damp shirt, from the sex or from the truth—she wasn't sure which.

Poppy was chopping tomatoes for a salad when Gina came home that evening, pottering around the warm kitchen humming to herself and wondering whether they should have steak or salmon. She loved this kitchen. Everything about it, the smooth granite worktops, the neat stack of chopping boards. It was perfect. One of the few rooms that really felt like hers. She spent most of her time in here. She'd asked Drew the other day if he thought it was odd to have so many rooms and use so few of them. "It'll come alive when we have people to stay," he had told her. "Houses like this were meant for parties."

It wasn't clear whether they were going to be open now, whether the fact that Drew had grown up at the house would be a part of their lives or whether it was going to be a quiet secret between them. Poppy guiltily hoped for the latter. It didn't bother her. Not really. She understood more than anyone—more than Drew could possibly realize— what it was like to want to go back and rewrite the story, to have another chance at the past. But she didn't want to tell Gina. She couldn't face the rise of her left, perfectly angled eyebrow, the tilt of her head, the *And you're OK with that?* that would inevitably come.

Gina crashed through the front door, dropped her handbag—a huge leather thing covered in chains—on the kitchen table and pulled her shoes off. "I am sweating like a priest in a brothel," she said, pulling a glass from the shelf and filling it with water from the tap. It was as if she had been gone for a couple of hours, not the whole weekend. "What's up with you?"

"Drew's outside," she said, hoping Gina would catch the hint and not bellow *So what were you so upset about earlier?*

Beads of water ran down Gina's chin as she gulped the entire tumbler down. "He's home already?"

"He came home at lunchtime. To surprise me."

"Nice," Gina said, picking her bag back up. "I'm going up to my room. I've got, like, an entire weekend of sleep to catch up on. What were you calling about earlier?"

"Oh." Poppy scraped the fat red tomatoes off the board into a bowl. "It was a misunderstanding."

Gina took a slice of tomato out of the bowl. "About what?"

"Nothing."

"Didn't sound like nothing."

Poppy pulled the purple skin from an onion. Then she

sliced the top and the end off, cutting through the lilac flesh and dicing it deftly. The knives were new and gloriously sharp, slipping effortlessly through anything Poppy used them on. She sprinkled the onion over the tomatoes. Where was the rock salt? She had had it the other day.

"Poppy?"

"Oh, it was stupid," she replied, still looking for the salt. "It makes me sound like such a dick. Basically I found this photo of Drew . . ." She paused. There it was. She put her hand into the white box and pulled out a fat pinch of rock salt, sprinkling the flakes over the bowl. It was so pretty, with the green basil, red tomatoes and purple onion. She'd never dreamed when she was a kid, washing dried-out chicken nuggets down with weak fruit juice, that food could be exciting or beautiful. It wasn't until she had started working for the Walkers that she'd even realized food was supposed to be enjoyed.

"Was it with another girl?"

"What?"

"Jesus, you're out of it this evening. Was the photo of Drew with another girl?"

Poppy wasn't sure what she had been intending to tell Gina, but she wouldn't have to decide now. A photo of Drew with another girl. That was easier. Neater. "Yeah," she said. "I lost it over nothing."

"Was it an old picture?"

She nodded. "I feel like a complete dick."

"Was he OK about it?"

"Drew?"

"Yeah. He wasn't angry or anything?" Gina looked

worried. "He didn't . . ." Was she being paranoid or was Gina looking her up and down for signs of a fight?

"God no," she said. "He was fine. It was just me being paranoid. I was such an arsehole."

Gina laughed. "We've all been there, babe." She went to the larder and grabbed a bottle of white wine.

"That's not cold."

"It's fine."

"There's a cold one in the wine fridge?"

"Can't be fucked."

"It won't be that nice like that."

"Jesus, Poppy, I said it's fine."

Poppy dropped the knife she was chopping garlic with, feeling as if she had been stung. "Sorry," she said, avoiding Gina's eye. "I didn't mean to—"

"It's OK." Gina was heading for the hall door. "It's me, I'm just tired and grumpy. I need some sleep." She still had the bottle of tepid white wine in her hand.

"Do you want supper?" Poppy asked as Gina disappeared.

"No thanks," she called back. "See you tomorrow."

CHAPTER 28

It was such a cliché to try on seven different outfits and then land back at the first one. But that was exactly what Poppy had done. She'd tried on jeans, skirts, dresses and even a pair of shorts before landing right back at the dress she had started with. It was navy, came to her mid-thigh. The fabric was silky. It had been expensive, one of the few things she'd bought herself since she'd been given the credit cards. She spritzed perfume over herself. Should she put lipstick on? She dismissed the idea as she thought it. No more makeup. She had a habit of adding more and more to fill time and distract herself from nerves, which was how she had ended up on various dates with raccoon eyes and red lipstick. She looked at the clock. They would be here soon. Drew had told them to come at five o'clock. "That way," he'd said, "they can nosy around the house, then shower and change before we start drinks." He'd been doing that all week. Saying things as if she already knew them, finding ways to tell her how to handle this without making her feel stupid for not knowing how to host a weekend in the countryside. As if that was just something that people knew.

There was a knock at the door as it swung open. Gina's

knock was an announcement of entry, not a request. "I don't know what the fuck I'm supposed to wear," she said, dropping her towel.

For the thousandth time in their friendship Poppy admired the length of her limbs and the concavity of her stomach. "How do you look like that?" she asked.

Gina looked down, as if her body was a surprise. "Like what?"

"Urgh, like that," said Poppy, getting up.

"You are joking, right? Your body is sick. I would commit actual murder for your rack."

Poppy pointed at the walk-in wardrobe. "Help yourself to anything you want. It'll all be too big for you, though."

Downstairs she found Drew in the study, looking at the crossword. "Regard highly," he said as she closed the dark wooden door behind her. "Six letters."

"Esteem?" she asked.

"Esteem," he repeated, filling the letters in. "Very good, Spencer." He looked up. "What's that face for?"

"Face?"

"You look miserable."

"I'm not." She paused. "Do you think they'll like their rooms?" she asked.

"Of course they will. You've done an amazing job on this place, you know that. You could make a fortune as a designer. And if they don't like their rooms then they can bugger off."

She knew he meant it as a reassurance, but all she heard was him admitting it was possible that they might disapprove of her taste, that Drew might finally realize what she'd told him so many times, that she was different from him, and not in a way that she was proud of. What would Caroline tell her? She closed her eyes and imagined her, tall and tanned with masses of curly dark hair. *Make sure there's enough loo roll and enough wine.* That's what she would have said. *If you've got loo roll and wine then everything else is window dressing.*

An hour later, Poppy watched Drew's face light up from the inside as his friend got out of the sensible, midsize family car. So this was Ralph, the miracle worker who had fixed everything about the house, made it so that they could move straight in. He wore a pink-and-white-checked shirt tucked into jeans. Poppy knew he and Drew had grown up together, but Ralph seemed older than Drew. And there was more than that. Something undeniably "dad" about him.

Drew had said that the three of them had been at boarding school together. What must that be like? An expensive sort of orphanage, she supposed. Rafe, the oldest Henderson, would have been shipped off in September. They had had an appointment booked at Harrods to go and have his uniform fitted. Thinking about Rafe—irritating, aggressive, naughty Rafe—being packed off to school in a blazer a little too big for him raised a tightness in the back of her throat. What must it have been like for Drew, being there with all those boys, who all had families to go home to for the holidays? But then she supposed that really this was his family. She straightened up. That was why she had to make a good impression. There would be no "meeting the parents" with Drew. So this had to work. She had to make them like her. *Drew loves me,* she told herself, trying to ease the feeling inside her stomach. *They love Drew, and Drew loves me.*

"Hi," she said, smiling up at Ralph. "I'm Poppy. Thank

you for everything you did for the house. We really couldn't have done it without you."

He pulled Poppy in for a hug and then clamped his hands either side of her arms. "Wonderful to meet you," he said, sounding sincere. "I've heard so much. This is my wife, Emma." He gestured to the woman holding the bunch of flowers before turning toward Drew.

Emma was just what Poppy had expected. Her skinny legs were encased in neat jeans, which she had paired with a long-sleeved striped T-shirt. Her hair was thick and blond and almost brushed her shoulders. The kind of woman whom Poppy met at school pickup, though they'd never have spoken, not with the unofficial nanny versus mother divide that ruled southwest London's playgrounds.

She smiled. "Great to meet you."

"You too," said Emma. They bumped their cheeks against each other, Poppy's cheek soft against Emma's razor cheekbones. Emma handed her the flowers. "These are for you."

"Oh wow, thanks." *Wow?* She bit the inside of her lip. This was not the time to start talking like a six-year-old. They had probably already spent most of the journey guessing how old she was going to be.

"How was the drive?" she asked, reaching for an adult question.

"Oh, fine. Shall we go inside?"

Poppy felt her eyebrows rise. "Oh. Yeah, of course. Drew?" she called. "Shall we go in?"

"I'd leave them to it," Emma said, picking up her neat leather bag. "They're always like this when they haven't seen each other for a while."

Drew was rubbing Ralph's head, saying something about his receding hairline.

"Looks like you've been struck by a case of the love chub," Ralph shouted, patting Drew's stomach, which was marginally less washboard flat than it had been when he had met Poppy.

"Good plan, we can make some tea. Blokes, right?"

Emma said nothing.

"They're all the same," Poppy tried again. "Eight or eighty, always taking the piss out of each other."

"Mmm," said Emma. "I suppose so. Shall we put those in some water?" She put her handbag down in the kitchen and started opening cupboards. "Where are the vases?" she asked.

Poppy pointed to the larder, the long cold room at the side of the kitchen where most of the food lived. There was a shelf, high up on the wall, running the length of it, full of vases that had survived her and Gina's cull. Poppy allowed herself a moment to remember the glorious feeling of throwing the cushions from the drawing room on the bonfire at the bottom of the garden, watching them smolder and burn and take the last traces of that dated room with them.

"Very neat shelves," Emma called into the kitchen, almost sounding impressed. "Is that you or the cleaner?"

"We don't have a cleaner at the moment," Poppy replied. "My friend Gina is staying with us and helping me out until I find something more permanent."

Emma emerged, holding a vase.

"That one has a crack in it," Poppy lied. She heard the words come out of her mouth and wondered why she had felt the need to say it, why she needed Emma to have gotten something wrong. "There's a green one at the back that would work," she added, feeling guilty. "I need to clear them out really." She pulled herself up to her full height. "Most of them really aren't to my taste."

Emma disappeared back into the larder and came out holding a tall clear glass vase. "I'd be careful with doing that," she said, filling the vase from the tap. "That tall white one was Drew's mother's."

"His mother's?" asked Poppy, taking the huge metal kettle and putting it on the hob. "Are you sure?"

Emma nodded. "Quite sure. It was her favorite. I remember seeing it when I was little," she added. As if that was an explanation.

"Little?"

"Didn't he tell you? Our mothers were best friends. I spent half my life with him and his brother."

"No," said Poppy weakly, pouring milk into a jug. "I knew he was at school with Ralph, but he didn't mention that."

Emma snorted. "Typical Drew. Scissors?"

"In that drawer," said Poppy, "but honestly, I'll do it in a bit. Just let me finish—"

"It's fine," said Emma, yanking the drawer open. "They'll wilt if you leave them too long."

They wouldn't wilt in the next fifteen minutes. But there was no point in saying that. "That's so kind of you."

Poppy put the kettle on the hot plate of the Aga. Why hadn't Drew mentioned that was one of his mother's vases? She could have dropped it without knowing, or chucked it. Was he embarrassed because he'd kept hold of something so feminine? Surely he was more evolved than that? It was sweet. So sweet that she almost wanted to go and wrap her arms around him. She searched in the cutlery drawer for the sugar tongs, listening to the click of Emma's scissors as she sliced through the stems of the flowers. She should say something. Fill the silence.

"How was the drive?" she ventured. She had already asked that.

"Fine," said Emma. She had lined the flowers up on the counter in a perfect stack. Each severed stem—identical in length—had been placed in a bowl. "Bin?" she asked, holding the bowl up.

"If you leave them there I'll take them to the compost later."

Poppy watched a little quirk appear at the left corner of Emma's mouth. "Quite the country mouse," she said.

Poppy took the kettle off the hob and placed it on the side.

"Isn't that a bit hot?" asked Emma from the other end of the long kitchen, where she was arranging the flowers into a military configuration.

"It's OK," said Poppy.

"You'll scorch it," said Emma. "Put a mat underneath it."

"It's heatproof," said Poppy. "That's why I chose it."

"You redid the kitchen?" Emma's eyebrows disappeared into her heavy blond fringe.

"Yep." Poppy nodded. "It was the first thing we did."

She watched Emma drink in the butter-yellow cabinets and brass taps. Was Poppy being oversensitive, or did she look surprised to see that Poppy had taste? "I'm thinking about retraining in interior design," she added, hearing how stupid the words sounded as they fell into the room.

"Well," said Emma, "you've got a great eye." She picked up the vase and placed it at the center of the wooden table. "We can move it later, when we eat," she said. "Nothing worse than being unable to see across the table."

"We're eating outside this evening," Poppy replied. "Because it's still quite warm, and we've got the heaters, we thought it might be nice to eat on the terrace. Drew is barbecuing."

"Gosh," said Emma. "I hope everyone's packed appropriately."

"Oh, I wouldn't worry about that. It's just nice to be out there while the weather holds. And we've got blankets and spare sweaters."

Emma made a noise with her lips sealed together, a noise that didn't mean anything. "How else can I help?" she asked.

Poppy managed to smother the smile pulling at her mouth. "Honestly, it's all under control. I don't need anything. Why don't you go and get ready for supper?"

Emma shrugged and turned for the kitchen door. As she reached for the handle, she stopped. "You know," she said, her words slow and flat. "Drew is very special to all of us. We . . ." She paused. ". . . love him."

"I know. That's why I'm so glad that you're all here. In our home."

Emma did not mistake Poppy's meaning. She gave a tight smile, which Poppy read as an admission of defeat, and closed the kitchen door behind her.

CHAPTER 29

Cordelia and Mac arrived half an hour later. Poppy was just about to slip upstairs to check her makeup and spray yet more deodorant under her arms when she heard a voice in the hall, calling hello. Running from the kitchen, she saw a dark-haired woman with muscular arms wearing a sleeveless shift dress.

"Hello," she said, not unkindly. "Could you let Mr. and Mrs. Spencer know that Mr. and Mrs. Wren have arrived?"

It was a moment before Poppy processed what was happening. In fact, she was just about to wipe her hands on a tea towel and run down to give the message when she realized that she was, in fact, Mrs. Spencer.

"You've just told her yourself," said a voice from the staircase. Gina's endless legs were appearing above her, eventually covered by denim shorts. What a moment to have chosen to finally appear downstairs. Her torso was long and lean in a cropped T-shirt. Poppy fought off the fact that Gina had gone through her entire wardrobe and hadn't found anything she wanted to borrow. Were her clothes really that boring? "That's Poppy," she said. If she was trying to repress her laughter, she wasn't doing a very good job of it.

Poppy stepped forward and offered her hand to shake, just as Cordelia leaned in to bump her cheek against Poppy. Poppy's fingers sort of stabbed Cordelia's toned stomach. Gina laughed.

"Gina," said Poppy, "any chance you could get everyone a drink?"

"Sure," she said, turning for the kitchen. "Drew and Ralph have already started."

Poppy looked out of the hall window and saw that Gina was right. They were both sitting at the wooden table with beers in their hands. It was fine, Poppy told herself. That was good. They were having fun.

"Typical Ralph." Cordelia laughed. "Always such a bad influence on poor Drew."

Poor Drew seemed like an odd thing to say, but Poppy couldn't think of a response.

"Dilly, did you have to pack everything you owned?" came a voice from the door. Looking up, Poppy saw a man, no more than five foot five, with a great deal of curly ginger hair. He dropped the suitcase heavily on the floor. "That's it, I've definitely got a hernia."

"Hi," said Poppy, looking from Cordelia to the man, wondering if it was possible that these two people could be married to each other. "I'm Poppy."

He looked her up and down, which should have been offensive but somehow from his crinkly brown eyes felt friendly. "Well," he said. "You were quite right, Dilly."

"Right?" asked Poppy.

"She said you'd be gorgeous."

Poppy laughed, sure that when Cordelia—Dilly—had said it, it wouldn't have sounded like a compliment. "Thank you," she said. "Shall I show you to your room, and then you can play catch-up with the others? They're already a few beers deep."

She could hear herself doing it, playing the cool girl. Something about Cordelia's starched dress and sprayed blow-dry was making her want to be the polar opposite. Any resentment she had felt at Drew for sitting outside drinking beers rather than making the cocktail she'd found a recipe for drained away. There was no way Cordelia would let Mac sit outside getting gently pissed and not helping. So that was exactly what Drew was going to be allowed to do. She remembered Drew saying something before they came back to England about his friends' wives. How diligent and reliable they were. Two words that no woman ever wanted to be described as.

"Follow me upstairs," she said as she turned to show them their room.

In the kitchen, Gina was taking a long slug out of the vodka bottle.

"What are you doing?" asked Poppy gently as she walked in. It was warm in here. Too warm? It would be lovely to eat outside. That was what she had told Emma they were doing. But then, people might get cold. There was a basket of neatly rolled blankets by the back door, specifically for anyone who got cold, yet there was the strong chance that that was the kind of thing Emma or Cordelia would consider tacky.

"Sorry," said Gina, putting the bottle down. "I had a feeling I wasn't going to be able to cope with that one"—she gestured toward the front of the house—"sober. By the way, I found that on the floor of the larder." She pointed to the kitchen table at the far end of the room where the tall white vase was lying in two neat parts.

"Gina! What the fuck?"

"What? It's one of the old ones that came with the house, no?"

"How did you break it?"

"I didn't!"

"You just found it on the floor?"

"Yes, I just found it on the floor."

Poppy picked up the two halves and took them into the larder. She wrapped the pieces in newspaper and hid them in the recycling bin. "Don't tell Drew," she said.

"It's a vase, not a dead body. Why are you so worried about him finding out?"

"Just don't tell him, OK?" Gina gave her a look. "What?"

"Why are you so worried about what he thinks? It's like you're scared of him."

Poppy wanted to stamp her feet and scream. "Gina, do we really need to do this right now? I'm not scared of him, I don't know why you keep asking that, but you really don't need to. I love him, he loves me, I just don't want him to find out that the vase is broken when his friends have just arrived. OK?"

"OK." Gina held out the vodka bottle to Poppy.

She shook her head. "I can't smell like booze."

"Vodka doesn't smell."

237

It was an olive branch, so Poppy took the bottle and drank from it. "You make a good point."

"Did you see that one's arms?" whispered Gina, gesturing upstairs toward Mac and Dilly's bedroom.

"I know. That's six hours a week of boot camp, I reckon."

"Imagine doing that when your pelvic floor's been ripped out."

They both laughed, but the laugh brought Poppy a wash of guilt. They were Drew's friends, and they hadn't done anything wrong. Thinking she was the housekeeper was almost certainly an honest mistake. "I shouldn't be a bitch," she said, taking another sip from the bottle. "They're nice. Really. She liked her room."

"Well, that was big of her."

"She's not that bad."

Gina raised one perfectly angled eyebrow. She didn't need to say a word.

"OK, they might not be nice," Poppy said. "But they're here, and they love Drew, and they might be nice when I get to know them?"

Gina's eyebrow didn't move. She picked up the jug of Moscow Mule she had made and then headed for the kitchen door. Poppy stood by the long window that ran the length of the kitchen, watching as Gina padded across the lawn and reached the table where the boys were sitting. Mac's and Ralph's eyes widened as Gina appeared, playing to her audience and swinging her slender hips. A little warmth swelled in the middle of her chest as she watched Drew's eyeline. He barely glanced at Gina. She shouldn't feel smug, she knew that. The other two had been married for years, to impressive, successful women. They had children and

238

whole big lives together. Of course they wanted to sneak a look at Gina's thighs. She was young and vibrant and the shorts she was wearing were designed to show that off. It didn't mean Drew loved her more than those men loved their wives. But she couldn't help feeling just the tiniest bit triumphant.

BEFORE

Later that night, Caroline lay awake in bed.

They were sleeping on the first floor, the kids on the second and Poppy had a cool, spacious wing on the ground floor—the room that she and Jim usually slept in. Caroline had insisted that Poppy take it so that she had some space from the kids. She was terrified that Poppy would look back in a decade and think that she and Jim had somehow taken advantage of her despite paying her her full salary to be there.

This room felt foreign to Caroline. The bed was huge and squashy and must be almost a hundred years old. The ancient fan spun determinedly in the corner, giving out the ghost of a breeze.

"Poppy said something about her passport earlier," she said into the darkness, careful to sound offhand.

"What?" Jim turned over.

"Poppy. She said something about you helping her with her passport?"

"Oh," he said. "She didn't have one."

"She didn't have a passport?"

"Not everyone does, Caro. I didn't have one until I was her age. We don't all grow up going on holiday every year."

His tone stung her. She turned over, feeling for the cold side of the pillow.

"Sorry," he said. "I'm being chippy."

"It's fine," she said. "But why didn't you tell me?"

"She was embarrassed," he said, his voice gentle now. She felt his hand on her lower back. "She's completely in awe of you."

"What?"

"Oh come on! You've seen how she looks at you. She thinks you're the best thing since sliced bread. She wants to be you when she grows up. Is it any wonder that she didn't want to admit to you that she doesn't even have a passport?"

His hand was on her thigh now, pushing up the sensible, comfortable nightdress that she'd started wearing after Grace was born. "Mm?" he asked.

She didn't say no, so he continued his determined quest.

"Have you got a condom?" she whispered.

He got up, clearly irked, and returned from the bathroom holding it aloft, like a trophy. She smiled, disappointed. She'd hoped that he might struggle to find one, giving her a reason to pretend that she wanted to, that she was sad they hadn't managed it. But still, it was a good thing really. It meant they had already done it once this holiday. And the fact he felt like doing it was a great sign. When he was in one of his low patches he'd barely lay a finger on her for weeks at a time.

She felt him against her and wrapped her ankles around his back, running her hands through his hair. The same movements she had made a thousand times, the same movements that had brought them countless orgasms, orgasms that had brought them three children.

"Good?" he whispered, pushing into her.

It wasn't bad. "So good," she replied.

Why hadn't he told her? Even if Poppy was ashamed, she didn't have to know that Jim had told her. Wasn't it strange that he hadn't told her? She pictured Poppy walking into his office while the kids were watching *Phineas and Ferb* downstairs. Saying, with that gentle voice, "Can I ask your help?"

He would have pushed back his chair, put down whatever he was doing without a second thought. Of course he would. What middle-aged man could resist offering help to a girl like Poppy? She would have blushed, probably. She blushed a lot. When she dropped something, when she mispronounced something, when she had to ask how to do anything. She'd have looked at the floor too, probably. And Jim would have coaxed it out of her, got her to admit what was wrong, just like he did with the children. She wouldn't quite have sat on his lap and rested her head on his shoulder, but it wasn't so far off.

And he had made it all OK. Just like he used to for her, when they were younger and she had problems that he could help with.

They weren't like that anymore. He couldn't help when it looked like she was going to lose a case. She couldn't help him when he was trying to fit more bathrooms onto the fifteenth floor of a building. There wasn't any room for each other in those cracks of their lives anymore.

Jim grunted. "Are you close?" he whispered.

"No," she said, "I've had too much wine. Don't worry." Almost as the words were out of her mouth, he came.

"Thank you," he said, running his hand over her hair and kissing her forehead. "That was great."

When did they start thanking each other for sex? As though it was a favor. She kissed him back. "It really was," she lied. "I love you."

CHAPTER 30

"So, what's the plan for tonight?" Ralph addressed the group, who were gathered around the outside table.

"Well," Poppy said, pulling a cigarette from the packet on the table and rolling it between her fingers. She hadn't smoked for weeks, not since they came back to England. But it smoothed the jagged edges of her nerves, giving her something to do with her hands. Emma had said something to Drew about it earlier, a snitty comment about how she would have thought he would have given up by now and Poppy had lit up, almost in defense of him. "I was thinking we would eat out here."

"Lovely," said Mac, just as Cordelia said, "You don't think it'll be too cold?"

"Nah," said Gina, dismissing her. "It's still warm and we've got heaters. And what about food?"

Gina was the best wing-woman a girl could have. She knew how badly Poppy would want to seem cavalier, like she hadn't been planning the menu for this weekend since the day that Drew suggested his friends come to stay.

"We're having sea bass," Poppy said. "But I was thinking

we could barbecue it. Drew, d'you fancy being manly with fire?"

Drew seemed younger since his friends had arrived. Sillier. He got to his feet, still laughing at something Ralph had been saying. "Absolutely, my darling," he said, stopping to kiss her neck as he ambled across the lawn.

"Isn't it funny," said Emma, refilling her glass, "how they show no interest in cooking indoors, but when it's outside you can't stop them?"

The women laughed, Gina loudest. "You're so fucking right," she said, getting to her feet and picking up an empty wine bottle. "Shall I bring the fish out?"

Poppy nodded. "I'll come help you."

"No, it's fine, babe, stay here."

She watched Gina wind her way back into the house, still barefoot. She'd looked cold, so despite her protestations Mac had offered her his sweater. She wore it now over her shorts and it looked like she wasn't wearing anything underneath it, just endless legs, almost as thin at the top as they were at the bottom.

"She's a real treasure," said Cordelia, who unlike Emma didn't seem to have relaxed yet. "You'll have people all over Wiltshire trying to poach her."

"Oh, she's not like that—" Poppy started.

"Everyone thinks that." Cordelia gave a flat laugh. "But when the offer's good enough, you can't blame these girls. She's gorgeous too. So exotic. That's your saving grace, I guess, lots of women won't want her in the house!"

"She's not exotic, she's from Crystal Palace. And she's not one of 'these girls' either."

"I thought she was your housekeeper?"

"No. Well, yes, technically. But she's my friend."

Emma and Cordelia exchanged glances. "Friend?"

"I told Emma earlier. She's a friend from London, helping me out until we hire someone full time. We worked for families on the same street, back in London."

"Oh," said Dilly.

"That can be difficult," said Emma. It seemed like she was trying to be gentle but her tone was infuriating.

"This isn't *Downton Abbey*," said Poppy, getting up. She could hear her voice getting louder. How many drinks had she had? Three? Four? Too many. She put a smile across her lips and forced her voice back into its normal tone. She was saying this stuff to them because she hadn't said it to Drew, because his skepticism had hurt her more than she had let on.

"Sorry," she said, picking up the empty jug. "It's just that Gina is a great friend. I don't want her being treated like 'staff.'"

"Of course not," said Emma, before Cordelia could speak. "I completely understand."

"I'm going to go and help her," said Poppy, turning to the house.

"Could you ask Ralph not to burn his eyebrows off?" called Emma.

Poppy laughed. "I'll try!" she called back, grateful for Emma's olive branch.

"This all looks beautiful, girls," said Ralph, as if Gina and Poppy were the two sweet teenage daughters who had put together supper for their parents. They smiled politely, and

Drew dropped his arm around the back of Poppy's chair, like a tiny reminder that Poppy was his wife.

He wasn't wrong, though. It did look beautiful. The air smelled like sweet pollen and sunshine, stronger and heavier with scent now as the sun went down than it had been all day. It mixed with the smoke of the barbecue, the perfume of people and the faint smell of sun cream. How many generations had sat in this garden, shielded from everything in the real world by the heavy green hills and ancient trees?

"Please start," said Poppy, looking down at the food. She had stuffed the sea bass with lime, chili, garlic and red onion, and thrown salt and olive oil over it. It was beautiful fish, bought from the fishmonger on the other side of Linfield. No need to smother it with sauces or overwhelming flavors. Just an arugula salad, roasted new potatoes, homemade mayonnaise and a salsa verde that Gina had made that was vibrantly green, though hotter than Poppy would have made it.

"Who did the fish?" asked Emma.

Poppy half raised her hand, shyly.

"Really?" said Cordelia.

"She's a wonderful cook," said Drew. "As is Gina, if you can hold your spice."

Everyone laughed.

"You've got quite the setup here," said Mac, spooning mayonnaise onto his plate. Poppy watched Cordelia lightly place her hand on his arm as he reached for a second spoonful. He said nothing but put the bowl down.

"Have you got enough mayo?" she asked Drew, looking at Cordelia.

"Like a little harem," laughed Cordelia, returning Poppy's gaze. Poppy looked from Gina to Drew, and then back. Was that what people thought? That she and Drew and Gina had made some sort of threesome?

"It's not like that," she said, too fast. Too loud. Drew's arm stiffened on her shoulder.

"Of course not," he added, his tone light. "I can only just keep up with this one."

Everyone laughed again.

"Plus," said Gina, leaning over, "no way would he be able to afford me."

The laughter rang out again, through the garden. Poppy imagined the sound wrapping around the branches of the trees and floating into the purple sky. It really was like no one else in the world existed. Sometimes, in the week, when Gina hadn't come home from the pub the night before and Drew had gone to work, it scared her. The immensity of it. The silence. She missed the smallness of her room at the Hendersons' house. Cramped as it was, it housed everything she had ever loved and if she sat with her back against one wall, she could see it all. That was impossible at Thursday House. She didn't believe in ghosts or anything like that, but sometimes, when she walked around the house entirely alone, there was a feeling. A feeling like the house was watching her.

She realized now that the house was built for this, for people and parties and lots of noise. It was never designed to be lived in by two people; it had been designed to overflow with children and grandchildren and dogs and servants and guests. So perhaps she and Drew should get on with it. Maybe the house would like her more if she gave it a child.

Reading her thoughts, Emma and Cordelia broke through her distraction.

"Poppy?"

"Yes, sorry," she said. "I was a million miles away."

They both made noises about it not mattering. "So, are you?"

"Am I what?"

"Gosh, you really were somewhere else. Thinking about having children?"

Poppy turned to Drew. She must have looked horrified because he intervened. "Rather a personal question, don't you think?"

"We're amongst friends," replied Cordelia.

"Poppy is a new friend," said Drew. His voice was calm, but cold. Poppy wouldn't have pushed back against it.

Cordelia smirked. "She's a new lots of things."

"So perhaps we could afford her some privacy? Just while she gets to know us."

"Of course." Cordelia folded her napkin in her lap.

"Anyway, you're young. There's no rush with these things for the boys, not like there is for us. You probably want a little time to adjust," Emma interrupted.

"To living in the country?" said Poppy, trying to change the subject.

"Yes," said Emma, "and being married, all of that."

"And making the jump from downstairs to upstairs," said Cordelia, her voice just low enough that Poppy wasn't sure whether she was supposed to have heard the comment.

"I'm sorry, Cordelia?" she asked.

Cordelia gave a tinkly little laugh. "Call me Dilly; everyone else does."

"What did you say?" Poppy repeated. She could feel the heat in her chest that meant she was about to lose her temper.

"I said call me Dilly?"

"Is everyone finished?" asked Gina, getting up. "Shall we clear?"

"What a good idea," replied Cordelia. "I'll help you, Gina."

Poppy took a long gulp from her wine glass and rested her head against Drew's shoulder. He was always so warm, his heat radiating through his shirt. The rage was still pumping under her skin, but the opportunity was lost. If she tried to bring it up when Dilly came back to the table she would look petty.

"She doesn't mean to be—" started Mac, sotto voce. Did he have to do this often? Follow behind Dilly, apologizing for her?

"A bitch?" Drew said, looking at Mac.

Emma laughed, and the boys joined in. Poppy reached forward to top up everyone's wine glasses, and as she did, music poured out of the kitchen. Gina came running out, looking delighted with herself. She'd opened every window and let the song come spilling over the lawn. Poppy jumped up. "Amazing!"

"Come on," shouted Gina at the assembled group. "Come dance."

She and Poppy grabbed hands and spun together; then Poppy was being twirled around by Drew, and Gina was jumping up and down with Mac. Even Emma was self-consciously tipping from side to side and singing along. Poppy was almost too out of breath to follow suit, but she dragged air into her lungs, forming the familiar words.

"Thank fuck you don't have any neighbors," exclaimed Gina just as Cordelia, a perplexed expression on her face, came back out. There was a little wet patch on the front of her dress where the tap of the downstairs loo must have caught her off guard and splashed her. Poppy decided not to say anything about it.

The song finished and Poppy dropped to the ground, lying on the cold grass. Gina collapsed next to her and everyone else followed suit.

"What did I miss?" asked Cordelia, sounding perplexed.

"Nothing, Dilly," said Poppy, laughing on the ground. "Just having fun."

It was two o'clock in the morning when Mac and Ralph decided that they'd had enough port. They'd made the "any port in a storm" joke four times each, and Poppy had watched them lurch up the stairs to their rooms, desperate to collapse on her own bed and tangle her body around Drew, to talk about how it had gone and what had worked and what they'd do differently next time. She'd have to be up before eight the next morning to make breakfast. How did everyone know what time to get up?

"How do you think that went?" asked Drew, unbuttoning his shirt. "I think everyone had fun."

Would she ever stop being impressed at the way his body was built? A little glow swelled inside her, thinking how much more attractive Drew was than Mac or Ralph.

"Good, I think. I like Emma a lot. And all of them, really. Though I don't think Dilly likes me very much."

"I wouldn't worry about that." Drew had changed into a pair of cotton pajama bottoms and settled on the bed, the last of his Ibiza tan still clinging to his skin. Something about the fact that Drew told her not to worry, rather than reassuring her that everyone thought she was great, stung.

"But I want your friends to like me."

"They do like you."

"Did they say that?"

"I can tell."

"You think Dilly likes me?"

Drew put a pillow behind his back, seeming to accept that this was going to be a conversation. "Things are complicated with Dilly."

"Why?"

"We were together. Years ago."

Poppy dropped the coat hanger she was putting her dress back onto. "What?" She half laughed. "You and Dilly?"

Drew dropped his gaze to the floor, a bashful smile on his lips. "Yes, me and Dilly. Is that so strange?"

"But she's so . . ." Poppy trailed off.

"Conservative?" he suggested.

"I was going to say cold. Didn't you get frostbite on your dick?"

Drew surprised her by snorting out loud, racked with real laughter that came from the stomach. "Oh God," he said. "I can't wait to tell Ralph that."

"You can't!"

"He'll think it's hilarious."

"Don't tell him I said it."

"I thought you wanted him to like you?"

"I thought he already did?"

Drew held his arms out and when she capitulated and crossed the room to him, he pulled her into his chest.

"Look, you were amazing this evening. I can't tell you how grateful I am."

"Grateful?"

"Yes," he said. "You've put in so much thought, so much effort. I love seeing you with them. They really like you, and honestly I just couldn't have done this without you. It's . . ." He paused. "It's pretty special to have everyone I care about in one place."

He was wrong. Any of the Henriettas he went to school with could have done this. Any of the women that Dilly and Emma probably threw at him whenever he'd come back to England. It wasn't exactly hard, not with so much money and time and good looks. He could have popped a ring on a much longer, more aristocratic finger than hers and had the exact same thing, only whoever this fantasy woman was wouldn't make a fuss about it, or burst into tears when she dropped a vase of flowers, or prep supper in her knickers and a T-shirt because she couldn't be bothered to get dressed.

"I love you," she whispered, still feeling the words odd on her lips.

"I love you too. And I'm wiped."

"Me too. I'm going to take my makeup off and do my teeth and then I'm passing out on you."

In the bathroom Poppy tipped her bottle of cleanser upside down. It was empty. Had she finished it earlier? Maybe Gina had used it when she was getting changed. Poppy took her dressing gown off the hook on the back of the bathroom door and padded down the corridor to the guest bathroom. She'd put a new bottle of cleanser there that morning. The door was shut. She reached to twist the handle when she realized that there was a strip of light under the door. Had someone left the light on, or was there a person in there? Terrified she'd open the door to reveal Cordelia, or Emma, with her knickers around her ankles, she pressed her ear to the door. Could she hear voices? Dropping to her knees, entirely aware that her behavior was bordering on psycho, she looked through the keyhole. It was a huge Georgian door just like the rest of them, with a decent-size hole punctured halfway up. The locks stuck, so Poppy had taken all the mismatched keys away, temporarily replacing them with bolts, meaning to have them fixed. Through the little wooden frame Poppy saw a long, tanned thigh. At the top of the leg was half a pair of denim shorts. It was Gina. And there was something else. White fabric. It looked like the bottom of a nightdress. It moved. Someone else was in the bathroom with Gina.

Poppy saw a slender, pale leg. Was it Emma or Cordelia? What the fuck was happening? She got to her feet and stepped, silently, several paces back. Then, walking normally, she approached the door and twisted the handle. It didn't open.

"One second," came Gina's voice.

"Gee, it's me," she said. "I've run out of cleanser and I know I put one in here. Can you see it?"

"Course," came Gina's reply.

A moment later Gina's face appeared between the wall and the door. "Here you go," she said, passing it out.

"Is everything OK?" Poppy asked. Should she just push the door open? Should she ask if anyone was in there?

"Yeah," said Gina, closing the door. "Totally fine. See you in the morning."

CHAPTER 31

There were few things Poppy hated more than oversleeping. It was her least favorite feeling: waking, grabbing for her phone to check the time, praying that her instincts were wrong and then discovering that they weren't, that the time she had needed was gone forever. Which was exactly what had happened that morning. She'd woken to see Drew, showered and dressed, standing by the window looking out to the garden. Poppy had noticed the time and ripped herself from the warm comfort of bed. "Why didn't you wake me?" she had demanded, grabbing a bathrobe and heading for the shower.

Drew had turned, seemingly distracted. "Wake you?"

"Yes, wake me. We've got guests. I've got to do breakfast, remember?"

"You looked so happy sleeping."

She rolled her eyes. "What are you looking at?" She followed his eyeline to the table and chairs on the lawn. Outside, Gina was clearing the ashtrays.

"The lawn needs mowing," he said, moving away from the window. "Mind if I go down?"

"To breakfast?"

"Well, yes."

"Can't you wait for me?"

Drew's eyes went to his wrist but he seemed to think better of checking the actual time. "It's fine," she said. "I'll have a lightning-fast shower. Just make some coffee and if everyone is starving then get Gina to start making food. There's bacon in the fridge, sausages in there too. I bought nice bread, that's in the bread bin, and proper butter, that's in the fridge too—"

"Go and have a shower." Drew laughed. "We'll work breakfast out. You're not running a hotel."

He was right. She wasn't running anything. Dilly was.

Poppy arrived downstairs half an hour later, her hair towel-dried and clothes sticking to her damp skin, to find Dilly standing at the Aga in pale pink jeans and a white linen blouse.

"It's all right," Dilly was saying to Emma, "give Drew that bit. You know he likes his bacon cremated."

Drew picked the bit of bacon up between his fingers and popped the almost-black meat between his neat white teeth.

"You know burned bacon gives you cancer, right?" Emma poked Drew in the ribs. "As does smoking."

Drew wrapped his arms around her. "You are such a sodding killjoy."

"Poppy!" said Dilly. "How did you sleep?" It was an expression of greeting that anyone normal, anyone like Drew or Mac or maybe even Emma, would think of as a pleasantry. But Poppy wasn't stupid. She'd worked for women like Dilly for years. "How did you sleep?" didn't mean good morning, or any genuine interest in how she slept. It meant

"You're late for breakfast. I've had to help myself to your kitchen, because your guests were hungry."

"Shall I take over?" she said to Dilly in a tone that stripped the question from the question.

"Oh, it's all right, I'm almost finished now."

"Really, I'd like to."

"You deserve to relax! Besides, cooking Drew breakfast brings back such happy memories."

"Oh God, not that!" shouted Ralph from the other end of the kitchen. "Please don't remind us!"

"Remind you of what?" asked Gina, coming in with a heaving tray of glasses. She put the tray down on the counter.

"Oh, Gina," said Dilly, pointing with her spatula, "put those in the butler's pantry, so they're out of the way."

"The what?" asked Gina, who was still wearing her sunglasses.

"She means the utility room," said Mac.

"Right," Gina said.

Poppy tried to catch Drew's eye, as if he'd be able to telepathically send her a message about how to handle this situation, about how to tell Dilly to back the hell off and stop treating Gina like staff without being rude. But Drew was picking up a copy of the paper and a mug of tea and heading over to the kitchen table.

"Remind you of what?" Poppy asked Ralph, trying to sound as if she didn't care.

"Dilly and Drew used to be a thing, about a hundred years ago," said Emma. "The worst couple of all time."

"Yes," said Poppy, raising her eyebrows. "He mentioned

it." There was no point in seeming rattled. "Though he was rather evasive. How bad were you?"

"Oh, we weren't so bad." Dilly laughed. "Though even I couldn't cope with how tidy he kept the flat."

"You lived together?" Poppy asked before she could stop herself.

"Didn't Drew tell you?"

Drew smiled. "No. I didn't think she needed to hear a blow-by-blow of our six-month domestic car crash."

"You're far too dramatic." Dilly took plates from the Aga. She'd remembered to put them in before everyone ate, so they were warm. Just the sort of thing Drew would do. Just the sort of thing Poppy always forgot to do.

"We would have been fine if you hadn't insisted on moving across the Pond," said Dilly.

Poppy cocked her head to one side, wearing a smile. "Should I be worried?"

Everyone laughed, loud enough that Dilly didn't get a chance to answer. She was still smirking though, and standing by the Aga, looking like it was her kitchen. Her house. Poppy wanted to snatch the spatula out of her hand, to slam her perfect manicure in the hot heavy lids of the Aga. She took a little breath, and then crossed the kitchen to where Drew was sitting. She perched neatly on his lap, wrapping one arm around his broad shoulders. "Hello," he said. "You're friendly this morning."

Mac snorted. "Get a room, you two."

Ralph put his newspaper up like a screen in front of Emma's eyes. "I'm saving you, darling."

"Dilly?" Poppy called from the kitchen table. "Seeing as you're doing breakfast, is there any chance you'd do Gina and me some bacon too?" She turned to the rest of the table. "It's just such a treat to be cooked for," she said.

Drew pinched her side gently and murmured in her ear, "Look who's boss."

"You guys go and relax; Gina and I will wash up," said Poppy, who had eaten an entire bacon sandwich while sitting on Drew's lap. She had a cramp in the leg she was using to take most of her weight, in case Drew found her too heavy, but it had been worth it. It was exactly what she'd never had the balls to do as a teenager.

She'd spent years at school, standing nearish the popular girls, not exactly being bullied, not on the outside, but on the fringes. Invited if someone else dropped out. Asked to be a partner on a trip as a second option. Not lonely, not left out. Just never at the center of things. She had realized, watching mothers in the playground, that people never grew out of it. There was always a queen bee, always a social hierarchy. And the people who claimed they were too mature for all that might have missed out on the drama, but they missed out on everything else too. Poppy was done with missing out. She liked Emma, and Ralph. She even liked Mac. Dilly wasn't going to be allowed to cut her out in her own home, to make her look stupid in front of Drew.

Drew and the boys peeled off to go and set up croquet on the lawn. Emma said she was going to put a sweater on and Dilly either couldn't find an excuse to resist Poppy's dismissal or didn't want to stay in the kitchen alone with them.

"Fucking hell, Poppy," said Gina as the kitchen door closed behind Dilly. "Good work."

"Was it obvious?"

Gina nodded heavily. "Like a period in white jeans. But she got the message, and that's what matters."

Poppy stacked the plates in the dishwasher and ran the hot tap. It took forever to get hot water here. "By the way, who were you in the bathroom with last night?"

"What?"

"Last night. When I came to get cleanser. Who were you in the bathroom with?"

Gina scraped the dish of dried-up bacon into the bin. "You need to get a dog. It's a waste throwing these bits away. Bathroom?"

"Yeah, I thought you were in there with someone?"

Gina shook her head. "Just me."

"Are you sure? I was certain there was someone else."

She laughed. "You think I'd slipped one of those two some Viagra?"

"No! I thought it was Emma. Or Dilly."

Gina put the dish in the hot soapy water. "Why would I have been in a bathroom with one of them?"

"Well, that was why I was confused."

"Nope, just me."

"How come you were in that bathroom in the first place?"

"What?"

"The guest bathroom on the second floor. You've got your own bathroom, upstairs."

"So I'm not allowed to leave the servants' quarters now?"

Poppy shook her head, trying to take back what her words had implied, how she had sounded. "No, no, it's not that at all. I just wondered if there was something wrong with that bathroom. You can pee wherever you like. Come pee in our bathroom if you prefer. I'm not trying to be—"

"It's fine," Gina interrupted. "I just wanted some makeup remover, so I went down there."

"Sorry," said Poppy, plunging her hands into the scalding water. "I didn't mean to be a bitch, I was just—I thought maybe she was telling you something."

"It's fine," said Gina. "Really. No big deal."

"Sorry," repeated Poppy.

"Anyway, what would she have been telling me? Who's the best yoga instructor in Chelsea? The best place to buy a diamond pony?"

Poppy laughed. Maybe she had been wrong about last night, about what Dilly or Emma could have been talking about in the bathroom, what home truths they might be spilling. But Poppy had been at least five glasses of wine down, and tired. Could she have imagined the second pair of legs in that bathroom? Could it have been a trick of the light? Maybe. She shuttered off the thought into a little corner of her brain.

BEFORE

It was a classic case of right place, right time. Or rather, exactly the wrong place at the wrong time.

Grace hadn't woken up from her nap by three o'clock, which was unlike her. Usually she started chattering away two hours after she went down.

Grace had always been a perfect sleeper, nodding off as soon as she was placed in her crib—a source of resentment in the mother-and-baby group. "She has help," Caroline had heard one of the others say, once. She had wanted to pull her back by the hood of her yummy mummy parka and tell her that she only had help during the school holidays and that otherwise she and Jim managed entirely on their own. But she hadn't. Alienating yourself from the mothers who lived near you—no matter how irritating they might be—was never a smart idea.

At home Caroline used Grace's nap time to try to plug all the holes in her life, paperwork, housework, even an attempt at going to the gym. But on holiday it was her time, sacrosanct and reserved for lying by the pool, reading her book or enjoying the indulgent bliss of doing nothing. She had sat up, just after 3 p.m., and looked around, realizing that neither Jack nor Poppy were doing their usual afternoon sunbathing. Something like intuition pricked at Caroline.

"Where's Jack?" she asked Ella, who was sitting in the shallow end wearing her water wings and playing with a Barbie.

"Don't know," she said. "Maybe with Daddy? Or Poppy?"

Caroline got up. "Let's go and wake Grace up."

She climbed the twisting staircase up to the first floor with Ella's hand in hers. She turned the corner and sitting on the bottom step of the staircase up to the children's rooms was Poppy. She had tears streaming down her face.

"Poppy? What's wrong?"

To her horror, Poppy sprang to her feet and rushed past her, stammering something that Caroline couldn't catch. She watched as Poppy disappeared down the stairs.

"Ella," Caroline said firmly. "Go downstairs and get your iPad from my bag."

Delighted with the surprise screen time, Ella skipped down the stairs.

Caroline pushed the door open to Grace's room, and found Jim bending over the crib, talking to Grace. Surprise and confusion replaced her sense of fear.

"Who's my little Gracie?" he asked into the crib. "Who's my little Gracie-cat?"

"What's going on?" Her voice was concrete to his cotton candy. Jim stood up, apparently surprised.

"What?"

"I just saw Poppy."

His eyebrows rose in a way that said, "And?"

"She was crying."

Jim picked Grace up and jiggled her a little. She laughed, a string of spit dangling from her lip. "Crying? Why?"

Caroline's conviction was beginning to evaporate. "You tell me."

"I don't know." He crossed the room, heading for the door. "Didn't you ask if she was OK?"

"Jim, stop it."

"Stop what?"

"You must know what happened—you must know why she was crying, she was just outside this room."

Jim started down the stairs. "Caro, I don't want to get heavy-handed about this, but are you . . ." He paused. ". . . accusing me of something?"

Was she? Her scalp felt tight.

Was she accusing him of something?

"No," she said quietly. "I just thought you might know what was going on. She talks to you."

Jim was below her on the stairs, looking up. "Well, I don't. Are you coming down?"

She followed after him, one bare foot on each step, until she caught up. She took long, slow breaths. Trying to convince herself that everything was OK was just like trying to sober up when you suddenly realized that you had had too much to drink. "Yes," she called. "I'm just going to get the sun cream."

Later that evening she asked Poppy to help her make supper. It was only pasta. Desperately uncomplicated. They both knew it was an excuse.

"What was wrong earlier?" Caroline asked, after she had waited as long as she could bring herself to. "When you were crying."

Poppy's neck was bent, her hair almost trailing on the counter. Caroline stood behind her and swept her hair into a bunch, then gently put four or five links of a braid in it. "You'll get food in it otherwise," she said, tying it with a hair tie from her own wrist. The gesture seemed to upset Poppy because when she spoke, her voice was thick with tears.

"I just tried to call my mum and she wasn't great. That's all."

Caroline wanted to hug her, but she couldn't decide whether that would be worse. When she herself was upset, being held in someone else's arms was the last thing she could cope with.

"I'm sorry," she said, going back to making the side salad. "That's tough."

Poppy made a noncommittal noise.

"My mother and I aren't close either."

Poppy looked up. Her eyes were tight from crying but the redness only served to make her eyes look even greener. Was it really any surprise that Caroline had had her suspicions? Even she, a straight woman, found a tiny part of her wanted to press her lips to Poppy's, though whether she wanted to do it for gratification or to comfort her, she couldn't be sure.

"Family isn't always the people you're related to, you know. You can go out and find your own," she ventured. It was a cliché, but it was true. And it was quite clearly what Poppy needed to hear.

CHAPTER 32

After breakfast Gina had retreated to her bedroom, and was not keen on the idea of joining the others for croquet.

"I'll be shit at it," she protested, lying on her bed. "I was just going to stay up here, babe. Sleep off last night. I feel like a pile of hot shit."

"Gross."

"Seriously, I may die."

"Come outside, it'll make you feel better."

Gina sat up. The idea of fresh air clearly appealed. "OK. But I'm doing this because the hangover needs it, not because I'm playing mummy-wars. OK? And by the way, everyone is going to realize that you're wearing that top to piss off Dilly. It's not even that warm."

Dilly took one look at Poppy's T-shirt and said, "I hope you're wearing SPF, with your complexion."

"It's, like, twelve degrees," said Poppy. She knew that because she was shivering in her skimpy T-shirt.

"I'm just so careful about sun protection." Dilly smiled. "I just live in fear of getting to sixty and looking like a leather handbag. Shall we go Poppy and Gina versus me and Emma versus you three boys?"

Poppy wasn't sure when the right moment was going to be to admit she had absolutely no idea how this game was played.

"Oh no, let's mix the teams up," said Mac cheerfully. "Dilly, you play with Ralph, Gina with Drew, Poppy, you go with Emma. I'll referee."

Poppy realized after watching Emma knock balls through hoops with an impressive ease, matched only by Drew's skills, that Mac had set her and Gina up so they wouldn't be embarrassed. She should be irritated, she supposed, that Mac had guessed she'd have no idea how to play. But he was right, and he had saved her the humiliation of a crippling defeat at Dilly's hands, so really there wasn't much point getting on her high horse.

Drew was lining up a shot, his face a picture of concentration.

"Fucking hell, they take this seriously," Poppy whispered to Emma.

"Oh, don't even get me started. Sometimes when I play tennis with Ralph I just let him win because it's not worth the sulk when he loses. They're like little boys."

Emma and Poppy laughed.

"If you think you're going to put me off, you're sorely mistaken," said Drew, still agonizing over the position of his mallet.

"Oh, hurry up and stop making such a fuss," Emma retorted.

Drew took his shot and knocked the ball neatly through the hoop. He whooped, stick in the air, like an overexcited child.

"Yes, Will!" shouted Ralph. Poppy watched as Ralph

looked around, as if he was checking to see who had heard him.

"Will?" Poppy asked. "Who's Will?"

Ralph laughed. "Drew. I meant Drew."

"How long have you known each other?" Dilly shook her head. "I swear, sometimes I worry about you, Ralph. Have you already been on the beers?"

Emma picked up a ball from the grass. "He's always like this when he's hungover. Sometimes I worry it's early-onset Alzheimer's."

Ralph got to his feet. "Please don't buy me a one-way ticket to Switzerland quite yet, darling. There's still some life in me. Anyone want anything from inside?"

"I'll have a Corona," said Gina, "with lime in it, please."

"I'll come and help," said Poppy. She had a sweater in the kitchen.

"Don't be silly," said Ralph. His voice was firmer than she had heard it all weekend. "You've been running around after us ever since we got here. Relax. I'm sure I can manage to slice up a couple of limes. Anyone else want a beer? Drew, mate?"

Drew shook his head.

"What a pretty bracelet, Poppy," said Emma.

"Thank you," said Poppy, looking at her wrist. "It was a present from Gina, and I haven't taken it off since she gave it to me."

"Really lovely. I bought one similar for one of my girlfriends when she had her daughter. Is it Tiffany?"

"I don't think so," she said, not wanting to be disloyal to Gina, who definitely didn't buy presents at Tiffany.

"Well, it's lovely." She put her mallet back in the

croquet box. "I'm getting my sweater from inside. Do you want one?"

Poppy shook her head. She twisted the bracelet around her wrist. The gold plate was surprisingly perfect, given that she'd worn it in the shower and the pool. Usually something plated would be turning her wrist green by now. But how the hell could Gina have afforded to buy her a real gold bracelet?

BEFORE

Poppy was different after the day that Caroline found her crying on the stairs. Skittish. She skipped the family trip to the beach. Sat on the side of the pool with her T-shirt over her swimming costume.

"Do you want to come and help me make supper?" Caroline put her head around the door of Poppy's room. It looked the same as it always had when she and Jim had slept there, but it smelled different: of Poppy's perfume. Nail varnish. Clean laundry.

"Um." She looked up from her laptop. "Do you mind if I don't? I've got a bit of a headache."

"Of course." Caroline backed out and closed the door gently behind her. Standing in the corridor, looking as if he had been caught doing something he shouldn't be, was Jack.

"Hello, darling," she said. "What are you up to?"

His sandy hair had been bleached by the sun and despite her liberal application of SPF fifty, which he had vehemently objected to, his skin was golden. He dropped his gaze to his bare feet, his hands twisted in front of him. Pain swelled up in her temples, squeezing her head. Watching

Jack struggle always hurt her physically. "Darling?" she repeated. "What's wrong?"

"Is she OK?" he asked, pointing one finger, with its bitten nail, at Poppy's door.

"Poppy? Yes, of course. She's fine, just a bit of a headache. Why?"

Jack shook his head.

"Darling, why? What's going on?"

"Dad yelled at Poppy," he said.

Caroline looked into his face. He'd shot up recently. Soon she'd have to look up at him when she was telling him off. But despite the height, the lengthening of his limbs and the widening of his shoulders, there was still something childlike about him. The worry etched across his brow hurt her. "What happened, darling?"

She had to sound calm; she had to sound as if she wasn't angry, like there was no big deal here. Otherwise Jack would spook. He hated trouble, hated raised voices or disagreements. He didn't even like family board games because they led to bickering.

"It was a couple of days ago. Poppy came into the kitchen and I was . . ." He paused. "I was taking a beer, and I knew she'd tell you or Dad. So I hid in the pantry. And then Dad came in. He was cross."

"What did Dad say?"

"He said she was being awful and she had to stop."

Caroline's eyebrows knitted together in confusion. "Was that all of it?"

Jack shook his head, avoiding her gaze. "I can't remember the rest, but he was angry and Poppy cried."

Caroline wrapped her arms around Jack. "Darling, don't worry. I'm going to have a chat with Poppy, and sort everything out. Will you take Grace and Ella to play outside?"

He nodded.

"Jack," she said. "It's going to be fine. Really."

Jack smiled. God, it must be wonderful to have your worries wiped clean like a whiteboard.

All the feelings she had been trying to compress were swirling in her chest. She felt sick. Not just a little nauseated, the proper gut-wrenching sickness of early pregnancy or a vicious hangover. She knocked on the white door again, the wood stinging her knuckles.

"Come in."

Poppy was sitting up on the bed, her cardigan pulled tightly around her. She seemed relieved to see that it was Caroline.

"Can I sit down?" Caroline asked.

Poppy nodded.

"I spoke to Jack."

Poppy's eyes widened but she didn't say anything.

"He said that Jim shouted at you."

Poppy shook her head. "He didn't shout. He just—"

"And when I saw you on the stairs the other day you were upset. Really upset."

She shook her head again. "I'm fine, really. It's nothing. I'm just being . . ." She seemed to run out of words. "I'll come and help with supper."

"Poppy." Caroline kept the same voice she had used with Jack. "What happened?"

"Nothing."

"I know that's not true." Caroline thought of Jim's face when he'd dismissed Poppy's crying.

"It was nothing."

"Did something happen? Between you and Jim?" Caroline heard the words before she realized she had said them. They had come from somewhere inside her, a place she had been trying to ignore. But as the question hung in the air she realized that what she had asked was the right thing.

Poppy froze. Then slowly pushed her hair out of her face. "I didn't want to . . ." Her voice trailed off.

"He forced you?" Caroline couldn't keep the shock out of her voice.

"No . . . He stopped when I said no, I just . . ." Poppy stopped to gather her breath. "I didn't want to lead him on or anything."

Caroline heard herself laughing, a cold kind of laugh. "Well, that's OK then," she said.

Poppy looked as though she'd been pierced. "I didn't mean that. I just meant—he wasn't—he didn't—he stopped when I said . . ."

Caroline looked into Poppy's face. She was so young and so vulnerable, and so completely incapable of wanting someone like Jim.

How could he have looked at her and seen something sexual?

Caroline wrapped her arms around Poppy. "I'm so sorry," she whispered. "I'm so sorry he did that."

She felt Poppy's body relax into hers and then, from the rhythmic shaking of her shoulders, realized that she was crying. Caroline stared up at the ceiling, which had a faint crack running across it. This would be the last time they came here. She wouldn't come back on her own with the children. It would be too tainted now, too full of these memories.

Jim had betrayed her. Or at least, he had tried to. He'd violated her trust, gone after a girl young enough to be his daughter, a girl who was in their care. Why wasn't she more upset? Caroline found that the swirling and churning in her stomach was only in defense of Poppy and worry for her children. The idea of a life without Jim in it? Perhaps it was too new to process. Or maybe, though she would never say the words out loud, the idea of life without the constant worry about Jim's black moods—his dark lows and his manic highs—was not so bad.

"You're not angry?" said Poppy weakly, eventually, her voice muffled.

"I am," said Caroline. "But not with you. He was the one who fucked up. Not you."

"I didn't think he was like that." Poppy's voice was so flat. So disappointed. Would this be it for her? Would Poppy spend the rest of her life thinking that all men were like Jim—weak-willed and unable to resist a pretty girl who made them feel like a big man? Or would she move on? Would she find someone better and kinder, with an iron-clad spine who would shudder at this story one day and tell her that he'd like to hunt Jim down and kill him?

"Me neither," Caroline replied.

Perhaps it was her own fault. Mel was right; it was ridiculous to put a man like Jim, so fragile and easily bruised, in such close quarters with a vulnerable, beautiful young woman and not expect him to try something. That was who he was. Always searching for the next thing, the thing that would finally cure his blues and make him the person he was half the time, the person he liked being.

"He said I'd led him on." Poppy's voice was so quiet that the words were almost lost to the ceiling fan, spinning round and round above their heads. For the dozenth time that day Caroline tried to trap the anger inside her. She had watched Poppy around the house and nothing she had done could have led Jim to believe she was into him; she looked to him as a father, for Christ's sake.

"Bollocks," said Caroline. "Absolute complete and utter bollocks."

CHAPTER 33

"Fucking hell," breathed Gina as she opened the double doors to the dining room. "It's incredible."

Poppy felt a warmth creeping up her chest onto her neck and hoped she wasn't going red. But seeing Gina's face as she drank it all in: it was the best feeling.

"You have got to start doing this for a job," Gina said. "It even smells amazing in here."

The dining room was a high-ceilinged glass room at the back of the house. Poppy had thought, when she'd first explored the house, how funny it was that this room served the same purpose as her mother's conservatory and yet it couldn't be more different. The glass panels here were hundreds of years old and mullioned. The glass was thicker in some places and one of the panes had letters on it, where someone, according to Drew, had scratched their initials with a diamond ring decades ago. Poppy had strung the ceiling with garlands of eucalyptus, mixed with white roses. She'd lined the room with trees, real trees in pots that would later be planted in the garden.

She'd filled dozens of jars with candles. The evening

was still light, but as it got darker they'd glow amongst the greenness.

"It's not too cold in here, is it?" she asked.

Gina smiled. "It's perfect. Literally perfect. The table looks amazing. Where did you find gold cutlery? And all the flowers, and the candles, and those glasses. When did you—"

"You're sure it's not tacky?" she asked. "Or over the top? And the dress is OK?"

She'd agonized about what to wear tonight. Eventually she'd gone into Bath and panic-bought a polka-dot dress.

Gina shook her head. "You couldn't be further from tacky. It's beautiful. Why are you stressing about this? You know you have great taste. Henderson might have been a bitch but she had a fucking nice house. You learned from the best."

Poppy laughed. "I guess it's just that we've got a whole lot of Hendersons with us tonight."

"Preach."

"It's not just me, right?"

Gina shook her head, switching her name card on the table so she was sitting next to Mac instead of Drew. Poppy opened her mouth to argue and then decided against it.

"Why is Drew friends with Dilly? I don't see it," Gina said.

"He's friends with Mac really, from school."

"I guess," Gina ventured, pulling out one of the chairs and sitting cross-legged on it. "He did marry a nanny half his age who he met on Ibiza. After, like, a week. Can you blame them for being a bit protective?"

"I'm not half his age! And it wasn't a week."

"How long was it?"

"Four weeks," said Poppy, trying and failing to sound dignified. They laughed.

"But seriously," Poppy went on, "I have to be on best behavior if I don't want them to think that I'm a gold-digging whore."

"I'm sure no one thinks that," said Ralph, pushing the doors open.

Poppy whipped around, running her hands through her hair. "Fucking hell," she said. "How much of that did you hear?"

Ralph smiled. "Nothing at all. Now, who do you have to screw around here to get a drink?"

Gina jumped to her feet and pulled a bottle of champagne from the huge silver bucket on the side. "Champagne, sir?" she asked, tilting the bottle forward to show him the label and affording him a peek down the front of her top at the same time.

"How could I say no to that?" asked Ralph, picking up a glass. Gina opened the bottle with finesse. "Very impressive," he said.

Gina smiled. "Not my first time."

Poppy pulled a packet of cigarettes from her clutch. Something about the way Ralph was looking at Gina, about the way he was allowing his eyes to roam over her long limbs while his wife, years older than her, was upstairs putting the finishing touches to her makeup, made her nervous. She didn't want to stay here and watch it. She slipped through the dining-room doors, which opened onto the neatest of Thursday House's lawns, and crept along a side path. Putting her champagne glass onto the ground, she lit a cigarette with a wobbling hand and leaned against the warm yellow stone of the house. She wanted just five minutes to herself. But she wasn't going to have it. Above her, there must have been a window open because she could hear voices. Someone that sounded like Emma.

". . . as bad as I had expected."

Poppy was filled with an overwhelming desire to rip down all the leaves and flowers and candles in the dining room. She had gone too far. What had she been thinking? Of course they wouldn't be impressed. She should have given them a casserole at the kitchen table, wine from Waitrose, and a store-bought dessert. Forced them to think that she didn't care, that she was at home here, that she knew how to behave in a house like this. That's what Dilly would have done.

". . . do you think she knows?" she heard. It was another woman's voice. It must be Cordelia. What was the start of that sentence? Did she know what? Poppy couldn't catch the rest. Dilly must have gotten up from the dressing table and gone to the other side of the room. Poppy took a long drag on her cigarette. What didn't she know? What was it that they were sitting upstairs talking about, thinking how stupid she was not to understand?

"Poppy?" She heard Drew's voice. Picking up her glass and grinding the cigarette butt into the ground, she forced a smile.

"Here," she said. "I was having a sneaky cigarette."

"What's wrong?"

"Nothing, I'm fine."

Drew caught her arm and pulled her back. "What's wrong?" he repeated.

She shook her head.

"Please tell me," he asked.

It occurred to her how few times Drew had asked anything of her, how rarely he had ever pushed her to talk about things she would rather not talk about. She could ask, she supposed. But what would she even say? She had heard someone, she didn't know who, saying that someone else, maybe her, didn't know something. It was hardly an accusation. "It's not a big deal," she said. "I just think your friends might think I'm . . ." She trailed off.

"Think you're what?"

"Tacky," she said quietly, looking down at her feet.

"Did one of them say something?"

Poppy shook her head. "No, no. It's me. I'm being stupid."

Drew wrapped his arms around her. "I can't wait to see what you've done."

If Drew's expression of delight was fake, then he deserved an Oscar for it. He drank in every detail of Poppy's decoration and then threw his arms around her. "It's beautiful," he said. "You are so clever."

"Told you so," said Gina. "Drink, Drew?"

Drew had been wrong about Gina, Poppy decided. It was because he'd never worked in a job like theirs, never had to straddle that middle ground between family and servant. But Gina did it brilliantly, filling up the glasses and passing around the canapés they had made that morning. She glanced at her watch and then caught Poppy's eye. *Yes,* Poppy said to her silently. *They're late.*

Ralph, Drew, Gina, Poppy and Cordelia's husband, Mac, who had apparently gotten bored of waiting for her to be ready, were standing on the terrace sharing Poppy's contraband cigarettes when Emma and Cordelia came down.

"Are you smoking?" asked Cordelia, catching sight of her husband with a Marlboro between thumb and forefinger.

"Whoops!" He laughed, dropping the cigarette and covering it with his shoe.

"He was just holding it," said Ralph, also laughing.

"For you?" asked Emma, arms folded across her boyish chest.

"I think we're in trouble," said Mac, pulling a silly face.

"Not at all," said Emma. "Is there any chance I could have a drink?" she asked, looking at Gina.

"Of course," she said, striding into the dining room to find two more glasses.

"It looks lovely in there," said Cordelia, looking back into the room. The sun was setting and the jars of candles glowed gently. "I'm afraid we're a little underdressed." She gestured at her pale blue trousers and white blouse. "I didn't realize it was quite so . . . formal."

Poppy took a slug of champagne and gave Cordelia a wide smile. "Oh God, we don't worry about things like that here. You can come to supper in your pajamas if you like. I probably would have done, if it weren't for the fact that Drew prefers me in dresses."

Drew came up behind Poppy and wrapped his arms around her waist. "Actually, darling, I prefer you in nothing at all."

"Drew!"

CHAPTER 34

Poppy hadn't eaten much of her supper. She was too consumed with watching the others eat and panicking that it wouldn't pass muster. But everyone had made appreciative noises and the buttons on Mac's shirt were straining over his stomach, which she had decided to take as a win.

"So, Poppy," said Cordelia across the table. "How are you finding life in the country, really?"

"I love it," she said.

"You're not bored?" asked Emma. "Ralph and I spent the summer at our place with the kids—it's a couple of miles from here. We thought it would be wonderful but honestly, they were just bored rigid. It went like *Lord of the Flies* after about a week. We all had to flee back to London for phone signal and PlayStations."

Everyone laughed. Apparently they were all going to ignore the suggestion that Poppy was of a comparable age to Emma's teenage children.

"Poppy's been working like a Trojan," said Drew. "You haven't had the chance to be bored, have you, darling?"

"It's been amazing though," she said. "And I couldn't have done it without Gina."

Gina looked up from her plate and grinned. "You didn't really let me do anything but I love you for saying that."

"And the house is finished now?" said Cordelia.

"Looks pretty finished to me!" Mac tipped the bottle of red wine into his glass, not offering it to anyone else. "Looks like a hotel."

"A fucking fancy one," said Gina. "I can't believe how much you transformed this place. Honestly, you should have seen some of the décor before. It was like a time warp. You could have charged for it, like a museum."

Poppy caught her eye and gave her a grateful look.

No one replied to Gina. The knives and forks were loud on the plates.

"So what will you do, now that you've finished the house?" said Emma, who was apparently fascinated by Poppy's plans for the rest of her life.

"God," said Poppy. "Big question. I don't know."

Emma smiled kindly at her. "Drew says you're thinking about training in interior design?"

"Maybe. I'd love to do up other houses. But I'm not sure if I want to go back to studying."

"Back?" said Mac.

"Poppy was at Durham," said Gina.

"Really?" asked Cordelia.

"Yes," said Poppy, putting her glass down. She must have been a little bit drunk because her teeth felt numb. "I can read and write and everything."

Drew and Gina burst into laughter and, seconds after them, so did Ralph and Mac. Cordelia gave a tight smile, but if you'd covered her lips you'd never have known that she was smiling.

"She's funny," said Ralph, talking to Drew. "You didn't tell us she was funny."

"It wasn't on the press release?" asked Poppy.

"She's good at lots of things," said Drew. He looked shy. This mattered to him, she reminded herself. Them liking her mattered to him. Poppy slipped her hand into his lap, squeezing his leg. She shouldn't drink much more. It would only be a couple of glasses of what Gina called "fight fuel" before it was almost impossible to resist the temptation to tell Dilly to go fuck herself. She shifted in her seat, sitting up straighter.

"What did you study at university?" said Ralph.

"History."

"History? Really?" Emma sounded impressed.

"Arabella is thinking about studying history," said Cordelia. "She's choosing her options for GCSE. Perhaps she could pick your brains about Durham?"

"It was such a long time ago," said Poppy. "I'm sure it's changed a lot."

"Nonsense," said Ralph, "these places never change. It'd be good for her to chat to you—she never listens when we go on about our college days."

"Maybe," said Poppy. She looked at her glass of wine. If she knocked it over she could jump up, make an excuse to get away from the table.

"You must have been in the same year as Ralph's cousin's daughter. Didn't she do history?" said Emma.

"Yes!" said Mac, smiling. "What's she called? Sophie King?"

Poppy's hand shook on her glass of water. Sophie had been in her tutorial group. She tried to catch Gina's eye, urging her to send the conversation in another direction.

"Can you imagine how in demand she was as a nanny?" said Drew. "With a degree from such a good university."

"Well, not a degree," said Poppy quietly. Better they heard it from her. Better they were embarrassed enough that they didn't get in touch with this cousin and start asking questions about her, picking at old scabs.

"What?" asked Dilly.

Poppy couldn't meet Dilly's eye. She squeezed Drew's leg again, this time asking him for help. "I didn't graduate," she said.

"You didn't?" asked Cordelia. "But you just said . . . ?"

"I didn't finish," she replied, looking down at the tablecloth. "I dropped out after my second year."

"Still, two years is a long time . . ." Drew faltered. Was he embarrassed for her, or embarrassed by her? Emma and Cordelia made a sort of sighing noise, as if suddenly everything made sense, as if order had been restored to the world around them.

"Didn't you know that, Drew?" asked Dilly, clearly enjoying herself. "You said degree?"

"Much of a muchness," said Drew.

"More wine?" said Poppy, picking up a decanter of wine, blue-black in the half light.

"She worked for Hengist Henderson and his wife, Amanda," said Gina from the other end of the table. Poppy watched as the two women perked up. "Do you lot know him?"

"Yes, worst luck," said Emma. "That must have been interesting."

"Nightmare," answered Gina, speaking for Poppy. Poppy got to her feet, slowly circling the table topping up glasses.

It was a view she'd seen from this angle so many times. Empty places, a tablecloth dotted with drops of red wine and candle wax. "Amanda's on so many pills she practically rattles. Isn't that right, Pops?"

She'd have to sit back down. Standing up was a tactical withdrawal, a sign of weakness. Gina was keeping it afloat; she had allowed her a few essential seconds to compose herself. But that was over now.

"So was he," she said, sitting down and pushing her face into a smile, forcing her voice into a conspiratorial whisper. "Little blue ones mostly."

The table tittered obligingly.

"The night I met Poppy," said Drew, his voice quiet. The rest of the conversation dropped. How did he do that? "Those vile people had kicked her out of the house."

"Why?" asked Emma.

"I'd asked her not to come home six hours late again, because it upset the kids. And Drew rescued me." She looked over at him. "I was sitting on the side of the road wearing someone else's shoes, and he whisked me away."

"And then you rescued me back," he said, as though there were only two of them in the room.

"It's true," said Ralph, breaking the spell. "He was a bloody train wreck before he met you."

"Really?" The idea of Drew being anything less than perfect was mad. "A train wreck?" She looked to Drew. "You didn't tell me you were a train wreck."

"He wasn't a complete mess," said Emma.

"Oh come on," said Mac.

"All right, he was quite a mess." She laughed. "We used to take it in turns to go and see him, to make sure he was eating—all he ever did was work. Eighteen-hour days at the office, no social life. Barely had time to see us on the weekends. Almost never came over to visit."

"We caught him on a conference call at the back of the church at Maya's christening!"

"Drew!" Poppy put her arms around him.

Drew's skin was pink under the olive tone. "They're exaggerating."

"They're not," said Ralph.

"I think we should have a toast," said Gina. "To Poppy. For doing all of this."

Poppy fixed her gaze on her napkin. There were crumbs in it. She couldn't look up as she heard the clink of glasses and her name chanted, but she allowed herself a small, embarrassed smile.

CHAPTER 35

The jars of candles were just pools of wax now, and the last of the light was gone. Only the little lights twisted in the garlands of leaves and the pillar candles on the tables were left. The tablecloth was stained and Drew was standing by the open doors, smoking a cigarette.

"Shall we get coffee?" Poppy asked Gina.

Gina nodded. "And dessert. Hold tight, guys, this is going to blow your mind."

"Oh really?" asked Mac. "I must say, the food has been quite amazing."

"Wasn't it? Mind you, no surprises there, Poppy did work in a kitchen when she was growing up."

"Did you?" asked Drew from the doorway.

"Yes," said Poppy. "Nothing fancy though, just the French place on the local high street. Most of it came in frozen."

"You didn't know that either?" asked Cordelia. "You need to start paying attention, darling. Doesn't sound like you know anything about your new wife at all!"

Before Poppy could answer, Gina did. "It's part of their whole *Eternal Sunshine of the Spotless Mind* thing."

No. No, no, no. It had all gone so well. The food had been perfect, the conversation mostly OK. She hadn't embarrassed Drew, or said anything stupid, and if she stayed here long enough and kept smacking down the snarky little comments then they'd probably start to accept her eventually. Surely it wasn't going to fall apart now?

"What?" asked Emma, turning away from Ralph. This conversation was clearly more interesting than school fees or second ponies or whatever it was they had been talking about.

"Gina, can you help me with these?" Poppy got to her feet, taking one empty water jug in one hand and gesturing to the other.

"Their deal thingy," Gina went on. Was she doing this on purpose, or was she just drunk? Poppy caught Drew's eye across the table. His lips were tight with frustration. "Shut her up," his expression seemed to say. "I can't," she tried to tell him, silently.

No one was trying to hide their curiosity anymore.

"What deal?" asked Mac.

"It's not a deal," said Poppy. "It's just . . ." She trailed off. What was the end of that sentence? What was she supposed to say? She looked up through the glass above her head and to the night sky above. The stars here were astonishing, like crushed diamonds on navy velvet. "It's just something Drew and I decided. We don't ask each other about things that happened before we met. How many of us want coffee?"

"I'll get the dessert," said Drew, getting to his feet. "Gina, will you help me with the bowls?"

"I'll come," said Poppy.

"No," said Drew. "You've done so much this evening. Gina doesn't mind, do you?"

From the way that she stuck her bottom lip out it looked like Gina did mind, very much. She gave him a nasty sideways look as they left the room together. Why was she being like this?

"I'm probably being very slow here," said Cordelia. "You'll have to help me out. You and Drew don't ask each other about anything that happened before you met?"

"Um," Poppy said, "yeah. That's about the size of it."

Silence fell around the table for the first time that evening. It rang in Poppy's ears and she wished ardently that she had put some music on in the background.

"So you've got no idea about each other's pasts?" Cordelia said.

Poppy was starting to lose her temper. The swipes at each other earlier had been one thing, but this was turning into a ritual humiliation. Cordelia was a guest. She should act like one.

"You make it sound very 007," said Drew, coming back into the room. "I'm afraid it's nothing as exciting as that. Only that Poppy and I agree there's no real benefit in quizzing each other about every brokenhearted disaster that happened before we met, so we agreed not to. We focus on the here and now."

"Extraordinary," said Emma, almost under her breath.

"I've never thought that total disclosure toward a spouse about every little thing that one has ever done is the way to make a relationship work," said Drew.

"Oh for God's sake, Drew," said Emma, "you know that's rubbish. Honesty is the most important part of a marriage."

Poppy traced his stare, across the table, right into Emma's eyes. "I'm surprised to hear that you're such a stickler for honesty, Emma," he said. Poppy watched as Emma pushed her hair back from her ears and pulled it around onto one side, twisting the ends around her finger. She could see now—this was why they paid Drew the mega-bucks. Because he could work out exactly where to apply pressure and how hard to push. "Gina," he said. "Thank you."

"Weren't you supposed to be helping?" Poppy asked.

"He was just in my way." Gina gave a laugh that sounded fake. "Easier to do it myself." Poppy knew that smile. It was the "fuck you" smile that they gave their bosses when they suggested a last-minute Saturday babysitting slot. "I'll just go and get dessert wine and some clean glasses."

"I should go and help her," she whispered.

"Stay," said Drew in a voice that sounded warm but absolutely wasn't.

"It's fine," said Gina. "I've got it. You stay where you are."

"I meant to say," Emma called across the table. "I've got a friend who runs an interior decor magazine. Country houses—that sort of thing. I'm sure he'd love to do a feature on this place."

"On Thursday House?" Poppy was grateful for the change in topic.

Emma nodded. "And on you. It could help if you're serious about doing this professionally. Would you be interested?"

"That would be incredible," she replied. "Drew, did you hear that?"

He smiled. "Brilliant idea."

"I've got loads of before photos too," Poppy said, pulling her chair around next to Emma.

"I'll go and see where Gina's got to with that coffee," said Drew. Poppy wanted to tell him not to nag Gina, that she'd get it done in her own time. But just as she opened her mouth to do so she found a picture of Emma and Ralph's bedroom before it had been wallpapered. "Look—this is where you're sleeping, before the work," she said. Emma's gasps of surprise sounded genuine.

"Drew is quite right," she said. "You really have got an eye for this sort of thing. You could make a fortune."

Mac got to his feet, swaying slightly. "Right. Time for a swim, I think."

A roar of objection went up across the table. "It's freezing," said Emma.

"We're far too old for that," added Ralph.

"Speak for yourself." They all turned to look at Dilly, who was, to Poppy's enormous shock, peeling off her neat cashmere cardigan as she headed for the door. "It's heated, isn't it, Poppy?"

Poppy nodded.

"Well then."

Dilly unzipped her neat trousers and stepped out of them. Her underwear was nude lace, matching but deliberately unexciting. Poppy watched in utter bemusement as the rest of them followed, skipping across the dewy lawn toward the pool, which glowed aquamarine in the darkness. She trailed behind, fiddling with a knot on her dress where she had tied it.

"Come on, Pops!" called Ralph from the water. "It's bloody lovely."

If someone had told her earlier that day that these people, these civilized, proper grown-ups in their forties, would be naked and splashing each other in the swimming pool at midnight she would have laughed in their face. "Let me get Drew and Gina."

"They'll be out any minute."

Gasping, she looked down. "You bastard!" she shouted. Mac had splashed her, soaking her legs and the bottom half of her dress. He looked guilty, worried he had gone too far. Poppy grinned and pulled the dress away from her body, leaping into the blue water and soaking Mac in the process.

"Oh Christ," she heard Drew's voice from above them. "My eyes!" He pointed and Poppy saw Ralph's skinny, hairy legs sticking out of the pool, leading down to his soft, square arse. Also hairy.

"He's doing a handstand!" said Emma.

"He's scarring me for life," called Dilly from the deep end, where she was treading water, apparently without effort.

"Aren't you coming in, darling?" Poppy asked Drew.

By way of answer he stepped out of his trousers, pulled his shirt over his head and dived, long and graceful, into the pool. Poppy still couldn't dive. She hadn't told Drew, for fear that he would insist on teaching her. The ease with which he did it—no fear, no horror that he would misjudge it, knock his head on the bottom and crunch his spine—impressed her.

"Very good," she laughed as he surfaced.

"Seven out of ten," called Mac.

Poppy took the steps, relieved to find the water warm, and wrapped her legs around Drew's waist and her arms around his neck, letting him carry her as he bobbed up and down in the water. "Where's Gina?"

"She went to bed."

Fuck. She'd left Gina to do half the clearing up, disappeared down here to have fun with Drew's friends whom Gina had spent most of the evening saving her from. "I should go and check on her." She untangled herself from Drew's body and swam toward the steps, but he caught her arm.

"Don't go. She'll be asleep by now."

"I should just see if she's OK."

"She's fine! Just said she'd had a lot to drink and needed to go to bed. That's all. Stay out here. Please?"

Poppy looked guiltily over to the house.

"Mr. and Mrs. Spencer, out of the way, please," yelled Ralph. "Mac and I are about to set a new speed record for the butterfly."

She had meant to go inside and check on Gina, really she had. But instead she'd found herself sitting on the steps in the shallow end, arms crossed over her naked chest, water lapping at her torso, laughing so much that she had to struggle for breath as Mac and Ralph attempted an utterly shambolic butterfly stroke, smacking into each other, the sides of the pool and finally the wall of the deep end. By the time they finally heaved themselves out of the water, shivering and giggling, it was too late to check on Gina. She'd have been long asleep. It was too late to do anything other than follow Drew, laughing all the way, back up to the house to go to bed.

BEFORE

"Where's Daddy?" asked Ella as Poppy strapped Grace into the car seat.

"Shh," she said. "Remember? We have to be quiet? That's the game."

Guilt flushed through Caroline. But there really wasn't another way. Asking, or telling, or explaining: all of it would have led to shouting and screaming and possibly being stuck here. He wasn't himself when he was angry, he'd make threats about taking the children, say things about what kind of a mother she was. It was cleaner this way. Jim would get a taxi to the airport and a flight. He would calm down before he reached England and then they would be able to talk about it. And, she told herself sternly, she wasn't the one who had tried to force herself on the nanny.

"He's staying here, darling," she said, turning the engine on.

"Why?" asked Jack.

"It's complicated," Poppy replied. "We just need you to trust us for now. OK?"

Jack shrugged and went back to his mobile. He'd do anything for Poppy.

Caroline's stomach tightened; the engine seemed a thousand times louder than it did in the daytime. But nothing. No movement from inside the house. No lights. Grace was still sleeping in her car seat, Jack was playing with his phone and Ella's eyelids were flickering shut. They'd managed it. She pushed her foot toward the floor and looked out over the long, sliding road and the red sky.

"Red sky in the morning," she said, almost to herself.

"Are you OK?" whispered Poppy from the passenger seat. She'd brought her feet up, twisted them underneath her body.

"Yes," said Caroline. It was at least half true. A part of her—quite a big part—wanted to believe that waking up to find all of them gone would shock Jim straight, that he would be so horrified at experiencing life without them that he would come home changed.

And, when Jim had apologized and when Poppy went back to Durham, they would try again. He'd finally agree to go to therapy. They would do all of those silly magazine-advice things that people did, like taking solo trips away and going out for dinner and having whole evenings where they weren't allowed to talk about the children. All of the things that she wanted but felt embarrassed to admit to.

"I think so, anyway," she went on. "I feel guilty. I keep wondering if we should go back."

Poppy shook her head. "Can I say something?"

"Of course."

"You always put him first. I think maybe it's time to think about yourself."

Caroline gave a half smile. Poppy wasn't wrong. It had been nearly two decades of trying to predict Jim's moods and understand what triggered his dark patches. This was the first truly selfish thing she'd done since walking down the aisle at the Islington Register Office eighteen years ago.

"Caroline?" Poppy sounded worried. The road was long and wide and totally empty.

Caroline turned to look at her drawn face. "Yes?"

"Do you want me to leave when we get back to London?"

Caroline shook her head. "God no."

"Are you sure?" There was a note of hope in there now.

"Yes. I won't be able to cope without you."

Poppy twisted in her seat. "Does anyone want a sweetie?" she said, clearly testing to see whether the children were really asleep. She was a smart cookie. Caroline's children were not above faking slumber to overhear what the grown-ups were talking about. But for once they were fast asleep.

"I would understand," Poppy said, "if you didn't want me around?"

"Well, I do," Caroline said. "I need you."

"He'll be so angry."

"He should have thought about that."

"What if he says—" She stopped.

"What if he says what?"

"What if he says that I'm making it up? That he didn't really come on to me?"

"Poppy." Caroline put a hand on Poppy's arm, holding the wheel steady with the other. "I get that maybe this hasn't always been the case for you, but I need you to understand. I believe you. I think you're telling the truth. You have no reason to lie to me. I trust you. OK?"

Poppy nodded as a tear spilled down her freckled cheek. "Thank you," she said.

Caroline nodded, not trusting herself to speak in case her voice cracked. Instead she reached for the radio, putting it on. The gentle hum of Europop filled the car, stripping away the silence.

Two hours later, Caroline's phone buzzed and she handed it to Poppy.

Poppy silenced it, but it kept ringing. Again and again. Eventually, Poppy put the phone to her ear. "She doesn't want to speak to you, Jim," she said. There was a crackle of voice from the other end, saying something that Caroline didn't catch. Poppy hung up the phone.

"Thank you," said Caroline.

"It's OK," said Poppy.

CHAPTER 36

Poppy's eyelids were pulling down, as if her eyelashes weighed several pounds. The chlorine from the pool had made her skin stiff and dry. As she reached up toward the lamp, wondering if she could reach it without sitting up properly, she heard a noise at the door. Was it a knock, or just the movements of an old house? There it was again. A knock.

"I need to talk to you," said Gina, standing in the fuzzy darkness.

Poppy pulled her dressing gown tighter around her body. "What is it?" she asked.

"Not here," said Gina. "Upstairs."

Poppy rolled her eyes. "Gee, I've got a house full of people. I'm tired. Let's do this tomorrow."

"Please," said Gina, raising her voice. "Please."

Poppy turned to look at Drew's sleeping figure, long and lean in their beautiful new bed. "Shh," she said. "You'll wake everyone up." Poppy pulled the heavy white door of her bedroom shut behind her.

She followed Gina around the square landing, looking

over the banisters down to the beautiful floor, quiet and dark below them.

"Let's go to my room," said Gina.

"Fine," whispered Poppy, checking the doors of the two bedrooms next to her own for a bar of light, a sign that they had woken one of the guests. The stairs to Gina's room had a little door on the main landing, and then a twisting staircase. A stark contrast to the huge wedding cake stairs in the hall.

Gina pushed her door open and Poppy looked around, struck with guilt that she hadn't been up here for weeks. Gina had covered the bed with a silky Indian blanket and put pictures on the walls. There were bottles of nail varnish, perfume and body lotion scattered across each surface. Somehow she'd managed to make this stark room feel like a home.

"So," said Poppy as Gina sat on the bed and pulled her knees up to her chest, "what's going on?"

In the light from the single ceiling bulb, Gina looked about fifteen. From the twisting of her lips it was clear that she was wrestling with how to say what was coming.

"Gee," said Poppy, "I have to go back down in a minute. If Drew wakes up and I'm not there—"

"Drew said things before—when we were inside, when you were in the pool. He said . . ." Gina trailed off.

"What did he say?"

She shook her head.

Poppy stood up. If Gina didn't care enough to tell her, then it couldn't be important. She didn't want to hear it. She didn't want Gina to say yet more things that made her life feel precarious, not now when she was starting to feel safe.

"Fine," she said. "If you don't want to talk to me, I'm going back to bed."

"He paid me," said Gina, the words spilling out into the room.

"Who paid you?" said Poppy. "Drew? For what?"

A silence.

"For what?" she asked again. "Gina. What did he pay you for?"

"To meet you," Gina whispered. "He paid me to help him meet you."

There was something tight and hot constricting Poppy's head.

"Drew?"

Gina nodded. "Yeah."

"We met in a bar. On the side of a road . . . How? You couldn't have done. You—"

"You told me where you were. And I told him. He went there to meet you."

Poppy sat down on the bed, trying to slow everything down so that she could process what Gina was saying.

"Why?" she asked. "Why would he do that?"

Gina shook her head. "I don't know."

"You didn't think to ask? You didn't want to know why he was offering you money to meet me? Or you just decided to take the money and not give a shit what it meant?"

Gina's eyes were full of tears. "It wasn't like that," she said. "He—you know how he can be. He said he'd seen you at a party and he liked you. He was so charming about it."

"I'm sorry?" Poppy said. "What did you say?"

"I said you know how he can be—he's so—"

Poppy got to her feet. "I know how he can be because

301

he's my husband. What the fuck do you know?" She looked down and caught sight of her wrist. "Wait," she said. "Is that where this came from?" She held the bracelet to the light. "You bought this with the money he gave you? Because you felt guilty?"

Gina opened her mouth and then closed it. "I'm sorry," she said weakly.

The pathetic tone of her voice only made Poppy angrier. "Why are you telling me this now?"

It was clearly a question that Gina had predicted, and didn't want to answer. She twisted the silk blanket in her fingers, unable to meet Poppy's eye.

"I think he might be dangerous," she said slowly.

"What? Why?"

"Dilly told me some stuff last night. She said—"

"So you were in the bathroom with her?"

Gina rolled her eyes. "Yes, OK, I was, but that's not the point. Dilly asked me not to tell you that we were talking—"

"The same Dilly who treated you like a servant all weekend and keeps treating me like I'm Drew's teenage daughter? You've got secrets from me with her now?"

"She said he'd had problems in the past—she asked me if you knew but I didn't think you did. Do you? Because of this stupid fucking deal."

Poppy shook her head, trying to find the words to make Gina stop.

"Poppy, she seemed really worried for you. Don't you think there's something off about him?"

"Dilly's just jealous."

"Maybe." Gina looked away. "But the way she said this stuff—I just—"

"You've never even given him a chance. You decided you didn't like him from day one."

"Poppy, for God's sake, listen to me. I'm not trying to burst your bubble, I'm telling you he's not who you want to think he is. He's not who I thought he was. There's something bad going on. When we were inside earlier he was saying all this stuff."

"What stuff?"

"Like . . ." She paused. "Argh." She let out a frustrated noise. "It was how he said it. It all sounds normal when I say it but when he was saying it, it was scary, all right? It felt like he was dangerous, like he would . . ." She left the sentence hanging. "Look, you need to talk to him. Ask him what he's playing at. Ask him about life before he met you."

Poppy gave a cold laugh. "And then what happens when he asks me to return the favor? I tell him all about the Walkers? I love him. I love my life with him."

"You really think you're going to be happy with someone who won't even tell you where he went to school or what his mum's name was? You think that's normal? You think that's how marriages work?"

"We don't need each other's pasts, we've got a future."

"You sound like you're in a fucking cult."

"Are you just angry that he's stopped paying you? You didn't have a bad word to say about him when you were making money out of him. When I rang you from Ibiza and asked you if I should marry him, you told me it was a great idea and we should go for it. You didn't think he was dangerous then, did you? When there was something in it for you."

"You said you were happy. I didn't know what he was like."

"Like? What do you know about him? You've hardly spent five minutes with him since you arrived."

"I told him that I wanted to tell you and he threatened me. Not even three hours ago—in your fucking kitchen."

"Keep your voice down," Poppy hissed. "I have people sleeping downstai—" She stopped. Was there movement in the corridor? Had she heard something? She turned to the door and threw it open. The corridor was empty. She closed the door behind her and looked at Gina.

"I'm sorry. I lost my temper. I just—I know it might sound odd to you, but none of this has exactly been conventional." Poppy sat back down. "I think it's romantic, he wanted to meet me that much. But yeah, he should have told me that he paid you. He's a rich businessman. He pays people for services. That's what he does."

Gina shook her head. Her eyes were shiny. Was she on the brink of tears? "You know it's not normal."

Poppy ran her hands through her hair, twisting it up into a knot on the top of her head. "Gee, I love you and I want you to be here, I want you to stay. I get it, this isn't conventional but none of this is and actually . . . I'm OK with that. He should have told me but I'm not going to throw away my relationship over this."

Gina put her head to one side, eyes wide with infuriating sympathy. "How can you love someone who's done nothing but lie to you?"

Poppy could feel herself becoming frustrated again. "You wouldn't understand."

"I get it," said Gina, her voice getting higher, "big house, loads of cash, never have to work a day in your life. I'd take it too. But, Poppy, he's not a good guy. If something seems too good to be true, that's because it is."

Poppy took a slow breath, looking at the floor, and then, slowly getting to her feet, found Gina's eyes. "Leave."

"I'm sorry?"

"I'm tired of this argument, and the way you treat Drew, and your total lack of respect for our relationship. I want you to leave." Her voice was perfectly calm.

"You're throwing me out?"

Poppy nodded.

"In the middle of the night?"

Poppy didn't respond.

"You did learn from the best, didn't you?" Gina pulled her suitcase out from under the bed, flinging the lid open, and started to throw clothes into it. "How very Mrs. Henderson of you."

Poppy slammed the door behind her.

CHAPTER 37

Drew was sitting up in bed. He noticed her tears. "Darling, what's wrong?" he asked.

"Is it true?" she asked, trying to sound calm. "Did you pay Gina? Did you pay her to help you meet me?"

Drew nodded as if she'd asked if he'd finished the milk. "Yes, I asked her to introduce us."

Why didn't he seem more upset? Guiltier? He held his arms out toward her. "Come here."

"No."

"Please?"

Her anger choked her, her words fighting to get out, tangled. "You lied," she said, her voice high and loud. To his credit, he didn't shush her or remind her that they had guests sleeping next door.

"I suppose I did. Yes. A lie of omission."

His total calm was making it impossible to vent. She wanted him to shout back, to lose his temper, to let her open her mouth and scream everything that was swirling in her head. But he was so resolutely unmoved by the situation. It made her tone and pitch seem ridiculous.

"Why?"

"Why did I lie?"

"Why did you get her to help you?"

"Oh, I see." He held his arms out to her again. She couldn't bring herself to lie on his chest like he wanted her to, but he looked hurt enough at her rejection that she found herself sitting on the bed next to him, one foot under her body and the other on the floor. A nasty little voice was screaming at the back of her mind. *Don't fuck this up. Don't lose him. Does it really matter what happened?*

He ran a finger gently along her arm. "I've thought so many times about how I would tell you this." He paused. "I didn't want it to sound strange."

"It is strange," she snapped. "It's fucking stalking."

"I realize you could see it like that."

"So why did you do it?"

He sighed. "A while before I met you I went to a party at some friends of the Hendersons, and I saw you. You were the most beautiful woman I'd ever seen in my life, and I wanted to talk to you. But you were the nanny. I didn't want to be some sleazy older bloke hitting on you. So I didn't introduce myself. And then after that I kept thinking about you, and anytime I went on a date with someone else I'd think about you more. And then, one day, I realized if this were a business deal, I'd go out and get it. So why wouldn't I go after you? So I looked for you. I found every other nanny at that party, but I couldn't find you. And then I saw a picture of you on Gina's Facebook."

"And, what, you told her you'd seen me once and wanted to sleep with me?"

"I know how it sounds," he said. "I asked her if you were the redhead who was at the Waterworths' party. She offered to introduce us. For a fee."

Poppy turned to face him. "She asked for the money?"

Drew looked nonplussed in the half light. "Yes. I thought she just told you what happened?"

"She said you offered her money."

"I thought she'd do it for free, because she was your friend. She wanted cash. A thousand quid, to be specific. But she said you wouldn't take well to a blind date, that I should make it look like an accident, like I bumped into you."

"She suggested it?"

He nodded. "Did she not just tell you that?"

"No," Poppy said quietly, lying back down, relishing the cold of her pillow against her warm cheek. Gina had no shame. She could just imagine her purring down the phone to Drew, half-cut: *How much is this favor actually worth?*

"No," Poppy went on. "She left that part out."

Drew's arm snaked around her torso, his body following the curve of hers.

"I fired her," she said into the darkness.

Drew didn't reply, but he shifted slightly, and she felt his heart quicken, his chest pressed against her back.

"Fired her?"

"Yes. I told her to get out."

She felt his lips on her shoulder blade. "You did the right thing," he said. "She wasn't happy for you. For us. She—" He stopped.

"She what?"

He sighed. "I don't want to overstep."

"No, go on."

"It may be difficult for her, seeing you like this. You're going places. You're beautiful and clever and"—he swallowed, sounding self-conscious—"I think we're happy."

"We are."

"Well, she doesn't have those things."

"I guess." It was odd to think that after years of standing slightly behind Gina while guys chatted her up and spoke across Poppy pretending she didn't exist, Poppy was the one with the enviable life.

"I didn't want her to go," said Poppy. "I just got so angry. She was saying all this stuff about you . . ."

"Like what?"

"She said you were threatening. Intimidating." Poppy regretted it as soon as she'd said it.

He pulled her tighter into him. "Tonight? I would never have intended to be," he said, his voice gentle. "But she had had a lot to drink. Maybe she saw it that way?" He paused. "Have you ever found me aggressive?"

"No," Poppy said, horrified. "Not at all. Never. Maybe it's a good thing she's leaving."

Drew nodded. "Maybe. And it doesn't mean that she's going forever, she's still your friend. She'll still come to stay with us. But working with friends—I did say I was worried about it."

Poppy sniffed. "I know you did. I know. I just—we've been friends forever. I love her."

"I know," said Drew. "I know you do. And I'm so sorry for my part in all of this. I should have been honest with you." He rocked Poppy gently, she didn't know how long for, and eventually her eyelids began to drop. He was right. It would be OK. She and Gina would apologize to each other, agree that trying to work together was madness. Gina would admit that Drew was just as perfect as he seemed, that she had been jealous—not intimidated.

The next morning Poppy padded across the hall and up Gina's little staircase. She was surprised that she wasn't angrier at Gina for trying to make money from Drew. At Drew for paying, and for not volunteering that information. But Gina had been her lifeline for as long as she could remember. It was hard to imagine a life without her as her best friend.

The room was empty, as Poppy had sort of known it would be. Gina wasn't the kind of person who waited around for an apology. The bed was unmade, magazines and crumpled tissues filled the wastepaper bin, and on the desk was a piece of paper. She saw her own name in Gina's round writing and turned it over.

When you realize I'm right, call me. G.

Typical Gina. So self-assured, so completely convinced of her own righteousness. But this time she was wrong.

"I gave your friend a lift to the station," said Mac when Poppy came down to the kitchen. He was the only one there, reading the newspaper at the kitchen table. "She seemed to have all of her things with her?"

"Yes," said Poppy, taking a bottle of water from the fridge. "She got a call about another job, a last-minute one. Someone's nanny dropped out just before a two-week trip to the Maldives." She was such a good liar these days. Six and a half years of practice made perfect, she supposed.

"You'll miss her," said Mac. It wasn't a question. There

wasn't anything to say in response. Poppy made a noncommittal noise and started to hunt for the bacon. There was no way Dilly was going to annex the Aga and do breakfast this morning.

"It might be nice for you and Drew to have some privacy, though, I suppose," Mac added from behind his newspaper. Without seeing his face, it was hard to read what he was really saying.

"Yes," she replied tentatively.

"He's a good man."

"I know."

"I'm not sure Gina was so sure."

Poppy missed her bottom lip with the water bottle and a dribble of water trickled down her neck into her cleavage. "What?"

Mac put the newspaper down. Poppy wished he had kept it where it was. It was easier to talk to him when he wasn't looking straight at her. "He's a complicated bloke."

"I know."

"I know you know. Six months or six years, you're still his wife. I know Dilly has given you a hard time this weekend. She likes to think she knows best. But she's not married to him. You are."

Poppy smiled. "You couldn't have told her that?"

"You think I didn't?"

There was a bead of condensation running down the bottle of water. Having really cold water constantly available was one of her favorite silly luxuries about life with Drew. It felt indulgent.

"If you'll let me, I'd like to give you some advice." He paused, clearly waiting for an invitation.

"OK," said Poppy. Whatever it was, she didn't want to hear it. It seemed everyone had come here and trampled over the delicate, recently planted seeds of their relationship, saying and doing things that knocked their fragile equilibrium off balance.

"This 'deal' you made, this thing about keeping your pasts in the past . . ."

"I know it sounds mad—"

Mac lifted his hand and to her own surprise, Poppy fell silent. "Ask him. About the past. He deserves a partner who knows everything about him and still wants to stick around. You both do. He's not the judgmental type, you know. And I don't think you are either."

As a child Poppy had often worried that certain people—priests, teachers, her mother—could see inside her mind. For a moment that ancient fear came flooding back. Did Mac know? It was the first time that weekend she had seen his creased face in anything other than a laugh or a smile. His eyes, the same auburn color as his corkscrew curls, weren't smiling anymore. Not unkind, but hungry. As if this really mattered to him. Mac dropped his gaze back down to his mug of tea. "Lecture over."

"What lecture?" asked Emma, coming into the kitchen with Ralph.

"I was just telling Poppy here that those plastic water bottles are all ending up on the bottom of the ocean, choking sea turtles and circumcising dolphins." He smiled. "And she was very politely pretending to listen."

"I was listening!" she replied, adding a laugh. She clearly wasn't the only one who was proficient in dishonesty. Did Mac lie like that often? Perhaps he had someone else, someone who wasn't Dilly. She'd be plump, Poppy decided. Nicely so. Someone he'd met through a work event, younger and sweet with big eyes and big hips and big breasts. "Can I get anyone tea or coffee? I was just going to make a French press, but I can't find it in any of the cupboards. Gina must have put it somewhere." She realized, too late, what she had said.

"Where is Gina?" asked Dilly, who had come down to breakfast at just the wrong time.

"She's gone back to London," said Poppy, dropping to her knees to search another cupboard.

"Already?"

"I took her to the station while you were all sleeping off your hangovers," Mac said. "She's got another job starting tomorrow. Maldives trip, wasn't it?"

Poppy got up. She'd found the French press wedged at the back, behind a stack of little bowls. "Yep. All right for some."

Everyone laughed. She caught Mac's eye and sent him a silent "thank you." He was, however much she hated to admit it, right. Drew deserved to be with someone who knew everything about him, even the things that hurt.

Asking him about his past, she reasoned, didn't mean that she had to tell him anything about hers.

CHAPTER 38

Everyone was gone by midmorning. That was the unofficial rule of a weekend guest, to be gone before eleven o'clock on Sunday. Poppy had read that online. She deleted her search history afterward, as if it were hardcore porn she'd been bingeing on beneath the covers at night, rather than top tips for hosting. She and Drew had stood on the front steps of the house and waved everyone off, listening to the crunch of gravel and watching their neat SUVs disappear up the lane into the greenness of the countryside. Then they had retreated to the kitchen. The house felt emptier than it had before everyone had arrived.

"Are you all right?" asked Drew from the doorway of the kitchen.

"Yeah. Fine," she replied, looking down at her hands in the washing-up bowl.

"You look sad. Is it Gina?"

Poppy gave a little nod, not trusting herself to speak. Gina. Mac. Everything else. It was too much to wrestle into a sentence. "I'm fine, really," she tried. "I just want to get the kitchen cleaned up." Even as she said it she was aware of how weak it sounded. The kitchen was pretty much spotless. Dilly had insisted on loading and running the dishwasher because, in her own words, "Poppy must be exhausted, she's not used to entertaining." So there was nothing to do. If Gina were here then the three of them would have sat outside and drunk beers with wedges of lime in them because they'd had so much wine already that weekend. Gina would make outrageous comments about all of the guests and even Drew wouldn't have been able to help finding them funny.

"I just feel bad," Poppy said, a little sob cracking through the sentence. Drew came up behind her, wrapping his arms around her waist and peeling the washing-up gloves from her hands. "She doesn't have anywhere to go; there's no space for her at home. But I'm angry with her too. She didn't know you before she offered to help you. You could have been anyone—she could have been selling me to a complete psycho."

His arms were too tight around her torso. She pushed them away, trying to seem casual.

"Come and sit down." He steered her to the window seat and guided her head into his chest. But the tears she had been holding back all morning wouldn't come.

"You will sort it out eventually, you know."

"I don't know," she said, her voice little against his chest. "She's so fucking stubborn."

"She just needs time to adjust, that's all."

She nodded. "I suppose. I just miss her."

"Is there anyone else you might want to see? Different friends? From university, perhaps? You could come up to London with me tomorrow to see them?"

Poppy sighed. How was she supposed to explain? There

was no explanation, even if she could allow herself to lie to him, that would make the words "I only have one friend" sound reasonable. She wasn't that type of person. She'd had friends. Proper, real friends. People she'd shared a house with and gotten ready before nights out with and shared secrets and uncharitable comments about mutual friends with. She just didn't have them anymore.

After she'd left the Walkers she'd lived in fear that she would find herself in the papers. So she'd closed her social media accounts. All of them. Hoping that they'd be gone before one of her friends' faces ended up on the front page, slightly blurred next to her own face. She got messages. Calls and texts. One morning she walked calmly to the boardwalk and threw her phone into the churning water.

The girls emailed her eventually, when their texts went unanswered. All along, Poppy had craved their support, but when it came, she couldn't take it. It was like the feeling of being so hungry you no longer wanted food.

The more distance she put between them and her, the lonelier she felt. And the loneliness, the pain of waking up each morning with no one to turn to and nowhere to go, made her guilt a little bit less sharp. It made her feel worse, which made her feel better.

"No," said Poppy, pulling her focus back to the kitchen table. "It's OK. Everyone's working anyway. And I've got so much to do to get ready for the photo shoot; Emma said they might even come this week. It's fine."

"You're sure you won't come with me?" Drew offered. "You could go to a gallery or get a massage or something and then I could meet you for lunch?"

She shook her head. "It's fine, darling. Really. I'm going

to spend tomorrow cleaning up from the weekend, and go and buy flowers to go in each room, for the pictures."

"All right," he said, slowly getting to his feet. "If you're sure."

"I'm sure."

BEFORE

For the first couple of days, Caroline didn't worry. Jim had always been a sulker. It was classic of him to act out, to put their disappearing act higher on the list of wrongdoings than kissing their twenty-one-year-old nanny.

After three days, she wasn't worried so much as angry.

Her texts weren't being read. His phone was going straight to voicemail. Was he trying to play her at her own game? Had he rented a car and taken off somewhere? Would he feel that he was entitled to kiss other women? Sleep with them even?

So, when the police arrived, three days after she and the children had left France, with community theater sad faces and soft voices, she assumed it must be her parents. Or his parents. Or someone else. Anyone. But not Jim.

How could anything have happened to Jim?

He had shot himself, they said.

The world went silent after she heard the words. Completely, utterly silent. She couldn't remember what people were supposed to do with their arms or their hands. She stood, swirling in a completely silent vortex, waiting for someone to tell her that it was a mistake, that they had the wrong person, that her husband was coming home.

But they didn't say that. Instead they told her that he had found a hunting rifle in the shed, and shot himself in the head. Caroline tried desperately not to imagine the peeling whitewashed walls of the cottage covered with his brains: every feeling and memory and experience they'd ever had together, splattered over the wall of the first house that they had ever holidayed in.

She had offered the police officers a cup of tea because that was what people did. Her hands shook as she made them. One mug came out too light, the other too dark. She handed them over, apologetic for the quality. They must get served terrible tea all of the time, she thought. Did the same police officers do all of the bad news delivering? Or was it a shift thing? Did they get training for this? Did they have to download a seminar about how to do that special singsong voice?

"He left a note," one of them said eventually. She was stony-faced as she uttered the words. Caroline couldn't help thinking: the worst is yet to come.

"The French police faxed it over. Would you like to see it?"

She nodded, and then shook her head. "Could you leave it over there?" she asked, as though it was a delivery. "On the table."

The woman police officer, dark and pretty, put it down. "Is there anyone here with you?"

"My children," she said. "And the nanny."

Nanny was the wrong word for what Poppy had become, really. More of a friend. Doing everything that Caroline couldn't face doing, reassuring her whenever she wobbled about what they had done to Jim. How was she going to take this untakeable news?

Eventually, once they were sure that Caroline wasn't going to slit her own wrists or run screaming into the street, the police left. They shoved all sorts of papers and leaflets into her hands, saying things about undertakers and funerals and repatriating the body. Jim had always been a stickler for getting the most expensive travel insurance. Though did it still pay out if you killed yourself? she wondered.

She waved the police off, smiling in the door frame so that everyone on the square could see that she hadn't been arrested. Then she went back into the living room, the room where Jim had pulled the carpets up himself when they had first moved in to satiate her desire for wooden floorboards, the room where they had first laid Jack in his crib when they brought him home from the hospital. These walls had held Christmases and birthdays and arguments and tantrums. Games of Twister. Sick children lying on the sofa watching the TV.

She picked up the piece of paper from the table, her head crushingly tight, and took a long, slow breath. Was there anything that he could have written here that would make this unfathomable choice any better? She flipped it over. This was what she was going to have to cling to when she told her children that their father was dead, when she lay awake alone at night, wondering whether what she had done was the reason that this had happened.

She looked down. His writing was as familiar to her as her own.

She kissed me. I said no.

CHAPTER 39

The flatness of the week following the party had come as no surprise. She'd seen it lots of times with the Hendersons. Beautiful, exciting weekends evaporated into nothing and left the same routine that had sat there before. The week dragged, full of tidying and organizing and finding things in completely the wrong place and wondering how they could have gotten there. And without Gina the house felt cold again.

She had thought that by painting it and decorating it, by waxing and sanding and varnishing it, she would stamp her name all over it, beat the place into submission. It hadn't worked. It was still too big. Aggressively quiet. And any creak from upstairs or door blown shut sent a pole of fear through her body. On the upside, the photo shoot had provided some distraction. Someone from the office of *Your Country House* magazine had called on Monday and requested to visit on Thursday—today. Apt, given the name of the house. The very grand voice on the end of the phone had pointed that out and Poppy had laughed dutifully. They were sending a reporter, a photographer and a stylist, apparently. She was surprised that they had the money to hire so many people for one feature. But then maybe looking inside other people's houses was the sort of thing people would still buy a magazine for.

She was grateful for the distraction of the photo shoot. But even the prospect of ordering flowers and fiddling with every frame and ornament in the house hadn't made her happy. The regret about how things were with Gina had lain cold and heavy in the bottom of her stomach. Could she call her? Probably not. For the thousandth time she wished there were more people to call. No. That was a lie. She wished she could call Caroline.

All Poppy had to do was close her eyes and she was back in the Walkers' kitchen. High ceiling, yellow cabinets, drawings and letters from school on the fridge. Mismatched plates, music on the radio, a larder full of brightly colored snacks and treats that all the other children at their chichi north London schools were forbidden. But those kids were so active, so fast, so everywhere all the time that it didn't matter how much sugar they scoffed, it was burned up immediately. Poppy remembered the warmth of their skinny little limbs, wrapped in a towel after a bath. The weight of a child on her lap, begging for a story.

She shut the memories down, like turning off the TV. The sounds and colors and smells disappeared. She was good at that. It had taken a long time, but she could put steel shutters around every single moment of that life and forbid it to seep into the rest of her mind.

The kettle. That was what she'd do. She'd boil the Aga kettle, which took three times as long as the electric one, but looked better. And get all the teacups out. That way, when they arrived she would have something to do, something to busy herself with. Would they be able to tell when they looked at her that she wasn't the sort of person who owned a house like this?

She shouldn't have worried. Paul, the artistic director who arrived half an hour later, was definitely not that "type." He fell through the front door saying, "So lovely to meet you, darling, where the fuck's the toilet? I'm dying for a slash." He ran inside, shouting instructions to his assistant Pippa. They followed behind him, carrying suitcases and lights and talking incessantly. Their noise made Poppy realize how right Drew was, how this house went dead when it was empty but came to life when it was full of voices. When they started a family, it would be like this all the time. She would meet people with children, and they'd have parties here, and it would be full of noise and life.

"Where shall I set up hair and makeup?" asked a blond woman with deep creases in her tanned skin. "Somewhere with natural light is best."

"Makeup?" asked Poppy.

"Yeah, makeup," she repeated. "You're Poppy Spencer, right?"

"Yes," she said, "but I thought it was just the house?"

The woman looked down at a piece of paper and then held it out. "Poppy Spencer, hair and makeup."

"I didn't realize." Was this a bad idea? What if someone saw it? What if someone made the connection, saw her living in the big house with the handsome husband and thought that she didn't deserve it? Wanted to make trouble?

"Didn't Emma explain?" said Paul, walking through the hall carrying a crate, as though it was his house rather than hers. "We shoot the house; then we do some piccies of you

323

in your favorite room, and ask you some questions. She said she'd talked you through it?"

"She had, she had," Poppy said. Was that true? She couldn't remember. She'd been drunk on Saturday night when Emma had first suggested it, and then when she had called to discuss it the day before she'd been so distracted, so worried about Gina, that she'd hardly taken any of it in. "I'd just sort of spaced. Sorry. If I'd remembered I'd have sorted myself out." She gestured at her jeans and sweater apologetically.

"It's fine." Paul grinned. "You look gorge. But if you want to go and change, there's plenty of time."

She didn't really. She didn't want to put on a dress and stand smugly around the house looking like all of her dreams had come true.

"I'll just go and put something else on," she heard herself say.

What was she supposed to wear for a photo shoot? She pulled her hands through her wardrobe, as if by looking again she could magically uncover the perfect thing, something that made her look elegant and chic without seeming twee or older than her age. The right dress would be pale pink or pale blue, with cap sleeves and a fitted waist and a little kick to the skirt. She didn't own anything like that. Eventually she found a pretty green dress, printed with white stars. It had buttons down the front and a collar. She had ordered it online and meant to send it back because it was a little too tight in the arms and gaped a bit over her chest. She slipped it on hopefully and found that it fit. She must have lost weight. She'd been drinking less since Gina left. Much less. And she hadn't bothered much with food. It seemed so pointless making herself lunch for one.

From upstairs she could hear Paul bellowing orders, telling the crew to move the flowers and open the curtains and shift a table. Maybe you had to be like that if you were going to do his job, to go into other people's houses and make them look even more beautiful than they really were. Funny, how Paul had taken command of the house. It seemed to be listening to him, offering none of the resistance it did to Poppy. When she went back downstairs, her limbs hastily rubbed with fake tan, feet shoved into a pair of ballet pumps, the rooms seemed to have bent to him immediately, without any of the fight they had given her. If only she were brave enough to ask him how he had done it, perhaps she could have learned the trick.

The photos were painful. Poppy, like almost everyone, hated having her photo taken. The makeup artist had curled her hair and added vast amounts of volume so it was like a sort of auburn halo around her head. She'd painted liner on her lids and covered her mouth with a pink lipstick that managed to make her lips feel both greasy and dry. Something about the lipstick made the back of her throat ache. She stood in front of the kitchen counter, pretending to use her KitchenAid.

"It's not a bit Stepford wife, is it?" she ventured after ten minutes or so.

"Oh, that's the idea," said the photographer without looking up from the camera. "You haven't got a pair of heels you could pop on, have you?"

"No," Poppy lied. "Sorry."

The next setup had her sitting at the head of the table in the dining room, hands folded on the table. It must look ridiculous. As the photographer fiddled with the white tent thing, bouncing light all around the room, making no discernible difference, Poppy was struck by the horrible thought that her mother might see this. The chances were slim, admittedly. But what if she had a Google alert on her name? Or what if her sister or her mother stumbled over the magazine in the waiting room at the GP? She could see the tightness of her mother's lips without even closing her eyes. The little noise she would give, somewhere between a tut and a sigh. A noise that said, "How could you show yourself off like that? It's like you're asking for trouble."

Maybe she was. Maybe she had decided that asking for trouble was the only way to get what she deserved.

"We've got the shot," called the photographer, as if it was an episode of *America's Next Top Model*.

"Now, we'll just whisk you away for some questions and then we'll be all done," said Paul in his singsong voice. Did he always talk like that? Poppy wondered. Or did he get home, peel off his jeans and slump on the sofa, talking four octaves lower?

In the sitting room she kicked off her flats and settled on the sofa, legs curled underneath her.

"So, you did the whole place without a designer?"

"Yes," she said. What was she supposed to say to that? She had chosen the colors and the prints and the textures without paying someone else an enormous amount of money to do so. Was that really so astonishing?

"I heard you did it in a week?"

Poppy smiled. "Most of it, yes."

"You and your husband?"

"Me and a friend. Drew was away for work."

Paul raised one perfectly threaded eyebrow. "He didn't mind coming home to a completely different house?"

"He was pleased."

"Pleased?"

"Well, the house was always beautiful but it was quite worn out. Everything we inherited from the previous owners was tasteful and chic, but it had had a lot of use."

"Did you know the previous owners?"

The skin on the back of Poppy's neck tightened. Stupid. Stupid, stupid, stupid. How could she have stumbled into that so easily? He wasn't even trying to trip her up, she was managing it all on her own.

"No," she said. "They moved abroad."

"Nice. Somewhere hot?"

"Dubai," Poppy answered, plucking an answer from the air.

"How did you choose it?"

"The house?" Poppy shifted. "It's quite a romantic story. My husband bought the house for me as a wedding present."

"A wedding present?" Paul seemed charmed. "My husband got me a tie. I feel shortchanged."

Poppy laughed, more from the relief of getting away from the previous-owner question than because Paul's joke was funny. "He's a very special person. I'd never had my own place before. It was amazing to come back here and realize that it was ours, and we could do anything we wanted with it."

"Which is your favorite room?"

"It's a tie between our bedroom and the kitchen. I love

the view from our room, and because it's all in very soft tones it feels like a really gentle place to be. But the kitchen is what I'd always dreamed of."

Paul nodded as she spoke. She wasn't sure whether that meant she was doing a good job, or whether that was just what he did.

"Anything else planned for the future?"

"I want to tackle the garden. It's beautiful, but a bit of a mess. I'd like to have it over two levels, with a sunken garden."

"And the house?"

"The top floor is still pretty spartan. I think it would make a nice nursery—at some point."

Paul laughed out loud. "Oh, you tease! Brilliant. You're a natural."

Poppy couldn't help laughing too. "I doubt anyone will care. But I love these kinds of features, nosing around someone else's house."

"You're going to have a lot of women out there very jealous."

What was she supposed to say to that? Thank you? Was making other people jealous a good thing? Something she should think of at night to give herself an insulating glow of smugness?

"Well." Paul got to his feet and flicked through his notebook. "I think we've got everything."

"Oh, great. Well, if you need anything else, Emma gave you my number?"

Paul stopped on a page of the notebook. "Ah, yes, last thing. Why did you change the name?"

"The name?"

"Of the house."

Poppy looked blank. "Sorry?"

"The records for the house say that it was called Eden Park, but you're calling it Thursday House. It was changed by a Drew Spencer—that's your husband, right? I was just wondering whether there was any special significance there?"

Poppy's throat stuck together as she tried to swallow. He was going to think it was strange that she didn't know that.

Why didn't she know that? "Oh yes." She smiled. "Drew, being romantic again. He called the house Thursday House because we met on a Thursday."

Paul made a high-pitched noise and smiled. "They'll be creaming their pants back at the office when they read that. Sorry," he added, mistaking her expression for distaste at his words.

Drew had said that the house didn't have a name before, when he lived there as a child. He told her he'd christened it Thursday House. Why would he tell her that?

Why would he lie?

BEFORE

Caroline pushed the door to Poppy's bedroom open and pressed the note into her hand. She was sitting on her bed, painting her toenails a bright coral color.

"Read it," Caroline said.

She watched Poppy's face as she went over the words, over and over them, apparently struggling to understand them.

"He's dead," said Caroline. She would save the kind, gentle words for her children later. There was no point in wasting them now. "He killed himself."

Poppy looked up at her, her eyes enormous.

"Is it true?" asked Caroline, pointing at the note. His shaky blue writing on faint-lined paper. "'She kissed me.'"

Poppy didn't answer.

"Is it true?" Caroline said again, her voice a whisper-scream. This was not how the children would find out. That much she could control.

"Yes," said Poppy. "It's true."

Caroline turned away. The white wall of the bedroom seemed to sink away from her and then come closer, back and forward. She wanted to be sick. "How could you?" she asked eventually, struggling to form words. "How could you do that to him?"

"I didn't know," Poppy replied, her eyes dropped. "I didn't know that he was—I didn't know he would—"

"Stop lying," Caroline shouted, cutting Poppy's sentence off. "You're seriously telling me that after all of the little chats you had, after all the times you spilled your guts to him about your absent father and bitch of a mother he didn't tell you that he had depression? You didn't see the pills in the bathroom? You're really trying to tell me that you didn't know?"

Poppy stammered an answer, but whatever it was she was about to say, Caroline had no interest in hearing it.

"I thought you liked it here? I thought you cared about us?"

"I did!" Poppy yelped. "I do. He said he was going to tell you I'd tried to kiss him when we got back here, he said I'd have to leave, and I—"

Caroline had had enough.

"Go," she said, turning from the room. "Get out of my house."

She stood outside on the landing, listening to Poppy cry as she packed her things into her suitcase, and then escorted her down the stairs, out of the front door. She watched Poppy trail her fingers on the banisters, giving lingering looks to the walls around her, as if she were being sent from her childhood home, not somewhere she'd lived for a couple of months. Caroline slammed the front door and then took the stairs two at a time, running to her bedroom window. She watched the small redheaded figure walk away. She had to be certain she was gone.

CHAPTER 40

Poppy waited until the crew had gone, standing on the steps and waving the cars off one by one. Then, once she was sure there would be no chance of anyone coming back to collect something they had forgotten, she reached for her phone. She drummed her nails on the cold granite of the kitchen surface, bumping her toe against the cupboard. *Please pick up. Please pick up.*

"Gina?" Poppy said, relieved.

Her voice was cold. "Yeah?"

"I know you're angry with me, but I think something is wrong."

"What?"

"Drew said the house didn't have a name before, but we just had this photo shoot, the one that Emma set up with the magazine, and the guy who came, he said that Drew had *changed* the name of the house." She could hear Gina's breath at the other end of the phone. "Gina?"

"What was it called?"

"What?"

"The house. What was it called before?"

"Eden something. Eden House? Eden Park. It was Eden Park. I know I should look it up but I've just got this feeling, I—"

"I'll call you back."

Poppy walked up and down the hall, waiting for her phone to buzz. She avoided the gold tiles, stepping only on the blue ones and taking steps in multiples of five and then of six. *If I can get to that end without stepping on a crack it'll be OK. If I can get across in eighteen steps then nothing is wrong. If there's an even number of steps between this door and that door then he hasn't done anything wrong.*

Her phone rang again. The time on the screen told her that it had only been seven minutes since Gina had hung up. It had felt like hours.

"Gina?"

"Google it."

"What?"

"You have to Google it."

"What are you talking about?"

"I'm taking Mum's car, I'll be with you as soon as I can. Just search it. Eden Park. OK?"

Poppy hesitated. "OK."

As she hung up the phone she heard wheels on gravel. Panicked, she turned on her heel and fled to the kitchen. Standing in the hall would arouse suspicion. She went to the fridge, looking for something to do, and found a packet of broccolini. She tipped it onto a chopping board and put a knife in her hand. There. That looked natural. They hadn't known each other that long. Surely he wouldn't notice that something was going on, that there was screaming inside her head? She could just ask him. She could ask, the second he opened the door. But something inside her was writhing, telling her not to.

"How was it?" asked Drew, putting his bag down on the sofa, taking off his jacket and folding it neatly. He did the same thing every evening. Bag down, jacket folded on the arm of the sofa, sleeves rolled up. Then he'd stand behind her, kiss her neck and ask, "How was your day?" Often he'd slide his hands up her dress and run his hands over her stomach, her hips, her thighs, kiss her neck, stroke her hair and gently inquire as to whether she was interested in sex. Not tonight, though. Every muscle in her body was taut. Her jaw ached from biting down on her back teeth. Could he tell? She thought of her phone in her dress pocket. As soon as he was distracted, she would go to the bathroom and do as Gina had instructed her. *Calm down*, she told herself. *It could be nothing. You love him. He's your husband.*

Drew had never scared her, never made her feel unsafe. He hadn't even raised his voice to her. There was no good reason for the thudding in her chest or the sweat underneath her hair. Or was there? Instinct was screaming that there was.

She flinched as he kissed her. Would he notice the tension in her muscles? The thudding echoing in her chest? "It was good," she said, sliding the knife through the green stems. "They seemed pleased with the house. I didn't see many of the photos, but they were nice people. They wanted pictures of me too."

"Ah, I see. Hence the makeup."

She had forgotten about that. "Yes. I'm not sure about it, though."

Drew smiled. "I quite like it. But you know I think you look best when you've just woken up, or got out of the shower."

He was sweet to her. No one could question that. Kind and sweet and loving. What could Gina possibly have found? What could change the way she felt about the kind, gorgeous man who adored her so much?

"I'm just going to the loo," she said, her voice far too high.

The downstairs bathroom hadn't changed much since they had moved in. The floor was the same warm yellow stone as the kitchen. The walls were lined with books so there didn't seem much point in painting it. It was always cold in here, even when it was warm outside. And despite the jar of fat roses sitting on the windowsill and the expensive room fragrance, it still smelled like cold stone. She sank down onto the wooden loo seat, colder still on the back of her thighs. Her finger shook as she entered her passcode, getting it wrong three times; *iPhone disabled*, it taunted her. *Wait one minute.*

One minute. How could it be, she thought as she watched the screen, that one singular unit of time could move so quickly or so slowly depending on the circumstances? A minute of orgasm felt like seconds. A minute on a treadmill lasted several hours. And a minute when you're waiting for your stupid phone to unlock itself so that you can find out what deep, dark, fucked-up secret is about to ruin your marriage? A lifetime.

She got the code right the second time. The background, a picture of her and Drew in Ibiza, her hair full of the wind, taunted her. Her index finger shook as she tapped the internet icon and then the words "Eden Park, Wiltshire."

She didn't even need Wiltshire. Eden Park would have come up on its own.

A message from Gina flashed at the top of her screen and she swatted it away, trying to focus her eyes, trying to make the words make sense.

The Eden Park murder.

CHAPTER 41

The Eden Park murder had taken place thirty-four years ago, according to the article. Poppy stroked down the screen, reading. Rereading. Clawing at the information, trying to force herself to understand it, to make the chains of words turn into sentences she could process.

The Eden Park Murder

On 2 July 1984, Lauren Watkins, aged five, went missing from the village of Linfield in Wiltshire. Her body was found, five days later, at the bottom of a well at the village's manor house, Eden Park. Her death was ruled as murder.

Lauren Watkins

Watkins went missing on 2 July. Her father, who worked as a gardener at Eden Park, had brought her to work for the day, as his wife was unwell and it was the summer holidays. He told the police that he last saw her around 2 p.m. No witnesses saw Lauren leaving the premises and there was no security footage. Police efforts were focused mostly on search rather than intelligence. Locals report that they seemed optimistic that Lauren would be found.

Search

By that evening, the village had put together a search party and combed much of the surrounding area, hoping that Lauren had wandered away from the house, gotten lost and been unable to find her way back to her home.

Several days after Lauren disappeared, one of the children who lived at Eden Park, where she had gone missing, came forward and volunteered information. What followed has since become a focal point in the ongoing social debate about criminal responsibility.

Arrests

Simon and William Campbell, aged eleven and nine, admitted to pushing Lauren Watkins into the well at the bottom of Eden Park's garden. William, the younger of the two, claimed that his brother had panicked after they realized how deep the well was, saying that they would be in trouble if they told the police. His statements claim that his brother threatened him.

Simon Campbell was tried and found guilty of the murder of Lauren Watkins. There were extensive calls for William to be tried, though at nine he was under the age of criminal responsibility. While ultimately these calls were unsuccessful, it was decided that the rest of the Campbell family should be given new identities to protect them.

Simon Campbell died by suicide after being transferred from juvenile prison to maximum security, aged eighteen.

Will. Ralph had called Drew "Will" during croquet on Saturday. So Ralph knew. Did the others? Had that been what Dilly and Emma were talking about when she had overheard them on the night of the party? Had one of them been in the bathroom with Gina trying to find out if she and Poppy knew? Almost certainly.

The bathroom walls suddenly seemed thick and heavy, tight around her head.

Her fingers shook as she tapped the button on the phone screen. Gina picked up instantly.

"You read it?"

Poppy nodded.

"Do you think—am I—safe?" She was whispering, though she wasn't sure why.

"No."

"But he wouldn't—he wasn't . . ." She couldn't find the words to finish the sentences.

"You don't know." Gina's voice was high. She sounded vindicated. A small, childish part of Poppy was angry with Gina for being right. Agonizingly, horrifically right.

"What do I do?"

Gina's voice was urgent. "I'm coming. I'll be there soon.

Get your stuff. If he comes home, act like everything is OK. If you feel worried, call the police. OK?"

"OK."

It was impossible to know where to put herself. She tried to remember what she had done on other, normal evenings. So she went back to the kitchen and picked up a knife. Took a bag of carrots from the fridge. Put jazz on the kitchen speakers and poured two glasses of wine. She crafted a Thursday evening for two people who had been married a couple of months. Drew was in the garden, looking out over the view. It was getting darker earlier now. She looked at the back of him; it was different now she could see him. What might he do if he found out that she knew the truth?

"What are you making?" Drew asked, coming back inside.

Her eyes had become comfortable resting on one spot. She pulled them away, forcing herself to look at him. What was she making?

"Poppy?"

"Carrots," she said weakly, looking down at them. Drew was going to the fridge for a bottle of water.

"OK," he replied. "Are you all right?"

"I don't feel—" She stopped, putting the knife on the board and turning from the kitchen, walking to the hall. Why couldn't she make the right noises? Why couldn't she be more convincing? Perhaps there were only so many lies a person could tell before their body stopped being able to put on the act anymore. There was a thudding in her temples, a tightness around her waist. The numbness was starting to fade.

"Poppy?" came a voice from behind her. She turned, slowly.

She looked through him, at the hall. This was where he had lived. But not, as he had told her, until his parents had died. Until his family were chased out of the village because he and his brother had done something so horrific, so unforgivable, it wasn't safe for them here anymore.

No wonder he hadn't wanted to go into Linfield.

He looked up at her, paused on the stairs. She watched his face. Confusion. And then something else. Resignation?

"You know," he said, his voice flat. "Don't you?"

She nodded, and then, turning, took the stairs two at a time. She wasn't sure what she had hoped for. Maybe a denial? She might have chosen to believe a denial. She heard him behind her and began to run, finally reaching her bedroom—their bedroom—and slamming the door. She slid down and sat with her back to it, her knees pulled up to her chest. There was no lock for this door. It was on her list of things to do, but right at the bottom. Why would they need a bedroom lock? she had thought. Maybe when they had children, children old enough to open doors, but not yet. There was no reason to have one.

"Poppy." Drew's voice came through the door, low and calm. "Poppy, please. Open the door. Talk to me." He wasn't pushing the door. He wasn't even turning the handle. There was no aggression in what he was doing, but still her skin felt tight. Her husband had killed a little girl. Years ago. Or his brother did. It could have been either of them. Or both. Whatever the truth was, she doubted she would ever know it.

"Please, Poppy," he said again.

She said nothing, smacking her head against the door over and over again. The words she had read screamed in her brain, scraping the inside of her head, hurting it. *Killer, killer, killer.* He was the man who woke up in the middle of the night and wrapped his arms around her, the man who gave her anything she wanted and told her that she looked perfect with a hangover and a bare face, the man who could make her laugh even when she was moody and hormonal. *Killer.*

CHAPTER 42

Gina had told her to pack. She felt for her weekend bag under the bed and began to fill it with clothes. She had bought the bag thinking about jaunts to London or popping over to Paris. Not this. She'd never imagined this.

"Poppy," Drew called. "Please, open the door."

What did she need? She wrapped her hands around her head, trying to quiet all the noise. Jeans. Underwear. T-shirts. Sweaters. Socks. Shoes. Her handbag was downstairs, with her credit cards, cash, checkbook.

"Poppy?" There was a break in Drew's voice. "Poppy?"

His credit cards. Her husband. A little girl was dead because of him.

That was why he had chosen her.

The realization hit her like a train ripping through a station.

Not because he had seen her across a crowded room and fallen for her.

"Poppy, I just want to talk to you. You don't even need to open the door, but please, just listen to me."

Not because she was funny or clever or because he liked the way her nose wrinkled when she was thinking. He must know about Caroline. About Jim. About everything that had happened there. He knew what she had done. And he thought they were the same; he thought they were both guilty. Dirty and stained and damaged.

That was the only reason he wanted her. He thought they were the same. But Poppy was not a murderer.

A beam of white light came through the window. Headlights. Gina was here. She must have broken every speed limit. Poppy got to her feet and pulled the door open, the bag hanging from one arm.

"Please," he exploded, following her down the stairs. Reaching for her arm to slow her. "Let me explain."

"How?" She turned halfway down, her voice high. "How can you explain all of this? You killed a little girl."

His face was blank while the words filled the room, bouncing from the walls and the ceiling. He must, she guessed, have been called terrible things. People must have said far worse to him before now. Why wasn't he reacting?

"That's why you wanted me, isn't it?"

He said nothing.

"Isn't it?"

Gina's voice came from the bottom of the stairs. "Poppy. Come on. Let's go."

"Gina?" Drew started, looking down at her. "What are you doing here? Poppy and I need to—"

Gina interrupted him, her eyes bright. "You don't need anything from her, you sick fuck," she said. "I can't believe you did this. I can't believe you made me part of your fucked-up little scheme. You—"

"You took the money, didn't you?" Drew shouted back,

his voice tight with anger. "So you can get off your high fucking horse."

"Poppy, we're leaving," said Gina with a shrug. Was she enjoying this? Happy to finally see Drew reduced to shouting and begging?

"Please don't go," Drew said quietly. He held his hand out, not grabbing at Poppy's arm, but hovering over it. "Please." His voice cracked.

"How did you know?" she asked, her voice not much more than a whisper. "How did you find out what I did?"

"Poppy, I fell for you, but I still had to be careful. I didn't want to ask for a prenup, you were using your middle name, I wanted to be sure—"

"How did you know?" She ground out the words.

He sighed. "I had someone look into your past."

"And thought I'd make a perfect companion for you. Mr. and Mrs. Murderer."

"That's not why I married you."

She looked away, trying to shut him out. "You're a liar."

"I never wanted to lie to you. That was what the whole deal was about."

She half laughed. "Oh come on."

"I know," he said again. "I get it. I understand like no one else could."

"Stop it."

"Are you ever going to meet someone else who'll understand what you did?"

Poppy stopped. "What?"

"I know you. All of you. Someone else might tell you that one day, might pretend he gets it but he won't." His voice was rough. Strained. "You know everything about me now. All of it. There's nothing you don't know. No more secrets."

Poppy looked down to the hall, where Gina was standing. Her bag dragged at her left arm, the hum of the car engine on the drive pounding in her head. He took a step down, one step closer to her. She could smell him again now, the scent of fresh, clean masculine him. "I admit that I felt lucky when I read it all, when I realized what had happened. I thought that you wouldn't push, that you wouldn't want to talk about the past, and I thought that might be the only way I'd ever meet anyone who took me for me. I admit that. But that's not why I married you."

She tipped her head to one side. Why did she want to hear this?

"I fell in love with you," he said. "You know that. You know that this is real, and you know we could stay this way. I know what you did and I still want to be with you. You'll never have to explain anything to me, you'll never have to talk about it if you don't want to."

"I'm not like that, that person you've read about," she said quietly.

Drew held his hands out, as if she were a frightened horse. "I'm not like that either, Poppy. We made mistakes."

"It wasn't my fault. I didn't want him to die." She had never said those words aloud. But she had repeated them to herself over and over and over again, like a prayer, in every silent moment where the thoughts swelled up inside her and tried to haunt her. *It wasn't my fault.*

Caroline had said it was Poppy's fault. She had said it calmly and slowly and like she meant it, while she watched her pack up her things. And at the inquest, the last time

Poppy had seen her. Pale and thin and chewing on her nails. "If it wasn't for her, my husband would still be here. He would still be alive. My children would still have a father."

It didn't matter how much Poppy punished herself. None of it changed anything. Jim was dead. And, in her darkest moments, she knew that Caroline had been right.

"It wasn't your fault," said Drew, looking through her eyes and inside her.

"Poppy, let's go." Where did Gina think they were going to go? Was she expecting Poppy to put a hotel on her credit card? Drew's credit card.

"Please," said Drew. "Stay. We'll talk. I'll tell you anything you want to know. Don't leave me."

She looked between them both. Drew's face hollow and sad, a gray tinge to his skin. She had never seen him look scared before.

Gina's jaw set hard, her eyes tight. "She's leaving," she said, crossing the hall and taking the stairs three at a time until she stood just below them.

"I don't know, Gee," Poppy said. "I—"

"For fuck's sake," Gina shouted. "He's doing it again, he's got this hold over you. You're not like him, OK? What happened to you is nothing like what he did. He killed a child—he's dangerous."

Poppy shook her head. "Gina, I—"

Gina reached out her arm and pulled at Poppy's wrist. "Come with me. I need to get you out of here."

"Gina," Poppy said, a little sharper this time. "I want to stay. I want to talk it through."

Drew sat down on the stairs, his head in his hands. His sinewy forearms were shaking.

"What?" Gina snapped.

"I need to talk to Drew. I need to understand what happened. I'm not saying that I'm going to stay forever, but—"

"I'm not leaving you here."

"I'm OK."

"Poppy, he *killed a kid.*"

"Gina, please."

"I'll tell."

"What?"

"If you don't come with me now, I'll tell everyone what he did. Who he is. All them lot in the village. His office. The papers. Everyone."

Poppy shook her head.

Gina pulled her phone out. "I mean it. I'll post it online. Who he is, who you are. About how he paid me, about what he did."

"You—what?" Poppy couldn't follow Gina's words.

"I don't want to do this, Poppy, but you're not safe here. You can't stay here with him. I know you think you're happy, but you're just distracted by all the clothes and the big house. He's a killer. How can you know he won't do it again? I love you and if it takes telling everyone what you did, what you both did, to get you to come with me then I'll do it."

Gina meant it. Poppy knew that. She never said anything she didn't mean. Never stopped, never thought about the consequences of her actions. Just charged forward.

"Gina, please, I just want to talk to him. Give me one night."

"I can't," she said, her eyes huge with concern.

"Give me an hour then."

Gina shook her head. "If I do that you'll stay. I know you." She took another step up, reaching for Poppy. "I know what you're like. You think the money makes it safe to be here, but it doesn't." She held her phone up, showing her the screen. But it was too close for Poppy to see the display. "Come with me now, or I'm doing it."

A rage, sudden and pure, shot through Poppy.

She watched as her arms lifted, her palms flattened against Gina's chest and pushed, her whole weight behind it, surging forward and shoving Gina as hard as she could. She watched as Gina's long, limby body tumbled down the stairs. She watched as Gina hit the bottom, the beautiful blue tiled floor, with a sickening crack, and then silence.

She looked up at Drew, whose face was blank. Then she stepped slowly down the stairs.

Gina's eyes were moving underneath her lids and her chest was rising and falling.

Not dead.

Drew walked down the stairs. She listened to the sole of his work shoes click on the stone. When Drew reached the bottom, he wound his arms around Poppy's torso and kissed the top of her head. "What shall we do?" he asked into her hair.

"We don't have a choice," she whispered. Why were they whispering? There wasn't another house for half a mile.

Drew nodded. "Go upstairs," he said. He searched the hall with his eyes and picked up a marble-based clock from the hall table. It was a mottled yellow-pink with sharp edges.

"No," said Poppy, watching his hand wrap around it.

"I don't want you to see this." His voice was kind.

She kissed him, full on the mouth and, looking up into his face, she smiled. It was easy to see how things would be different from now on. "I'm staying," she said. "No more secrets."

SIX MONTHS LATER

Spring had finally arrived. The sky was a kind of blue that Poppy had begun to doubt would ever come back and all around her she could see daffodils. It was going to stay like this, the newspaper said. A long, warm spring sliding into another endlessly hot summer. They'd be able to use the pool before long.

She'd left Drew back at the house, building the crib in the baby's primrose-yellow bedroom. He'd told her off for fussing, sent her into the village for dinner supplies.

She ran her hands over her stomach, feeling the reassuring flicker of life beneath her skin. She added a bottle of water to her shopping basket and waited her turn at the register. It was a lovely place. All cream wood and bright, fresh fruits and vegetables in neat rows.

"Is it your first?" asked the woman behind the counter, gesturing to Poppy's bump as she counted Sicilian lemons.

"Yes." Poppy nodded. "Not much longer now."

"I like your accent." The woman smiled. She was pretty. Her dark hair was piled up on top of her head and a gold stud punctured her nose. She wore overalls and a pale pink T-shirt. Poppy wondered if this was her shop. Perhaps they would become friends. People were so much nicer here than they had been in Linfield.

The playground where Thursday House once stood would be finished now. All traces of the house gone, covered over with pavement and wood chips and brightly colored metal. The people who had refused to help her with decorating or plumbing would bring their children there to play. They'd say it was the only decent thing to do with that house. They'd sit on the wooden benches, watching their children run around, pleased. Feeling like they had won. With no idea what lay beneath the pavement.

"Thank you," said Poppy.

"Are you here on holiday?" the woman asked.

"No," said Poppy. "We've just moved here. Me and my husband."

The woman smiled. "Welcome."

"Thank you," said Poppy. "It's all a bit of a change. We don't know anyone yet."

Sticking her hand out, the woman said, "I'm Lily. So now you know me."

Poppy returned her smile. "Nice to meet you, Lily. I'm Alice."

She relished the feeling of her new name on her lips. Things were going to be different from now on. She and Drew and their baby would be happy here.

Acknowledgments

When I wrote the acknowledgments for my first book, *Perfect Liars*, I felt as if I needed to thank everyone I had ever known. Which was probably fair enough, given how much all of those people contributed to the story. They say that your first book takes your entire life up until that point to write, so all those friends and teachers and people I drunkenly met at parties really did have a part in it.

A second book, as I learned quickly, is a very different thing. The first person to thank must be Darcy Nicholson, the best editor a girl could ask for. Not only did she give me the chance to write this book, she helped make it what it is today, and she's keen on ordering wine with lunch. Similarly, the entire team at Transworld, not least my publicist, Becky Short, and marketer Ella Horne, who have both been a dream to work with.

My agent, Eve White, has always been a rock of calm, something I need given that the business side of writing books makes me utterly loopy. She and Ludo Cinelli are both stars.

Friends too have been an enormous part of this process. Liv, Mel, Emily, Grace, Kathy, Chloe, Emma, Jon, Ian,

Aimee, Georgie, Carol, Madeleine (whose name I spelled wrong in the acknowledgments for *Perfect Liars*), Becka, Tiss, all the Amsterglam girls, Tristan, Natasha, Hannah, all the Metro.co.uk Lifestyle team (especially Ellen, Jess, Miranda and Faima). You've all kept me sane.

Family too. Lucy, George, Tim and Charlotte remain the best people in the world to tell good news to, and the most supportive when things aren't going your way.

Last but not least, my husband, Marcus, whose reticence to talk about The Past was the inspiration for this book. Steady, patient, kind and always there to remind me that no, the first book was not "piss easy" to write. Thank you for forgiving me this ultimate act of passive aggression.

About the Author

Rebecca Reid is a freelance journalist and the author of *Perfect Liars*.

Rebecca lives in north London with her husband.